Senseless Confidential

A Novel

Martin Bannon

Published in the United States.
ISBN: 0615639577
ISBN-13: 978-0615639574

Cover design © 2012 Marty Beaudet
Front cover photo: © Laurent Renault, lrfolio.com
Back cover photos: © 2012 Marty Beaudet

Dedicated to U.S. Census Bureau field
representatives everywhere.

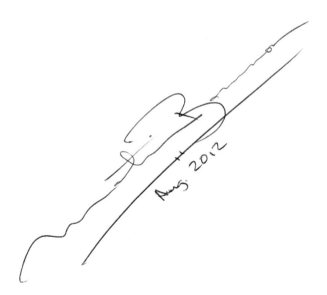

Aug 2012

ACKNOWLEDGEMENTS

This book would not have been possible without the invaluable input of the Laurel Writers' Group in Portland, Oregon. It would not appear in its current readable state were it not for the vaunted editing skills of my sister Judith, who scaled mountains to see that the work got done to perfection. Any remaining errors are my own.

As always, I owe a debt of gratitude to my husband, Chuck, who goes out of his way to make sure I have every opportunity to write, whenever and wherever I need it.

Many thanks to all who contributed, even if they didn't know it.

Title 13

TITLE 13 OF THE UNITED STATES CODE requires that data collected by the government from both individuals and establishments must be used only as statistical totals and no identification of individuals or establishments may be made.

I, _Nicholas J. Prince_ , do solemnly swear I will not disclose any information contained in the schedules, lists, or statements obtained for or prepared by the U.S. Census Bureau to any person or persons either during or after appointment. (Under Title 13, U.S.C. section 214, the penalty for disclosure is a fine of not more than $250,000 or imprisonment for not more than 5 years, or both.)

Title 1

HARDLY A DAY GOES BY WHEN SOME fuckhead doesn't want to shoot me. Today is no exception. I hear the pump action of the shotgun long before I reach the house. The thick forest obscures all but the clearing in which it sits, somewhere off to the right. At this point I'm only about fifty yards off the paved county road, but in this part of the county I could just as easily stumble onto a pot grow as a family farm. Not this time: there's no razor wire, no cameras, and—most importantly—no pit bulls attached to my ankles. I hate pit bulls.

I emerge into the clearing with hands raised to my side at about chest level. Not an actual gesture of surrender, but enough to let Shooter Dude know I'm a pussycat, not a crouching tiger. From my right hand I dangle the black computer bag on which the words "U.S. Census" are clearly stitched in white.

The clapboard farmhouse lies just beyond a late-model, black Ford F-250 Crew Cab, its meticulously polished chrome glinting in the sun. I've just been dodging muddy chuck-holes big enough to swallow a German shepherd, which means this truck has been spit-shined since it was driven in here. This confirms my suspicion that I'm dealing with a weekend cowboy here, not a real one.

I can see him now, standing on the covered porch with the shotgun leveled in my general direction, but not sighted on me. He holds it to his side at waist level rather than at shoulder height; intended to intimidate rather than kill me. Not that he could. Kill me, that is. I'm willing to bet, from his stance and handling of the gun, that he's not exactly comfortable with it. I continue moving closer.

"Can I help you?" he barks as I round the truck. His voice is at least a full octave below a normal speaking voice.

"Good morning," I say, all sunny bubbles. The goofier the better. It's never a good idea to piss on the turf of an armed alpha, no matter how badly aimed the gun is. "I'm from the United States Census Bureau," I add without breaking my stride. It helps to spell out the full name of the agency to these shooter-types, to avoid any confusion.

"Yeah?" Shooter says with a jut of the chin. "So what do you want?"

"We're conducting the American Community Survey," I say in my best Boy Scout, "and we weren't sure if your household received the questionnaire we mailed out last month." I know he has because there was a mailbox back at the highway and I confirmed the address.

The dude maintains his guard-dog stance. His blank look tells me he's contemplating whether he should bark some more or slip back inside with a macho slam of the door.

"Does that sound familiar?" I ask, trying to stimulate a response. Any response will do, so I can get to the canned spiel cleverly devised by government bureaucrats who have never personally been in such situations as these.

I'm now blithely ascending the steps in a manner that suggests I haven't noticed the Mossberg 590 in his hands. Never let a cornered animal smell your fear. Or, as my father used to say whenever I'd balk at some critter: *He's more afraid of you than you are of him.*

"Uh, I don't know," he says, the gun dropping limply to his side. "You'll have to ask my wife about that. She picks up the mail." I can almost see his tail tucking between his legs.

"Is she home?" I venture, knowing the answer before I ask. Of course she's home; the whole Rambo act is for her benefit. If she were gone he wouldn't have bothered to put down his beer to answer the door. He probably wouldn't even have been wearing pants.

"Honey!" he yells, sidling by me to the front door, pushing it open and ducking his head inside. "Darlene!"

A muffled female voice comes from somewhere beyond.

"Get out here, it's the Census guy."

More unintelligible vocalizations.

"I don't know! Just get out here!" Shooter stands aside and waits. He avoids eye contact, his duty done and the testosterone now ebbing.

Darlene swings the door fully open, drying her hands on a dishtowel. She shoots an annoyed glance at her husband before turning to me expectantly.

"Hi," I say, and repeat exactly what I told her guard dog a moment earlier.

"Didn't we do this already?" Darlene asks, sounding a touch annoyed. From all appearances she runs the household and has a lot to do at the moment. "I thought this was only once every ten years."

I explain to her, as I do to everyone I meet, that the Census Bureau has always done ongoing surveys, which, for some reason, they never seem to publicize. She checks my ID and looks skeptical until I give her the expensive glossy fact sheet that the government would rather not pay to distribute.

Ten minutes later I'm back in the Wrangler typing up my notes. *Personal visit. Completed interview w/*LOH. That's the "lady of the house." No mention of Shooter or his gun. Nobody cares what I went through to get the interview, as long as it's done. The bureaucrats will score one for me and move on. Despite Tea Party fears to the contrary, nobody's private property has been pillaged and burned. And no one has been arrested or thrown into a labor camp.

Not that crime doesn't figure prominently into my work. And no, I'm not committing them, I'm witnessing them. If anyone ever asks me though, I haven't seen a thing. That's because I'm sworn by the Federal Government to ignore what I see and hear. In fact, I could be fined up to $250,000 and spend five years in prison for reporting a crime.

Yep. Title 13 of the U.S. Code strictly forbids a Census field representative from divulging anything he learns about respondents during the course of executing his duties. You thought that rule only applied to priests and lawyers. But Title 13 confidentiality is sacrosanct in the Census Bureau.

What this means in real life application is that if I'm visiting your neighbor for a Census interview, and I happen to see you shoot his dog, I can report you—but if I see your neighbor shoot *your* dog, my lips are sealed, because I'm at his place on Census business. Same rule applies, by the way, if he's got you in his sights instead of your dog. Sorry, Bub. I'm not here.

Sounds crazy, I know. But the logic goes like this: no one will talk to Census workers if they think that what they say might get back to, oh, the IRS, their ex-wife's lawyer, or their parole officer. So, in exchange for the respondent's cooperation, the government promises not to rat them out. Even if they're Jeffrey Dahmer. Because getting Census data takes a much higher priority than body parts in the freezer. If you don't believe me, look up Title 13.

So yeah, I see a lot of shit in the course of my job that I keep to myself. Not my problem. It's just my job. A job I want to keep, even if it is part time without benefits. In this crappy economy I need every fucking cent I can earn. So I face down the guns and the dogs and the electrified fences, brazenly ignoring the "No Trespassing" and "No Solicitor" signs, and endure the idle threats of testosterone-oozing, self-styled sovereign citizens.

Title 13 also happens to prescribe the respondent's cooperation as well, not that any of them seem to care. And I value my life too much to remind anyone of this. The whopping $500 fine for failure to answer, if it were ever enforced—which it isn't—might sting someone who's struggling to get by, but it's never going to persuade an armed teabagger to cooperate with the Evil Empire that paves his roads, funds his children's education, and pays his mom's Medicare bills. No, if I'm going to get compliance, it's entirely up to me and my conversational skills.

Census work wasn't exactly my first choice of career. I was supposed to be a dot-com millionaire, but that bubble burst right about the time I graduated from Portland State with a useless degree in Computer Science. So I opted to extend my summer Census job until I found something more dignified. Here I am a decade later—at thirty-two—too old to compete with the latest crop of computer whizzes, even if there were jobs available. Computer skills have a shelf life of about eighteen months max.

Not that Census work doesn't have its advantages. I drag my ass out of bed at 9 a.m. I average only three hours of work a day. And I get paid to drive a thousand miles a month through four counties of scenic forests in the Oregon Cascades. What's to complain about? I love driving. Give me an open road and I'm happy. Unpaved ones into the outback are even more exciting. Even if they are unpredictable.

Title 2

MY LIFE HASN'T EXACTLY GONE AS I predicted either. And I don't just mean the career thing. I probably don't have to tell you, there's a woman involved. Isn't there always? This one was a girl, actually. I was in college at the time. And like all bartender-give-me-another-double sob stories, this one ends badly.

Beth and I met my junior year at Portland State University. It was a drizzly Saturday morning in the South Park Blocks and the Farmers' Market was in its second weekend of the season. I was there, not because I was health conscious, nor did I have a particular fondness for fresh vegetables, but because I heard it was a good place to pick up babes. Babes who *were* health conscious and therefore slim and trim. This was back before my beer belly would rat me out as a fraud.

"Excuse me, do you know what this is?" I asked the freckled redhead I'd been eyeing for the last half hour. Stalking, actually, though the crowds allowed me to mask my depravity. I was holding up what looked like the offspring of a beet and a Swiss chard: a purple bulb sprouting leaves all over.

"That's kohlrabi," she said with a smile like fire to my inner caveman. "It's a kind of cabbage."

"Whew!" I said in mock relief. "For a minute I thought it was Audrey 2."

She cocked her head and pursed her lips apologetically.

"Guess you're not a fan of *Little Shop of Horrors*," I said, feeling stupider than usual.

"No. It doesn't sound familiar."

I put down the kohlrabi; I didn't want her to feel threatened by it. The look on her face at that moment left room for doubt. I can't say I blamed her—I've kind of got an outer caveman, as well: I'm short, wide, and have a big head. And I'm one of those unfortunate guys who have to start shaving our faces from the collar line up—on a V-neck. Add thick, curly hair to the picture and I resemble an Airedale.

"I'm kinda new to this vegetable thing," I said, in an unscripted moment of candor, then added, to cover up my gaffe, "I mean, having so many choices. We don't have most of this...uh, these things where I come from."

"Where are you from?" she asked. It was too early to tell if she was interested or just being polite. That's always been a problem with Portland girls; they put up with a lot more shit than California girls, so it's hard to read the signals.

"California," I said, "but please don't hate me for it."

She sighed dramatically and did this little foot stomp thing that I would later come to love. "Why does everybody think we hate Californians? I mean, that gets so old!"

"Sorry," I said, cursing to myself, "I think it might have something to do with the bumper stickers that said *Don't Californicate Oregon*."

"Oh, so this is how we educate ourselves now? Bumper stickers?" Her sarcasm was tinged with humor, so I figured I'd go for broke.

"Well, if you don't hate Californians, how'd you like to get together next week for some kohlrabi and a movie—say, *Little Shop of Horrors?*"

She sized me up for a moment before replying. "Naw, thanks, but no."

My heart sank—I'd gone all-in and come up empty.

"Somehow I don't see you cooking exotic vegetables, and I sure as hell ain't gonna cook on a first date. What's your Plan B?"

And that was how it began.

Love at first sight? Maybe—if you believe in that shit. I just know that I spent every waking minute thinking about her for the next six months. And she couldn't get enough of me either. Friends—mostly hers—thought we were a mismatch: the coarse heathen with the foul mouth and the hippie-chick rebel from an evangelical Christian background. Most of my friends called us Fred & Wilma, as in Flintstone.

Those were easily the best six months of my life. Not only did I have more sex than in any six-month period before or since, but I loved waking up every day just to be with Beth. We would run away every chance we got, either to the coast, her favorite; or to the mountains, mine. It was only ninety minutes either way, so we ran away a lot. Sometimes we would study, but usually we'd just fuck.

Whoever tells you that doing it on the beach is romantic is full of shit. I got sand in orifices I didn't know I had and it chafed like a motherfucker, even after a shower. I much preferred it up on High Rock, with a view of Mt. Hood. We'd lie there on the precipice after a summer thundershower, amid the steaming stone, in a magical world all our own. It was enough to make me a romantic, if only for a few hours.

If I'd been a real caveman, that's when I would have dragged her back to my cave and made her fix dinner. And with her God-made-the-woman-for-the-man upbringing, she probably would have, too. Instead we'd go to Timberline Lodge for dinner and watch the sunset, or down to the Shack for Taco Tuesday. That's what was so awesome: it didn't really matter. We just loved being together.

This is where the movie script says she dies tragically in a skiing accident or something. In reality, it was nothing nearly that romantic. In fact, it was downright ugly. And I don't really feel like going into it; it's too fucking depressing. Suffice it to say that her parents discovered our relationship—God's Cherub cavorting with a Minion of Satan. They used everything in their arsenal to split us up, and they won.

The worst of it is, we were still in love. Let me tell you, it would have been a hell of a lot easier if we'd had some big, nasty blowout of a fight and vowed never to see each other again. This pining shit sucks.

Title 3

I TURN EAST OFF THE STATE HIGHWAY onto Elwood Road. Elwood's a pretty lonely place—not much more than a one-room schoolhouse, a pioneer church, and a cemetery. Unless it's Sunday or there's a wedding going on, you'd have a hard time finding a dozen people in one place. According to ALMI—the Automated Listing and Mapping Instrument—my destination today is at the farthest reaches of Elwood Road, where the pavement runs out and only logging trucks venture.

I double-check the listing on my computer. The "map spot" I'm seeking is the only residential entry in the entire Census block it occupies, sandwiched between two unnamed creeks and bounded by the Mt. Hood National Forest, miles from any other residential properties. It's got to be a mistake. There aren't even any services out that far: no phone or electricity. I barely get cell service here in Elwood, less than a mile off the highway. There can't be any at all where I'm headed. The only residence I can imagine there is a seasonal logger's trailer.

But hey, I get paid by the mile and I love the solitude. So I'm groovy. It's late summer, the soft top is peeled back, and Collective Soul's "Gel" blares from the stereo as I blow by the graveyard. I try whistling, but my lips are too chapped. I grab my big-ass Coke from the center console, take a swig, and downshift for the climb into the Cascades.

After about six miles the pavement becomes hard-pack with a thin dusting of gravel. It's been three days since the last thunderstorm and all but the deepest puddles have dried in the summer heat. I swerve breezily around the worst of the potholes, then, just for fun I start weaving the Wrangler randomly from side to side as I pound the steering wheel in time with the music.

I'm thinkin' I'm hot shit until a sleeper curve forces me to hit the brakes and my Coke erupts onto my government-issue keyboard while I slide into the curve. "Fuck!" I reach over to shove the PC out of the way of the deluge, but it slides off the seat, hits the floor, and slams shut with a *thwack*. And then I hear it. A sound that runs in the blood of every off-road driver in the Pacific Northwest: the air horn of a logging truck. It's coming right at me on the inside of the S-curve, where there's no shoulder and a fifty-foot drop into the forest beyond.

The law says the uphill driver on a single-track road has the right-of-way, but fuck that. This guy couldn't stop if he wanted to and I'm not pinning my hopes on a posthumous settlement. Besides, the Weyerhauser lawyers and their high-priced forensic teams would figure out I was the one who wasn't paying attention, so even when I'm dead the insurance money won't do anybody any good. My only hope is to get the fuck out of the way. *Now.*

I ditch the Jeep. Literally. I pop the clutch and crank hard right, throwing the vehicle into the three-foot ditch on the uphill side of the road. The transmission chokes out the engine and the Jeep continues up the opposite side of the ditch for a few more feet before seizing to a halt. I'm canted at a forty-five-degree angle. The Big Gulp, still in its cup holder, has poured its contents into my lap and the remnants drip into the fir needle carpet that is alarmingly close to my left cheek.

The logging rig sails by so close that the hair on my arms stands up and bits of fir bark pepper my face like buckshot. Instinctively I turn away, but not before a piece flies into my eye. For some reason it makes me think of the time in Kindergarten when Kenny Geraci threw tanbark in my face in the playground. It burns something fierce as I grope one-eyed in the back seat for a bottle of water. I finally release my seatbelt and climb over the seat to snag one. It takes a few minutes of flushing before my eye stops twitching.

By now the logger is long gone. I didn't expect him to stop and help. For one thing, he would have been at least a quarter-mile down the hill before he was able to bring the rig to a stop. And why would he want to hike back up the hill to coddle the asshole who nearly splattered himself across his grill? He's paid by the job, not the hour, so time is money.

I climb out of the Jeep and stand on shaky legs where only a moment before I was almost logged out of existence. I ponder my situation while I wait for my pulse to drop from the stratosphere. I notice something at my feet and bend down to investigate. It's what's left of the government-issue Garmin GPS that was once attached to my dash with Velcro, an apparent victim of five of the eighteen wheels that just passed by.

Fuck! is all I can think. Then I notice the PC. It's lying in the ditch under the driver's side door. I reach down and pick it up. With the exception of a couple of ugly scratches, it's intact. I'm glad now that it slammed shut moments before the wreck. I open it gingerly and breathe a sigh of relief when the blue log-in screen glows back at me.

I store the computer safely in its carrying case and turn my attention to the Jeep. I've managed to avoid colliding with any major trees, so the body is intact, if a bit scuffed up. Three wheels are on the ground, while the front right one hangs about a foot above it. The opposite rear tire has sunk into the mixture of duff and mud at the bottom of the ditch. Even with four-wheel-drive neither is likely to get much traction. I verify this assumption by jumping back into the driver's seat and firing her up. Sure enough, the one tire catches only air while the other flings mud and needles.

It's the winch that saves me. I extend the cable from the front bumper to the nearest tree and attach it, then fire up the motor. It takes a few tries and a few trees to get the Jeep back where it belongs, but forty-five minutes later I'm sufficiently chastened and back on the road at a slower speed, with more sedate Neil Young music playing. I now need the impending Happy Hour more than ever, though I've just delayed it by an hour. As soon as I confirm that the address I'm looking for is "Type C–Nonexistent," I'll be on my way back to the Safari Club in Estacada for some much-needed R-and-R.

The sixty-foot, second-growth Doug firs have closed in tight on both sides and I travel several more miles before there's any possible place to site a structure. Just before Milepost 15 the late-day sun begins to make inroads through the forest and I spot some clearing ahead. I slow as I pass through a recent clear-cut, but there are no signs of habitation. Finally I cross the first of the two creeks that define the boundary of the census block I'm looking for. Just fifty yards farther on, a road descends at an acute angle to the left. I don't need to consult the ALMI map to know I've found the right place. I swing onto the road and plunge back into the forest canopy.

The road winds around the top of the butte and I spot the wash of the second creek. Moments later my route is blocked by a gate. I roll to a stop, astounded. A typical rural gate in these parts consists of little more than a length of five-sixteenths–gauge chain strung across the road with a padlock. If there's livestock involved, then it's a swinging steel or wire-mesh gate. The accompanying fences are also usually made of wire on wood, not even barbed in most cases. Out here, even chain-link would be a luxury upgrade.

But what I'm looking at now are eight-foot–high, stuccoed walls. And protruding from the tops of them are some very nasty looking shards of glass. What the fuck? Somebody's really serious about security. Between the walls stretches a pair of equally high, electric-operated, wrought-iron gates. So much for there being no electricity out here; these folks must have their own. What the hell is this place?

I look around for some indication of who or what lies beyond the gate. I see no signs or nameplates, only an intercom box—just a button and a speaker, nothing more. I'll have to investigate further. The beer and strippers at the Safari Club are seeming farther away now. For a moment I consider heading back into town and calling it a day. I'm allowed two personal visits for each case, so I can always come back later when it's not so late and my mood is improved.

Then I remember the last ass-chewing from my team leader and I reconsider.

Title 4

I HATE THEM. YOU DO TOO. Those obnoxious telemarketing jerks who always call at dinnertime, disguising themselves as pollsters. They promise you a ten-minute survey that actually takes twenty because your answers don't fall among the multiple-choice options on their script. I usually end up hanging up on some sweet little minimum-wage worker who has a gun to her head, forced to ask all the questions, no matter what twisted answers I give her.

I know this because it also describes my own job. The first thing they teach you at the Senseless Bureau—and the one thing they repeat ad nauseum in every annual refresher training—is "Don't stray from the script. Read the questions verbatim." So, naturally, anyone with half a brain and the least bit of communication skills immediately strays from the script in real-world interviews.

I used to feel guilty about this. That is, until Angie Larsen, my team leader, accompanied me on a field observation designed to evaluate my performance. I was interviewing a mother of seven children. Of course, I was doing everything by the book so as to score a good review.

The questions dealt with handicaps:

Does Jane have any serious difficulty hearing? —No.

Does Jane have any serious difficulty seeing, even with glasses? — No.

Does Jane have any serious difficulty walking or climbing stairs? — No.

And so on for another five questions. Then I come to the next child: *Does Peter have any serious difficulty hearing?*

And on to the third child. The tedium of this is like nails on a chalkboard to me—and I honestly feel bad for the mother, who's trying to watch at least five of her seven while putting up with my questions—but I'm determined to read the questions verbatim.

Before I'm halfway through the third child, Angie can stand it no longer and interrupts. "She knows the questions! Just ask"—she turns to the woman—"Do any of the children have such difficulties?"

Way to go, Angie. Make me out to be the jerk for toeing the line.

The minute we're outside, Angie turns to me, "Listen, Big Guy"— she always calls me "Big Guy" and I hate it—"don't ever sit there and repeat all those questions like that! You're just asking her to show you the door."

"You think I don't know that?" I snap back at her in my own defense. "I was only doing it for your sake; reading 'as worded'!"

Well, that does it. I'm screwed. You don't contradict Angie, even if it's to tell her you know she's right. I go from "Big Guy" to "Mister" in two seconds flat—as in "Listen, Mister..." And I still have to drive her around for another two hours.

Angie, like all of my team leaders over the last decade, is a middle-aged empty-nester with dyed hair and a smoker's hack. She is easily the most difficult part of my job—right up there with the gun-toting "Type A" refusals. Only, the latter I never have to see again; Angie I have to check in with at least once a week. And it's always a crap shoot. On her good days she wants to dish the dirt on all the supervisors in the RO—the regional office. She loves to brag about the ones that she's able to manipulate and rant about the ones she refuses to deal with. My job is to agree with her—that, and ask her advice on doing things her way.

The idle chatter, I've learned, is Angie's way of co-opting me. Once she goads me into griping about a supervisor, she owns me. I'm her "Big Guy." We can shoot the shit for hours. But disagree with her and hellfire flares in her eyes. The caustic criticism comes in waves. She knows that I know that she's the one writing my performance reviews. Every deviation from the script and every dig at a supervisor is suddenly fair game for demerits.

So when I'm out in the field and find myself in questionable circumstances, I have to ask, WWAD?—What would Angie do? Because sure as shit, whatever I decide to do will be evaluated according to Angie's anything-but-uniform Code of Justice.

It is with this in mind that I roll the Jeep forward to the call box and press the button. This may, in fact, be a high-tech marijuana-grow operation, or something else illegal, but there's no way Angie would approve of my charging the bureau for two hours of wages and eighty miles of driving, just to wimp out and go home without making contact.

A youthful male voice answers. I have to strain to make it out.

"U.S. Census Bureau," I say into the box.

There's no answer.

I state my purpose. "I'm here for the American—" But the gates are already swinging open. "Thank you," I say to the box, determined to be as polite as hell. I watch the camera just beyond the gate swivel to follow me. It creeps me out.

For all the drama of the exterior, what's inside the walls is perfectly ordinary. About twenty acres of forest has been cleared; at least five have been planted with orchards, and another five with various other crops. As far as I can tell, there's no pot plantation. Of course, that could all be under grow lights in one or more of the clustered buildings I'm heading toward, about a quarter mile ahead at the bottom of the hill.

As I get closer I see what looks like a compound of residential buildings, almost identical in design. It resembles a barracks; I can't help but wonder what army is holed up here. Three white, wooden, two-story structures are stark and simple in design. They resemble traditional saltbox farmhouses—only larger—and all are of modern construction. The buildings and the grounds are immaculate, as if they were nothing more than a back-lot movie set.

Beyond the residences there's a large white barn, built in traditional style, and what appears to be a shop building as big as a commercial warehouse. The roof is laid with solar cells. This explains the electricity. I wonder if this is where the pot is kept. It's a natural question. What else would anyone with an operation this size be doing way out here with all this security? But if that's true, then why did they let me in? And where are the pit bulls?

I finally put my finger on what's so eerie about the place. There are no people. Farms don't run themselves. And a place this size is sure to employ a fair number of migrant workers. Yet I see no one as I arrive at the first house. This one differs from the rest only in the size of its covered porch and the landscaping in front. Behind a classic white picket fence lies a lush green lawn surrounded by rose bushes in full summer bloom. A large maple tree, about forty feet tall and several feet around at the trunk, shades one side of the yard. A cluster of white benches, perhaps a dozen or more, is arranged in rows facing the tree, as if ready for a meeting.

Besides a few odd pieces of farm equipment over between the shop and the barn, only one other vehicle is visible: an extended-length, white Econoline van, the kind they haul firefighters and road crews around in. It's parked next to the main house. I pull up beside it and park. Grabbing my computer bag, I check to make sure the ID card on the lanyard around my neck is facing outward, and pull out a business card before hopping out of the Jeep.

That's when I see him. A boy of nineteen or twenty, emerging from the shadow of the porch and loping toward me. He's tall, thin, and fairskinned, with a shock of dirty-blond hair sticking out from under a straw hat. I can't help but think of Tom Sawyer, all grown up.

"Hi there," I say, extending my business card. "Are you the man of the house?" I know he's not, but it sounds better and is less likely to offend than "Is your mom or dad home?" Besides, teenagers are flattered by the question and it usually makes them more likely to cooperate.

"Nick Prince, Field Representative," the boy reads from the card. He looks at me with alarm. "Wait. You aren't the septic guy?"

U.S. Septic Bureau. I kinda like that. On most days I put up with enough shit to make it an apt description. I think this, but don't say it. Instead I say, "No. The Census Bureau; it's part of the Department of Commerce—you know, the Federal Government?"

Tom Sawyer's eyes are suddenly wider now. He gives frantic looks over each shoulder. "Government? Uh, no," he stammers, "you— you shouldn't be here. I— I mean— Can you just go now?" He gives me an imploring look. "Please?" He's beginning to panic.

"OK, fine," I say, wondering how much pot they grow here. "If you give me a phone number, I can call instead of coming back." This is the devil's deal I offer everyone who tries to give me the bum's rush. It's a thinly veiled threat: give up those sacred ten digits, or I'll be forced to come back.

"I— I can't do that," he says with pleading eyes. "Please go." He looks back up the road like he's expecting to be arrested at any moment.

"All right. No problem," I say, climbing into the Jeep. "Can you tell me when I can find the man of the house at home?"

"He won't want to see you," the boy says nervously, again looking up the road. There's genuine fear on his face now.

"Well," I say, pulling another standard arrow out of my quiver, "I'm required by law to make contact. So please give him this and tell him I'll be back tomorrow." I hand him an informational brochure.

When this threat of a return visit fails to produce a phone number, I thank him and make my exit. I'm almost to the gate when it begins to open. I'm not sure whether there's a buried sensor or there's someone behind that creepy camera monitoring my position. In any case, I'm happy to get out of there and I'm already salivating over the coming beer and strippers.

But as the gates reach their full-open positions and I'm making my escape, two white vans, identical to the one I saw at the house, approach from the opposite direction. I pull over to let them by, wondering if I should turn back. Chances are good there's an adult in one of them that can complete the interview—or give me a firm refusal—and I won't have to come back.

The first van slows as it passes. The driver is an adult male, about 60, with a full, salt-and-pepper beard and no mustache—clearly the Papa Bear of the clan. He scowls at me so hard I expect to burst into flame. Then he guns the engine and shoots through the gate. The second van, right on his tail, is piloted by a kid about Tom Sawyer's age. He glances quickly at me but does not hesitate.

As he passes, I notice his passengers: nearly a dozen girls and women of varying ages, all with bonneted heads. Then it hits me. This must be an Amish community! *No, wait. The Amish don't drive. Mennonite! That's it!* No marijuana after all. And definitely no guns. I know this because I used to date a girl who was Mennonite. She was disowned by her family when she enlisted in the Air Force, because her religion detests violence. I spin the wheel and gun the engine; with a spray of dirt I pull the Wrangler back through the gates just as they begin to close.

Our procession reaches the main house, where the nervous boy stands stiffly in the same place I left him moments earlier. The first van pulls to a stop beside him, while the second goes around it and disappears among the other buildings out back. I pull up and park a respectable distance behind the van. I hop out of the Jeep and approach the driver. I want to introduce myself quickly to dispel any suspicions he may harbor.

But Papa Bear jumps out of the van and only looks at me long enough to shoot daggers before turning to Tom Sawyer. He's sharing some angry words, unintelligible from my distance. With a look of near terror, the boy stretches my brochure toward the man, who snatches it and turns back in my direction. He scans it only briefly as he marches toward me.

"Hi," I begin, "My name is Nick—"

"I know who you are," Papa Bear growls, "and we don't want you here." He shoves the now-crumpled paper toward me. "This is private property and I want you off it!" His voice is taut, barely under control, as he points up toward the gate.

"Fine," I say, nodding compliantly as I jump back into the Jeep. "I know you must be busy. We can do this by phone if you prefer."

"I prefer," he spits, lingering on the word, "that you get your ass off my property!"

"Sure," I say with a sunny grin. *Refusal letter*, I'm saying to myself, mentally writing up the notes on the visit. Since the Census Bureau never takes just one *No* for an answer, a letter will be FedExed to help Papa Bear "better understand" the importance of the survey. It will even mention the penalty imposed by Title 13, just to impress him. Then I'll be sent back to try again when things are clearer to him. *Right.*

I'm ascending the road back to the gate when I glance in the mirror. Papa Bear is in Tom Sawyer's face again. The boy is shrinking away from him. Then it comes. A backhand across the face so hard that I hear the *thwack* above the growl of the Jeep's engine. So much for Mennonite nonviolence. Instinctively I brake. I want to go back and put a stop to it. But, hey, I'm sworn not to notice, so I force myself to drive on.

The boy does not flee his assailant, nor does he strike back. Instead, he stands ramrod stiff as a second blow comes and knocks him to the ground. It wrenches my gut, but I still don't stop. The last image burned into my mind as the gates close behind me is that of Papa Bear astride Tom Sawyer, beating the living crap out of him. My appetite for beer and strippers has been obliterated. I wish to hell I could send a warrant instead of a refusal letter.

Title 5

"HEY, BIG GUY. HOWZIT GOIN'?"

It's my Monday morning phone call to Angina. I'm not sure what Angie's short for, but I've chosen to think of her as Angina because Merriam-Webster defines the word as "a disease marked by spasmodic attacks of intense suffocative pain," a fitting description of my symptoms when dealing with my team leader.

"I see you're seventy-three percent complete. Good job!"

She is not congratulating me; she is patronizing me. We both know that anything less than 92.1 percent of interviews completed by next week scores a "Level 1," the equivalent of "fail" on a five-level scale that is just one of the many absurdities of government bureaucracy. Of the 100 million or so American households, slightly more than 5 percent refuse the Census interview. So, the bureaucrats reason, if I have a 5.2-percent refusal rate, I'm a C-student.

What they fail to consider is that statistics are like physics: when you go from big to really small the rules need to change for it to make any sense. Which means this: since I get about twelve cases each month, just one slammed door leaves me at 91.5 percent completed—a failing grade. But nobody's going to give me any sympathy over this, Angie least of all.

"So, do you need my help with any of your outstanding cases?" she asks.

Yeah, bring some amply exposed cleavage out to Papa Bear's place and try the "Big Guy" routine on him. I'm sure it'll help. This is what

I'm thinking. What I actually say is, "No. I got it covered. I've got one refusal so far and I had the letter FedExed this morning."

"OK," she says, disappointed that I didn't need her help with that, "but have you checked with the tax assessor yet?"

"Roger that. The property is registered to Restoration Ministries. It's listed as a 'Seasonal Camp: Religious.' The tax bill goes to a P.O. box in Colton."

"Well, did you mail a letter there?"

Here we go. She's got to find something to correct, even if it makes no sense.

"Why would I do that? The FedEx goes directly to the respondent's door; he'll get it today. Mail would take two to three days, and we have no idea how often he gets into town to check the box." I don't hide my exasperation well, nor am I really trying.

"Don't get testy with me, Mister. Just have the letter sent."

"Fine."

"But you'd better hurry and call the RO. It's already 10:30 and they stop processing requests at 11."

If I can get you off the damn phone. I think this but don't say it.

Before I can think of something else to say, Angie adds, "Oh, I almost forgot. You've got an observation coming up next week. Let me look at the calendar."

Just shoot me now. I'm not ready to spend another six hours in the outback with this chain-smoking shrew.

"How about this Saturday, 9 a.m.?"

"You know, people like to sleep in on the weekend," I protest. This might be true, though it's only myself I'm thinking of at the moment. "Wouldn't afternoon be better?"

"Listen, Big Guy," she says, "I've got to drive from the West Hills, and I want to be back at a decent hour. Besides, all I need to see are two complete interviews."

So much for the spirit of the law. This is typical of Angie's passive-aggressive relationship with the Census Bureau rules. She's supposed to spend eight hours with me: two counseling me, and six observing my technique. But she only has to write up two interviews, and she'll do the "counseling" while we drive, cutting at least two hours from her schedule. That's fine with me. I just wish it weren't so damn early.

We confirm the date and a place to meet. It's ten to eleven when we hang up. I'm so exhausted from biting my tongue that I figure it's time for a long, hot shower, where the phone can't reach me. I forget all about the eleven o'clock letter-request deadline. But it doesn't matter. Papa Bear is not going to change his mind, no matter how many letters he gets. I figure I'm just going to have to eat a Type A refusal on that one. I'll still claim the mileage for a second visit though.

✳   ✳   ✳

It's 2:15 a.m. when Flight of the Bumble Bee shocks me from an erotic dream which, as usual, involves Beth. It's my cell. *Who the fuck?* Instinctively I grope for it. But without my contacts I can't read the caller ID, and I don't remember where my glasses are. I check the display anyway. Even without discerning individual digits, I can tell that it's not a phone number; it says "Private."

Fuck that. If you can't bother to tell me who you are, then I'm sure as hell not going to chat with you at 2 a.m. I don't care if it *is* an emergency. You can bleed until the sun comes up.

I switch the phone off and toss it on the floor. Within sixty seconds I'm dreaming again.

✳   ✳   ✳

I've already showered, had breakfast, and done my social networking before I remember to check voicemail. Sure enough, there's a message logged at 2:18 a.m. I punch ✳ to listen. There's some rustling and the sound of breathing before anyone speaks. *We got your letter,* the male voice says. *Please come today at 6 p.m.* More rustling. *You know, Elwood.*

That's it; the message ends. I punch 4 to replay it. I'm pretty sure it's Tom Sawyer. Or maybe the guy I saw in the second van; the voice is definitely too young to be Papa Bear.

Wow. I sure wasn't expecting a callback on that one. But why the fuck was it at 2 a.m.? The place still freaks me out, but if there's any chance I can get at least a "sufficient partial" interview, I'm sure not going to pass up the chance. I just wish the appointment weren't smack in the middle of Happy Hour again.

Title 6

PARKING IS ALREADY GETTING SCARCE in front of the Safari Club as I cruise by on my way to pick up the Molalla Highway. I can almost taste the Pabst that I'm not drinking there with the buddies I know only in the context of the bar. But I console myself with thoughts of the half-pound Viking Bacon Cheeseburger I'm going to have later at Fearless Brewing up the street when I get back from Elwood. I'm not a big fan of their fancy microbrews, but for a buck-fifty per pint, I'll drink just about anything.

For now I'm headed back to the Bible camp, or whatever the hell that place is. Today Chris Isaak's rocking out at high volume as I cross the Clackamas River and head south. I check my watch. I'm running a little late, but I might make it by six if I don't tangle with any more log trucks on the way. Once I'm beyond the Estacada speed zone, my foot gets heavy. The cool forest air splashes my face like a strong after-shave as the wind competes with the stereo. *Baby did a bad, bad thing...*

I roll up to the Pearly Gates at one minute past six. Everything looks as it did before. This time I'm aware of the camera pointed at me as I push the red intercom button. I check my face in the mirror, fiddle with the lanyard, and adjust the U.S. Census placard in the front window. I wait for a good two minutes before pushing the button again, wondering whether this is all in vain. I'm still puzzled by the middle-of-the-night call. Then the gates begin their slow traverse.

I roll into the compound at a respectful speed, careful not to raise dust on the now-dry dirt track. Anything I can do to put Papa Bear in a better mood than last time. The gates meet again behind me as I drop down toward the main house. Then I see him. Tom Sawyer is jogging up the road toward me. He's already covered 150 yards, his skinny, gangly arms and legs flapping comically.

Now what? We meet about two-thirds the way down the hill. I brake as I pull up alongside him. He surprises me by running to the passenger side and swinging himself up into the seat, from which I snatch away the PC just in time.

"Turn around!" he says hoarsely between gasps of breath.

"What?"

"Go!" he commands with more urgency. "Get out of here! Now!"

"But..." I begin, still paralyzed by confusion. Then I see the van. It's just kicked up a red cloud of dust as it jolts from its parking spot in front of the main house. Within a second it's racing up the road toward us. Without pausing to consider what the meaning of all this could be, I jerk the Jeep into reverse, and then into first as I execute a three-point turn, kicking up my own cloud as I race back toward the gates.

"Do you mind telling—" I begin again, but the kid cuts me off.

"Not now," he says with an authority that belies his yup-yup farmboy looks. "Just go." He holds up a remote and points it toward the gates, which once again swing outward.

I'm speeding toward the opening at a clip that will get us there before the process is complete, calculating how much I need to slow down. But when we reach the point of no return, I keep my foot to the floor, based more on faith than mathematics. With mere inches to spare we sail through unscathed. The kid's already clicking the remote over his shoulder and the gates reverse their course.

The van has closed to under a hundred yards but, apparently without a remote of its own—it occurs to me that the kid must have taken this one from the van before making his escape—the driver is forced to

slow to a stop and trigger the gate manually. I have the sneaking suspicion that all this can only end badly, but I've got to give the kid props
for the flawless execution of a clever plan.

So far, anyway. I have no clue what comes next. "Listen," I try a
third time, "can we—"

"Go-Go-Go!" Tom shouts, never taking his eyes off the van, which
by now is attempting to nose through the nearly open gates.

A moment later we're at the main road and I'm about to swing a
right toward town.

"That way," he barks, throwing an arm in front of my face. The terror on his face reminds me of my first visit to the compound. This kid's
seriously scared. By now, I'm wondering if I should be too.

Against my better judgment I follow his directions and career onto
the gravel of Elwood Road, deeper into the National Forest. When my
dust-wake settles, I estimate that the van is about five hundred yards
behind us. I balance this reality with the still-fresh memory of the
near-miss with the Weyerhauser rig days earlier; I'm clearly pushing
the limit of safety again as I negotiate the blind curves.

I've given up getting anything out of the kid for the moment, and
we speed on in tense silence, his gaze unbroken to the rear, and mine
alternating between the mirror and the road ahead. I'm thankful I
started with a full tank of gas today, and I wonder if Papa Bear—I
assume he's the one pursuing us—is similarly prepared. Will our fate
come down to the respective fuel ranges of our vehicles? I can't know.
But I take comfort in the fact that the Wrangler gets better mileage
and handles better than the rear-heavy Econoline behind us.

A rush of adrenalin shoots through my veins, making my extremities tingle. *God I love this fir-scented air!*

Title 7

OK, I LIED. SO SUE ME. TRUTH IS, I *have* committed a felony. Just one, mind you, but I'm marked for life because of it. I can't even leave the state without reporting my whereabouts. If you Google Nicholas J. Prince, one of the resulting links takes you to the Oregon Sex Offenders Database. Yeah, officially I'm a perv.

But, wait. Hear me out. You might even be one too, and not even know it. I just happened to be unlucky enough to have well-connected enemies with a grudge. As I said, Beth's parents didn't take kindly to my dating their daughter. As far as they knew, it was *only* dating, as defined in whatever fucked-up Nineteenth Century guide to etiquette they were using. Beth had told them that she was still a virgin and that we never spent the night together. This last part was true actually, since we both had roommates. But it also conveniently implied that there were no other opportunities for conjugal bliss, like High Rock and Crescent Beach.

Still, that didn't keep her parents from interfering in our relationship. Like inviting Beth out to Damascus every Sunday for church. "I have to say yes once in a while," she'd tell me. And then, when she would go, they'd find some excuse to keep her there all day. I was never invited, even if I promised to convert—which I'm ashamed to say I did more than once. Hell, I would have done anything for Beth, I was that into her.

I felt that way even after I found out she'd lied to me. When we met she told me she was 18. But she was only 17, a graduate of an accelerated high school program for "gifted" students. To be honest, that little detail probably wouldn't have changed my mind anyway. So I didn't blame her the day two vice cops busted into my apartment and slapped the cuffs on me: statutory rape. I was 22.

Like this stuff doesn't go on every day on campuses all over the country. Thousands of couples straddle the cusp of legal adulthood for a few months or years at any given time. Seniors graduate from high school leaving behind underage boyfriends and girlfriends. So for a year or two they're all statutory rapists, and nobody prosecutes.

I owe *my* arrest to the private investigator Beth's parents hired. A guy from their Evangelical congregation whose business card—I shit you not—said he specialized in matters of "chastity and fidelity." God's own sex police. The dick even followed us to Ecola State Park and took pictures of us going at it on the beach.

I spent 30 days in the county jail because I couldn't make bail. My dad had Alzheimer's at the time, so I wasn't about to hit my mom up for a loan. In fact, I didn't even tell her why I dropped out of school for a term. None of the people I hung out with had bail money just lying around, and my brother was off in Afghanistan. So I sat it out.

The upside—if you can call it that—was that I was able to work out a plea-bargain: I pleaded guilty, was convicted, and released on time served. The downside of the bargain: my probation required that I never see Beth again. That Devil's Deal haunts me to this day. I'd do five years hard labor for her, if I could take it all back. Hell, I'd even do Census work for the rest of my life—with Angie as my team leader.

So I finished out my last term, graduated, and moved thirty miles to Sandy, out in Clackamas County. My stated reason for this choice was to be closer to the slopes in winter. Privately, I hoped I might run into Beth. My house sits at the trailhead of the Bull Run Trail, her favorite place to hike. It hasn't happened yet. I don't even know if she's still in the state. But being there reminds me of her.

In any case, Sandy suits me fine; thirty minutes to Portland and thirty to the slopes of Mt. Hood. If you want my exact address, just look it up in the Oregon sex offender database.

Title 8

IT'S BEEN THIRTY MINUTES OR MORE since we've seen any sign of Papa Bear's van. I'm thinking he's given up. Whatever Tom Sawyer has done to piss him off, the old man probably figured he had better things to do than play tag in the wilderness. In fact, I'm thinking the same thing about now. Burger and beer. That's more like it.

But for some reason, I'm still driving deeper into the Cascades. By now Elwood Road has become Benzinger Road, then Jackson Lake Road, then 5-4E-18.2 Road, then Wherethefuckarewe Road. I'm sure we're lost, but the kid insists he knows where we are. Says his family comes out here all the time to hunt mushrooms. What a happy outing that must be. From the looks of the cuts and bruises on his face, I'm picturing a chain gang.

I finally decide to broach the subject. "Does he do that to you often?" I ask, nodding at the shiner under his left eye.

The kid looks away. "Only when I resist."

Jesus. I'm not sure I want to go there, so I steer in another direction. "He your father?"

"Stepfather."

"How long you been with him?"

"He took my mother when I was eight."

"Took? You mean, like kidnapped?" This may get ugly after all.

"Took her to wife," the kid says.

"Oh." I guess this is how they talk in these religious cults. "You got brothers and sisters?"

The kid looks at me as though he can't believe what he's hearing. He looks away again before answering. "Twenty-four."

I almost drive off the road. "Are you shitting me?" I ask, returning the look that he just gave me. "Twenty-four—no, *twenty-five* kids?"

The kid shrugs and mumbles, "Yeah."

"Christ on a bike!"

The kid jerks his head in my direction as though he's just realized I'm the Devil. It occurs to me he's not accustomed to hearing the Lord's name in vain. "Oops. Sorry," I say. "But twenty-five kids? Your mother must have been pregnant non-stop in her childbearing years."

"No," the kid says with annoyance, like, *Are you an idiot?* "They're not all hers. Some are from the sister-wives."

This shit is getting weirder by the minute. "Sister-wives?"

"Father John's other wives," he says with impatience.

A light goes on. "Oh, you mean, like, polygamy?"

"That's what you Gentiles call it. But it's just the Principle."

Principally disturbing. Who knew we had polygamists in Clackamas County? I thought that shit only went down in Utah and Arizona. "Principle of what?" I venture.

"Of Celestial Marriage. It was revealed to Joseph Smith back in—"

"Joseph Smith!? You mean you guys aren't Mennonites?"

"Mennonites? No. We're a Restoration Community. We believe in the Book of Mormon."

Mormons. Well that explains a lot—like the number of wives and kids, for starters.

I'm still taking all this in when the kid tells me to turn left. I do, and then he says, "Now watch for another quick left just up here. Forest Road 4510. That'll take us back to Estacada on Hillockburn Road."

And then what? I wonder as I make the second turn—directly into an active logging operation.

If you're like most people, you probably think the U.S. Forest Service exists to provide you and your family a place to camp and hike and hunt mushrooms in the summer. Like the Federal Government spends millions of dollars each year building and maintaining thousands of miles of roads through the nation's forests as part of a taxpayer-funded outdoor playground.

Hardly. The primary purpose of the USFS is to manage the sale of our country's natural resources—primarily its timber, but also its minerals. We The People are not its primary customer; the multibillion-dollar timber products industry is. And it's a real cash cow.

The vast majority of timber in this country is on Federal land, but it's not the government that gets rich off it. As with most of our nation's natural resources—oil, minerals, airwaves—timber is handed over to private-industry profit-makers, and at the same time generously subsidized by taxpayers in the form of infrastructure, such as roads, bridges, and fire mitigation.

Not that we aren't all happy to buy those timber products when they come our way, paying for what was already ours to begin with. Chances are you live in a wood-framed house, with wooden shingles, a wooden deck, and plenty of wooden furniture. And it's probably all neatly contained inside a wooden fence.

But it all starts with trees. Felled trees like the ones blocking our path right now. Logging takes precedence over everything else in these parts. It doesn't matter what the map says; if an active logging operation needs to turn a road into a sawmill or a staging area, tough noogies. You've got to find another way around or, if work has shut down for the day, pick your way through it.

Which is what we're about to do. It's after eight already and the crew is long gone. Odds are good that with the Jeep I can find a way through the tangle of eighty- to hundred-foot logs that lie every which way across what used to be Road 4510. The problem is, some of them are six or eight feet in diameter, so I can't see beyond the first few.

With the summer sun already low in the sky, I enter the maze cautiously, winding around the first of the downed trees. Even though the weather's been dry for days, the ground is muddy and soft in places. Workers routinely spray down the jobsite to minimize both the dust and the chance that sparks from the equipment might ignite a wildfire. In places, splinters of wood—some as big as small trees themselves—protrude from the mud at all angles, making the going treacherous, even for the Jeep. I proceed gingerly. This is not the time and place I want to be changing a tire.

It's after 8:30 by the time I spot the road again, emerging unobstructed just a hundred yards to the north of our position. My problem is the hundred-foot fir that lies between us and freedom. The way I figure it, I can drive eighty feet to the left, farther into the sticky mess of the operation, and circumvent the top end; or I can go twenty feet to the right, to the edge of the intact forest—where the trunk still rests on its base. I choose the latter. It'll be bumpier, and I'll probably scratch up the Jeep on a few small trees. But hey, it's a Jeep.

I pop the clutch and roll over a low berm of debris toward the base of the fallen tree. We make it to the stump, itself about twenty feet across when you count the exposed root structure. The way around it is clear of all but a few saplings, which I figure won't give us any problems. But the slope on the backside is greater than I realized. For a moment I consider going back, but rule it out due to the fading light.

"Hold on," I tell the kid, and ease the Jeep into the turn around the stump. A moment later the uphill wheels are beginning to lose traction due to the slope, and then the downhill wheels are spinning as well. I gun the engine and shoot farther around, now about 135 degrees through the turn. But that's as far as I can go. The combination of the angle and the large pieces of debris under the Jeep is preventing the front tires from making solid contact with the ground.

It's time for the winch. I've used the damn thing only half a dozen times in five years, and now twice in one week. I tell the kid to get out and grab the hook-end while I feed the cable out to him. I point to the tree we'll be wrapping it around and describe how to secure it. Then I fire up the winch. With a steady, reassuring whine, the cable plays out and the kid makes his way up the hill with it.

Then, with a loud crack, the Jeep shifts and slides a few feet downslope. The force of this jerks the kid to the ground with a grunt and a cry of pain. He's still holding the hook. "Let go!" I tell him, as I scramble to his side to see how badly he's hurt. "Are you OK? Let me see."

He lifts his head and lolls onto his side. His face was already so bruised I'm having a hard time telling if there are any new injuries. His arms are bleeding in a few places, but nothing looks like it'll need stitches. "Anything broken?" I ask, examining his legs. He slowly flexes both of them and I conclude they're intact.

The kid sits up and I offer a hand to pull him to his feet. Just then a cacophony of creaks and cracks erupts, and the Jeep begins a slow motion slide down the cleared slope. We watch in stunned silence until it finally comes to rest on its side on the road grade about a hundred feet below.

"Huh," I say, still staring numbly at the Wrangler. After a moment I turn to the kid. "It looks like we're going to be spending the night together. And I don't even know your name."

"Tom," he says.

"Huh," I say again, and look back at the Jeep.

Title 9

IT WAS THE SUMMER AFTER GRADUATION when I began working for the Census Bureau. Don't ask me why they hired a convicted sex offender. Maybe they didn't know. After all, I myself tell skeptical respondents every day: *The Census Bureau does not share any personal data with any other government agency, not even law enforcement or the IRS.* Maybe law enforcement doesn't share with the Census Bureau either. Or maybe they were just desperate, since ninety percent of applicants can't pass the Civil Service test: you know, things like finding yourself on a map, or alphabetizing a list of names. I've heard it said that the bureau will hire anyone who can manage to score a passing grade, no matter what kind of freaks they are.

In any case, once I was hired I was always careful not to raise any cause for concern. I made sure that when I knocked on a door and a woman answered, I stayed outside unless her husband was home. If not, I'd arrange to come back when he was. I wouldn't even ask for a phone number. If there was no GOH—gentleman of the house—I'd complete the interview while sitting or standing on the porch. The last thing I needed was an accusation of impropriety, which would undoubtedly raise the issue of my earlier conviction.

Despite such precautions however, I sometimes adopted a more pragmatic approach to interviewing, one that overrides all other methodologies: *The respondent is always right. Give 'em whatever they want if it'll get you the interview.* I've chased down escaped dogs, held crying babies, even stirred somebody's dinner on the stove while waiting for a respondent to settle in and prepare to answer my questions. And I've even broken the hard and fast rule against discussing partisan politics while on the job, learning to agree with any point of view—no matter how distasteful—if it would make the respondent my buddy for fifteen minutes.

So it should come as no surprise that when Mrs. X—remember, $250,000 and five years if I tell you her real name—insisted that I come in and make myself at home, I did as she asked. And you can't accuse me of any lurid intentions either; I hadn't even seen her yet when I acceded to her request. She simply called to me through an open bathroom window, "Go ahead and let yourself in; I'll be right with you."

Choosing pragmatism over caution, I step into the living room and take a seat on the couch. The home, situated on a one-acre view lot atop Scouters' Mountain in Happy Valley, is solidly upper middle class. Easily 4,000-plus square feet. The two-story windows in the great room offer views of five Cascade peaks: Rainier, St. Helens, and Adams to the north, Mt. Hood to the east, and Mt. Jefferson to the southeast. Hood and St. Helens seem close enough to touch. I wonder—and will soon find out in the interview—what these people do for a living.

I wait for at least five minutes before I notice that the furry white pillow at the other end of the sofa is moving. It turns out to be a cat, apparently unfazed by the idea of sharing its bed with a stranger. It crosses my mind that maybe I'm not the first strange man to sit here. I reach out my hand and make kissing noises—the kind you call a cat with—to see if it wants to be petted. It lifts its head, considering my advances, but remains undecided. "Kitty, kitty, kitty," I coax.

"You like my pussy?" The voice comes from behind me.

I withdraw my hand as quickly as if I'd been caught reaching for what she's implied. Her question, of course, is unanswerable in any polite fashion, and I instantly feel my face flush. "Uh, hello. I'm Nick

Prince," I say, jumping to my feet and turning to face her. "Here's my... uh—" My breath catches in my throat and I drop the business card I'm about to offer her, thankful that it gives me an excuse to look away as I retrieve it from the floor. Yet when I straighten up, she's standing even closer.

She's in her mid-to-late thirties, about five-foot-four, with bobbed chestnut hair that dips just below her ears. She's wearing little make-up and, to tell the truth, her buttercream skin doesn't require it. And there's a *lot* of buttercream showing on this little cupcake. A sheer, champagne-colored bathrobe—if you could call it that—cascades from her shoulders, underneath which she's barely wearing a black negligee straight out of the Victoria's Secret catalog. (I know this because I look at it often.) Her hands are behind her back, fiddling with a clasp or something, which has the effect of thrusting her tits unnervingly close to my face.

"I'm sorry to make you wait, but I was just getting out of the bath," she says, as though strange men are always waiting for her on such occasions.

"Uh, no problem," I say as I back toward the door. "We can always do this by phone whenever—"

"Nonsense!" she says, cutting me off. "Come. Help me hook this, will you?" She turns her back to me and lets the silky thing fall to the floor. She also lets go of the negligée's straps, which immediately fall to her sides. "Most of them are no trouble, but this one—my husband's favorite—is always a little tricky."

Yikes. Husband? I freeze. "Uh, really, I have no problem coming back later when your husband's home," I offer, lowering the computer bag to cover my raging boner.

"No, no," she insists. "We have to do this now. He won't be home until late tonight, then we're leaving for Hawaii tomorrow. Now just help me with this and we can get started."

She makes it clear that this is my one and only chance to get the interview, so what choice do I have? Like I said, whatever it takes. Being sure to keep the laptop between me and her, I approach on eggshells and gingerly snag the ends of both straps. A light floral and citrus scent fills my nostrils as I pull them together and quickly hook them. Instantly I step back to a safer position.

"Thank you so much," she oozes, turning back to face me. "I'd have been here all afternoon wrestling with that if you hadn't shown up when you did." She gives me a smile that, coming from a single woman, in other circumstances, would be a big green light. From her, on the other hand, it sets off sirens.

"No problem," I lie. "This'll just take five minutes, I promise. If I can sit here, I'll get started." I start back to the sofa, where her feline pussy commands less attention.

"Oh, no. I have to continue getting ready," she demurs. "I'd really appreciate it if you could come ask me the questions while I'm getting dressed." She says this without even a hint of a question in her voice. In fact, she's already disappearing through the double doors that lead to the master suite.

With my heart racing, I follow, keeping my eyes focused on the PC screen in front of me. "So, let me begin by verifying that I have your address listed correctly," I begin as we walk. I will prove no match for what lies ahead.

Suffice it to say, I went to the greatest lengths possible to assure that I left that home with a completed interview. And I'm not allowed to divulge anything I learned there, so don't even ask.

Title 10

WE'VE SCRAMBLED DOWN TO THE BOTTOM of the ravine, righted the Jeep, and winched it out onto a level spot in the road. Which road, we're not sure. Tom thinks it might be FR 45. I pull out the PC to look it up in ALMI. Darkness is already setting in. It may be summer, but up here it still gets damn cold at night.

The Jeep will run, but it lost both headlights on its way down the slope. I know that any route out of here will be circuitous and unpaved; not something I want to undertake in the darkness of the forest canopy without headlights. It's very easy to get lost on Forest Service roads. Trust me. I've done it many times.

ALMI is not known for its accuracy, especially in barely inhabited areas such as this. The Census Bureau counts people, not trees, so no one much cares if the wilderness maps are up to date. And with logging operations constantly altering the landscape—and the roads—it's a sure bet that not every route on the screen in front of me actually exists. The mapping software, like everything else about my work, is covered by Title 13's confidentiality requirements, because it contains map spots that identify the locations of actual houses. I'm not supposed to let anyone without a "need to know"—including Tom—see it. Right.

Well, screw that. I have a need for him to see it; that's good enough for me. Besides, if the Census Bureau ever expects to see this laptop again, they need Tom's expertise as much as I do at the moment.

"I'm pretty sure this is Road 45," Tom says, pointing to the spot we've identified as our most likely location. This is good, since two-digit numbers indicate trunk routes that carry more traffic and are usually kept in better condition. Tom traces his finger northwestward along the road as I scroll up the map. "There. See?" he says, "Here's where it becomes Hillockburn Road, which will take us into Estacada." The mention of Estacada makes my stomach growl with thoughts of that Viking burger I won't be eating tonight.

With our morning route planned, I begin to pull what we'll need for the night out of the utility box on the Jeep. This isn't the first time I've tangled with the Oregon outback; I learned long ago to be prepared for any eventuality. "Know how to set this up?" I ask the kid as I toss him the pup tent.

"I can figure it out," he says, already untying it.

"Good. We'll camp in the road beside the Jeep. It's level, dry, and there are fewer creepy-crawlies there." While Tom sets up the tent, I gather wood and get a fire going. Once we've finished our dinner of crackers, tuna, and Velveeta, plus a few strips of salmon jerky from my survival kit, I get down to business.

"OK," I say. "Now you're going to tell me what the hell is going on. Why the hell are we here?"

He continues staring at the fire, but says nothing. Minutes pass. I'm starting to get pissed off now. "I swear, if you don't start talking, I'm leaving without you in the morning." I mean it, too. I've had it with this shit.

He turns to speak and I see little reflections of firelight dancing in the tears on his cheek. "I couldn't stay there another day," he says. "He's a monster."

"I can see that," I tell him, indicating his shiner.

"Oh, no. It's much worse than that," he says as he gets to his feet. He turns his back to me and pulls his hoodie and shirt up over his head.

I gasp involuntarily. The entire length of his back is red, blue, and purple with welts and bruises. "*Holy shit.*"

"I won't take it anymore," he says, lowering his shirt. "It's not so much what he does to me—it's how he treats *them* that raises the hellfire in me."

"The other kids?"

"My mother and the sister-wives," he says. "He doesn't hit the kids because they're his. But it's sinful how he treats the women!" He's getting worked up now. "There's no way God will forgive him for that," he says, shaking his head. "And I won't either," he adds with a sudden fierceness I wouldn't have expected from him.

"Jesus," I say, "Why haven't you reported him to the police?"

The kid gives me that WTF look again. "Don't you get it? It's only us there. There's no 'police.' We're set apart. Very few Gentiles ever come inside."

"Why do you keep calling us Gentiles?" I finally have to ask. "What, like you're Jews or something?"

"We're adopted into the House of Israel," he says, "into the Tribe of Joseph, through Ephraim."

This is some weird shit, but I decide to let it go. After seeing what Papa Bear's done to him, I can cut him a lot of slack. "So, you think he'll come after you?"

Tom nods. "There's no question. He won't ever stop looking for me. We've taken a blood oath to protect our secrets."

Like their own Title 13, I guess.

"He'll kill me if he finds me," Tom adds.

"Jesus. That's fucked up, dude." I'm looking around now, wondering if this madman is going to rush out of the forest and slit our throats while we sleep. On second thought, it seems a little preposterous—a bit of hyperbole, no doubt. "Well, I'll tell you one thing," I say. "I'm not puttin' up with that shit. We're going—uh, well, *you're* going to the police when we get out of here."

Of course, Title 13 won't allow me to talk to anybody about this. But Tom can talk all he wants. Which reminds me why I'm here in the first place. "Hey," I say, as I jump to my feet and retrieve the laptop, "you're gonna give me that interview now."

As I begin asking Tom the routine questions, it doesn't take me long to discover that government programmers have failed to consider polygamy when designing the interview software. I've created the household roster: John Allred as the primary resident, plus four adult females and ten children. The software can't accommodate the other fifteen names that make up the household's human inventory, so I'm forced to omit them.

Now, as I attempt to indicate the relationships among the names I've entered, I'm getting an error message: *A spouse already exists for Line 1.* That would be Father John's first wife, Marilee Head. For the other three, I'm forced to choose some other relationship category; I reflect on my options, then settle for "unmarried partner."

"So," I ask Tom, "just how did Father John end up with four wives anyway?"

"What do you mean?" he asks, scrunching up his face.

"I mean, it's not like he can get four marriage licenses. The records search at the county clerk's office will turn up the first marriage and a second license will be denied."

"That's not how marriages are done," Tom says, shaking his head. "They're sealed by the Spirit in a private ceremony."

"Well, that's not really a marriage, then. Not in the eyes of the law, at least."

"It is under God's law," Tom insists.

"Suit yourself," I say. "You're free to believe whatever you want. All I'm saying is that there's nothing illegal about a guy having a wife and three mistresses. As long as he doesn't try to get multiple marriage licenses."

Tom just shrugs.

I select "unmarried partner" for Deborah Murdock, Julia Bateman, and Rebecca Olsen—Tom's mother. I guess the government programmers got it right after all. These three women aren't wives, really, just live-in partners. It's not against the law for a guy to fuck his roommates. He can even father children by them if he wants. Of course, it is seriously fucked up to beat them, however.

I begin listing the children by age, eldest first, putting Tom, 19, and his brother Luke, 16, at the top. Like their mother, they have their biological father's surname: Olsen. The remaining eight that the computer screen accommodates range from 10 to 16 years old. Tom tells me they're all Father John's children.

"So they all go by Allred?" I ask, assigning the surname to the whole list of them.

"I guess so," Tom says with a shrug. "I mean, no one really uses last names."

"Yeah, but I need to enter the name that's on the birth certificates."

Tom looks confused. "What's a birth certificate?"

"You know, the form the hospital fills out when a baby's born."

"Oh, no," Tom says. "There's no hospital; babies are born at home."

Now that I think about it, that's not surprising; a reclusive group like this one is likely to practice midwifery. I take a different tack. "Do the kids all go by Allred at school?"

Tom's shaking his head. "No. Don't you see? School is at home. Births are at home. Work is at home. We grow our food and make our clothes. We don't take part in the Gentile world. Only my mother, Luke, and I are allowed to go into town for supplies—because we've lived on the outside before—but we can only go under Father John's supervision."

"Are you saying that there's no record of any of Father John's children?"

"I don't know how there could be," Tom says. "They only go outside the walls to gather berries and mushrooms and such, or when we go for hikes and bicycle rides in the forest. But they never go into town; they're not allowed to talk to Gentiles."

"And nobody ever asks about them?" I wonder aloud. "Like public officials?"

"Nope," Tom says shaking his head. "You're the first."

Title 11

THE FIRST THING I SMELL WHEN I WAKE at five a.m. is gas. My investigation reveals that the Jeep's tank has been punctured and all the gas has drained during the night. Which means we've got no choice but to hike out—an all-day proposition at best. I pull out the computer and consult ALMI again. Our intended route from last night is almost entirely uphill, about ten miles to the Molalla Highway, where we might get cell service, but more likely would have to flag down a passing vehicle.

I'm feeling a little less certain about this option. Not only would it be about five hours of climbing, but it would also take us through the territory of the man my little friend here says has sworn a blood oath to kill him. Presumably, the guy wouldn't have any qualms about offing the kid's government accomplice as well.

The alternative route, which I can see is partly uphill, but mostly downhill because it follows the Fish Creek drainage basin to the Clackamas River, is longer by about three miles, but would be a hell of a lot easier—maybe even faster. That would put us on the Clackamas River Highway where we could easily catch a ride into Estacada.

We strike camp and pack everything of value into the Jeep's utility box. Not exactly foolproof security, especially out here, but it's the best we've got. The one thing I keep out is the computer. Not only might we need the ALMI maps along the way, but I'd have a hard time explaining to federal bureaucrats how my laptop—loaded with top-secret Title 13 data—disappeared in the middle of a forest I wasn't supposed to be in.

I throw some trail mix and the remaining four bottles of water from my emergency six-pack into the computer bag as well. Not as much as I'd like to have for a five-hour hike, but it'll have to do. Then we set off down Road 45 toward the Clackamas River in silence.

The going for the first hour is uphill, until we cross into the Fish Creek basin. I'm trying to figure out how I can account for this day on my timesheet without having to say exactly what happened. I can only imagine what thoughts the kid must be lost in. Whatever they are, I don't interrupt them until we've dropped down to the creek and it's time for a break. We've been walking for two hours.

"So, do you have any idea where you're going?" I ask Tom, handing him the trail mix and some stale cookies I've just found in one of the bag's zippered compartments. "Or didn't you plan that far ahead?"

He shrugs. "I don't know. I saw a chance to get out and I took it."

No shit. "Well, I'm sure DHS will help you out."

"DHS?"

"The Oregon Department of Human Services. They provide all sorts of family services for people who are down on their luck."

The kid is already shaking his head. "No," he says. "No government. There would be questions."

"Well, sure. They can't really help you, can they, if they don't ask you questions?"

"No. You don't understand. If the government gets involved, he'll know it was because of me, and he'll hurt them."

"The government?"

"No. My mother and brother," he says with a look of desperation. "He'll punish them because of me." He shakes his head again. "No. No government."

I'm mildly curious about what goes on in the twisted world Tom has just escaped, but I decide against probing any further. I'd rather enjoy the scenery in silence. I really do love it out here, even if this isn't exactly a planned outing.

We've only been walking for another fifteen minutes or so, when I see the glint of sunshine off the windshield of an approaching vehicle. I stick my fore- and little fingers in my mouth, let out a shrill whistle, and wave my arms. This is silly, because the vehicle has nowhere else to go but right past us, but I'm so damned relieved that we don't have to walk another ten miles that I can't just stand still and wait.

A moment later a blue Ford pickup rolls to a stop beside us with the driver's window down. There's a woman driving. "Is everything OK?" she asks. Before I can reply, she cocks her head, a crooked smile forming. "Hey, wait. You're Nick, right? Nick Prince?"

For a moment I'm thinking, what are the chances a Census respondent has crossed my path and actually remembers my name. Then I realize who she is. "Laura?"

"Dude! Wow, it's been how many years? I haven't seen you since..." she trails off. "Well, you know, since you were arrested."

"Yeah, well, I couldn't exactly keep in touch," I say.

"I know. Sorry to bring it up," she says. "So, what are you up to now? And what the heck are you doing all the way out here?" She looks me up and down, then glances at the kid. "It doesn't look like you've got any gear. You're not crazy enough to come all this way on a day hike, are you?"

"Not exactly. My Jeep broke down," I begin. "Well, it kinda slid off the road, actually."

"Oh, man. That sucks," she says with a sympathetic look. "How far up?"

"Road 4510," I say.

"Oh, fuck! You've been walking all that way?" Laura says, eyes wide.

"Yeah," I admit with a laugh. "We camped out there last night."

"Well, come on, hop in," she says, already clearing a mess of dirt-filled Ziploc baggies off the seat.

"Thanks," I say, "but are we keeping you from something? I mean, you didn't come out here to rescue us."

"Oh, forget it," she says with a throaty laugh. "I'm just lookin' for fungus. Nothing that can't wait."

"Fungus?" I ask as the kid and I climb into the cab beside her— Tom first, with me riding shotgun.

"Yeah. I'm hunting mushrooms for my restaurant in Brightwood."

"Well, as I recall, you always did like 'shrooms," I say, reminding her of our college days.

"Ha! I don't do that shit anymore," she laughs. "Too old." Then, shifting her attention to Tom, "Hey, I'm Laura." She gives him a high-five, but he doesn't know what to do with it.

"Tom," he says with a shy nod. He's been staring at Laura like she's from another planet. It occurs to me that Laura, in her tattered jeans and Everclear **T**-shirt, isn't exactly the gingham-clad variety of female he's used to hanging out with.

"Jesus," Laura says to him, noticing his shiner. "Did you get that in the accident?"

Laura, I remember, was never one to keep her thoughts to herself.

"Uh, no," Tom answers. "Just some trouble at home."

"Oh," Laura says, regarding him sympathetically. "Sorry to hear that."

Immediately her tone brightens again. "Well, Tom," she says, throwing the truck into a whiplash-inducing spin, "Hang on, 'cause I'd hate to give you another black-eye, and I'm one hell of a driver!"

Title 12

MRS. X AND I CONTINUED TO SEE EACH other for the next eight months. And since none of it was on Census business, I may as well tell you about it. I'd show up every Friday from two to five, while her husband was down in Salem on business. Go ahead—judge me. We both had what the other needed. I needed to forget Beth. And she needed, well, an Airedale, I guess.

Whatever it was, it had been her idea to make it a regular gig. I hadn't even thought of her again after the initial interview. At least, not until Angie called to give me the results of that month's reinterviews. Reinterview is the process whereby your supervisor calls random respondents you've already interviewed and says something that sounds like, *Hey, since we sent some slob out who we can't trust, we're calling to see if he actually visited you, or whether he just stayed home and made up all this shit.* Then the supervisor proceeds to put the respondent through the same set of questions all over again.

And they wonder why people hang up on us.

"Great job, Big Guy," Angie enthuses as she reports my August stats. "I just completed reinterview with a woman in Happy Valley and it sounds like you really knocked her socks off!"

I'm tempted to reply that she wasn't wearing any. Instead, I shrug it off. "Yeah? Good to hear, I guess."

"Hey, take credit wherever you can," Angie says. "This woman was really impressed with your performance."

"Huh."

"When I asked her *Was he courteous and professional?*, she said, 'Absolutely. He was a perfect gentleman and knew exactly what he was doing.'"

"Huh."

"And when I asked *Was the interview too long?*, she said, 'Oh, no. Not at all. It was just as long as it needed to be.'"

"OK, Angie!" I say with a sudden need to move the conversation along. Anything else we need to discuss? I mean, I was running out the door when you called."

"No, that's it, Big Guy. Whatever you're doing, I just wanted to tell you to keep it up!"

That, it turned out, wouldn't be a problem at all.

Mrs. X called me the very next day to give me her report of the same conversation. And to invite me back the next Friday, and every one thereafter. I didn't hesitate to accept, though I made it clear that I was no longer visiting under the auspices of the Federal Government and, please, don't grant any more interviews evaluating my "performance."

The arrangement worked well for as long as it lasted. I had something to look forward to each week and, at the same time, I saved a bunch of cash I would have otherwise spent on beer and strippers down at the Safari Club. Not that I didn't still drink beer on Fridays— but it's a hell of a lot cheaper at home. That, and I didn't have to dodge the sobriety patrols on Highway 211 between Estacada and Sandy.

One Friday in March of the following year the state legislature was called into emergency session for some reason I can't remember, if I ever knew it. If you're wondering why I would give a fuck, here's the upshot. The state senator with whom Mrs. X's lobbyist husband met every Friday canceled their appointment that day. And Mr. X did what any good husband would do: he came home early to surprise his wife with flowers and a reservation at the Waverly Country Club for dinner.

I made it out the back door with my pants in my hand, but just barely. I never saw Mrs. X again. Not that I cared at that point. It was Mr. X I was concerned with. For the next year I kept looking over my shoulder for him. With his political connections in Salem, I was sure he'd track me down, discover my sex offender status, and have the state troopers after me. In fact, I was so freaked I didn't go home for two weeks, except to pick up the few things I needed to get by. Then I moved in with the Jerrys for a few weeks.

The Jerrys are a gay couple that locals usually refer to as "the Boys from Boring." Jerry "Rigs" Thomas, from Riggins, Idaho, was my college roommate for two years. His partner, Jerry "Man" Wong, is a Chinese-American. Their nicknames derive from my habit of calling them Jerry-Riggins and Jerry-Mandarin. They own a place at the top of Wally Road, which we nicknamed WallyWorld. It sits at the top of a butte in the heart of the aptly named hamlet of Boring. Boring until they got there, at least. Never ones to hide in a closet—and a mixed-race couple to boot—they stand out in their conservative neighborhood in more ways than one.

Accustomed as they were to unannounced guests and freeloaders, Rigs and Man were more than happy to put me up as a fugitive from love and justice. My only fee was to babysit their two Lhasa Apsos, Zeus and Ganymede. Except for the dog hair I wore everywhere I went, it was a workable arrangement for as long as I needed.

I could only imagine what trumped up charges Mr. X had waiting for me: rape, home invasion, drinking his thirty-year-old Scotch. I'd already spent one month in the Clackamas County Jail, and that was more than enough. I'd be damned if I was going to end up getting raped in Coffee Creek Prison.

Title 14

"So, WHERE AM I TAKING YOU BOYS?" Laura asks as we reach the Clackamas River and emerge onto the state highway. "Or do you just want to get into cell range so you can call the auto club?"

"I wish it were that easy," I say. "The auto club doesn't cover towing from unpaved Forest Service roads."

"Oh, man. That sucks," Laura empathizes. "What're you gonna do, then?"

"If you can get me home, I'll call Rigs. He can take me back to the Jeep and we'll tow it out with his rig."

"You still see the Jerrys?"

"Yeah. Rigs has had my back ever since we were roommates. He comes in handy as a lawyer from time to time too."

"Man, I miss those days," Laura says with a wistfulness I can appreciate. "Those were hella good times."

"That they were." I say this with less enthusiasm than I intended and Laura picks up on it.

"Well, good until..." She turns to look at me with an apologetic expression.

"Nah, that's OK," I say, waving her off. "I'm good. That was a long time ago."

"And you haven't seen her since?"

"Court order," I remind her. "Those were the terms of my probation."

"Yeah, right," she says with a sigh. "I'd forgotten that part."

We drive on in silence for another minute or so, then Laura speaks again in a brighter tone. "So, Tom," she says as though she's just remembered he's sitting between us. "You don't say much, do you?"

Tom shrugs. "No, I guess not."

"Well, maybe you could get a word in edgewise if I'd shut up and give you a chance," Laura says with a guffaw. But she keeps on talking anyway. "Where am I taking you?" she asks Tom.

He glances at me, as though he's looking for permission to speak, or maybe for the answer to the question. He doesn't have a chance to answer before Laura's asking another one. "Do you live around here?"

Tom remains tongue-tied, so I jump in. "It's kind of complicated. Let's just say he's currently between places."

"Ah," Laura says, as though she understands. But she doesn't have a clue. I consider telling her the whole story, but five years in prison is more than I'm willing to risk, so I tell her only what I need her to know.

"Do you know of a good shelter out here?" I ask.

"What," Laura says with surprise, "you mean like a homeless shelter?"

"Yeah. You know, just for a few nights. Someplace with food and a bed."

Tom looks at me with trepidation, eyes almost pleading. Laura leans forward to look around him and shoots me an equally concerned expression. "What's with that? You'd put your buddy in a homeless shelter? That's seriously wrong, dude. Can't he stay with you for a few nights?"

I turn away from her, pursing my lips to measure my words before speaking. "Look," I say, looking only at the road ahead, "like I said, it's complicated. We only just met yesterday."

By the time we get to my place in Sandy, Laura's goaded me into telling her a cock-and-bull story about how Tom and I met. I told her he just hitchhiked in from Utah and a friend of a friend asked me to give him a ride to a job interview at a remote ranch in Elwood. It rings false, even to me, but she doesn't press for any further details, and Tom doesn't refute it.

"Awesome place, by the way," she says as we sit in the driveway of my little cottage on the Sandy River. "How'd you find it?"

"Beth and I used to come hiking out here. The trailhead's right over there, just past the gate at the end of the road. There was a little old lady living here then, and we used to stop and check out her garden. One day the woman invited us in for tea, and Beth fell in love with the place."

"So you had to buy it, even after you knew you'd never see her again," Laura says, finishing the story. "How romantic. Sick. But romantic." She laughs. "I don't blame you though. It really is awesome."

"Thanks," I say, climbing out of the truck and holding the door for Tom.

"You sure I can't take you to the MAX station, Tom," Laura asks as he scoots out the door. "It'd be more comfortable than riding bi-atch on Nick's bike!" she says with a laugh.

I answer for him. "No, really. We're cool. But thanks for everything. It was really nice running into you again. Even if we hadn't needed rescuing."

"Yeah, for me too," she says through the open window as I close the door. "Well, you've got my number now, so go ahead and use it. Come on up the mountain some time and we can catch up on old times."

I can't think of why I would call her. My only connection to Laura is through Beth, and I sure as hell don't need to stir those memories up after all these years. But, never mind; Laura does it for me.

"Hey, Nick," she says as she starts the truck. "There's something else you might want to know." She pauses as if seeking permission to continue.

"Yeah?" I say. "I don't really think I want to know anything but the inside of a coma for the next two weeks."

"OK," she says and puts the truck in gear.

"Well, shit. You can't just leave it hanging like that," I say, curious in spite of my claims to the contrary. "What?"

"Beth's staying at her folks' place in Damascus right now," Laura says. "She's going through a divorce."

The world stops spinning.

My heart begins to race. Beth. Local, soon to be single, and definitely old enough to make her own dating decisions. "What's she look like?"

"Pretty much the same. I mean, her hair's shorter and she's put on a little weight. But hey, haven't we all?" Laura says with a snort.

But the only thing I can see is the picture of seventeen-year-old Beth, a permanent fixture in my mind for the last decade. I try aging it ten years and applying "shorter hair and a little weight." It's still pretty damn hot.

After Laura drives off I pull out my keys, open the padlock on the barely standing garage at the end of the driveway, and pull back one of the rickety doors. The thing's probably been here since 1922 when the house was built. In this humidity, it's a wonder it hasn't rotted completely away.

The Ducati Multistrada 1200 waits patiently by the door, right where I left it last summer, the last time I rode it. I keep meaning to take it for a spin, but the wet spring didn't leave much opportunity, and it's not exactly suited to Census work, even in the summer. At the moment it's my only choice.

"Put this on," I tell Tom as I grab two helmets and hand him one. But he's in some sort of trance, eyes fixed on the matte black bike. I can't tell whether he's afraid of it or wants to make love to it. "Ever ridden a bike before?"

He shakes his head slowly.

"Well, just hold on to me and lean whichever way I lean," I tell him as I back the Ducati out of the garage.

The kid follows instructions a little too well. "Hey, not so tight! I need to breathe here," I shout back at him over the roar of the 150-horsepower engine as we shoot across the Revenue Bridge. "Just clasp your hands around my waist. You don't have to squeeze."

Then comes a real knee-dragger turn, a hairpin. I slow to a novice speed, but the kid still overcorrects, leaning to the outside of the turn instead of in. "Lean *with* me!" I scream into the wind, not sure if he can hear me. We wobble something fierce and swing into the oncoming lane before I manage to regain control. Fortunately, that's the last of the crazy turns on Ten Eyck Road before we reach the straightaway of the Mt. Hood Highway.

Twenty minutes later we pull up at the end station of the MAX Blue Line in Gresham. But the kid won't let go of me. "Hey, we're here," I say as I rock the Ducati onto its center stand. "You can get off now." I wrestle free of his arm lock and step off the bike. He slides off as well, but is unsteady on his feet. I brace him for a minute and help him off with the helmet. "C'mon."

We head to the ticket machine and I buy him a one-way trip into Portland. "OK, now keep this in your pocket," I tell him. "You get off at the second stop after you cross the river—the sign will say Skidmore Fountain. It's right under the Burnside Bridge—you can't miss it." The kid just looks at me. He hasn't spoken a word since we left Sandy. It's starting to irritate me. I'm trying to help him out, but he doesn't seem to appreciate that.

But hey, I tell myself, he's had a rough day too, and he'll be out of my hair in just a few minutes. "Anyway, climb the steps up to Burnside and you'll be right in front of the Portland Rescue Mission," I say as I lead him to the platform, where a train is already waiting.

I coax him onto the train and he stands there looking back at me. He looks like one of those dogs on a Sarah McLachlan SPCA commercial for abused animals. I'm starting to feel guilty as the doors close. The train lurches forward and the kid grabs a pole to steady himself, never once taking his eyes off me. He makes me feel like shit. But why? He's the one who started all this when he jumped into my Jeep. Besides, I've got my own problems to solve right now. Like getting the Jeep back.

Title 15

I WAKE UP ON MY BACK WITH MEATLOAF kneading my chest, signaling that it's time for his breakfast. Hey, it's not like I'm a cat-lover or anything; I just saved him from a little dust-up he had with a raccoon on the back patio shortly after I moved in. I mean, I couldn't just stand there and watch him get shredded like so much Mt. Hood powder. Have you ever tangled with a mama 'coon protecting a litter? Besides, Beth loved cats and he makes me think of her.

Which is what I've been doing all night; I've barely slept a wink. I'd love nothing more than to run over and see her right now—fuck the restraining order. But I need to focus on the Jeep today. I'll deal with the Beth thing later.

The forecasted "chance of rain" is actually a full-on thunderstorm by the time Rigs and I leave Boring in his monster Ford truck with a five-gallon can of gas. I've decided it'd be easier to just gas up and drive the Jeep out as is; the hole in the tank is small enough to get me back home before it runs dry again. I watch raindrops the size of quarters splatter the windshield, and I cringe to think how muddy Forest Road 45 is going to be by the time we get there. I hope the wind doesn't kick up; the Jeep's damaged soft top will already be leaking like a cheap diaper.

"Now how, exactly, did you end up out there?" Rigs asks between outbursts from "Jack," the annoying voice of his GPS, which we've programmed with the Jeep's exact map coordinates.

"Just trying to find a shortcut home from Elwood," I say with as much detachment as I can fake, since I'm not allowed to tell the real story and I'm not in the mood to make up a more convincing lie at the moment. "You know me, always looking for the next adventure."

"Yeah, but you're usually a savvy wilderness guy." Rigs laughs. "Not some dweeb who's gonna run off into the forest half-cocked without a GPS."

"I had one, but it got smashed by a logging rig during a little mishap last week," I tell him as I flip through his CD collection. "And you know government red tape; they won't replace it until they've held a full Senate investigation."

Rigs smiles wide and casts me a sidelong glance. "Why do I get the feeling there's a story in there somewhere?"

"Just drive," I say, popping Green Day's *American Idiot* into the player.

✳ ✳ ✳

"Goddammit! Can I catch a fucking break once in a while?" The rain has stopped, but the Jeep is gone.

"Are you sure this is the spot?" Rigs asks as we climb out of his rig. The mud makes a sucking sound with each step as we wrestle our boots out of its grip.

"Positive. Look at the slope. You can see where the Jeep slid down. And here's where I had my campfire," I say, kicking the remains of a half-burnt log. I make no mention of Tom. "And you can still smell the gas."

"Maybe the Forest Service had it towed," Rigs offers, trying to be upbeat. "Why don't we check with the ranger at Ripplebrook?"

"Yeah, right." We both know this is ridiculous. The USFS is too underfunded to tow its own rigs, let alone broken-down private ones.

Rigs moves on to the more obvious conclusion. "So, you think it was stolen?"

"Chances are," I say, already tracing the tire tracks in the mud. "Look here. These are the Jeep's tracks. I recognize the tread pattern. And here, another set of tracks interweaving."

"You think it was towed?" Rigs asks.

"I have no doubt," I say, walking about fifty yards farther up the road, where both sets of tracks turn up Road 4510. "See how the tracks diverge through the turn?"

"C'mon. Let's see where they lead," Rigs says, already heading back to the truck.

My first thought is that the Jeep and the jerk who stole it are probably long gone by now, but curiosity eggs me on to see how far the tracks go. Then a more obvious scenario suggests itself. "Shit."

"What?" Rigs asks, throwing me a worried look as the truck roars to life again.

"Uh," I stammer, "nothing."

I'm willing to bet my left nut that Papa Bear's got the Jeep. I mean, who else would have been poking around this far out in the woods in the last 24 hours? Besides hikers and campers, the kind of people whose only experience with Grand Theft Auto is on the Xbox. Besides, Papa Bear was right behind us when the whole thing went down. And he's got plenty of motive to want to screw me.

The sudden torque jolts me from my thoughts as Rigs throws the truck into four-wheel drive to make the climb up the steep side road. By the time we've reached the logging operation at the top, I'm back to wondering what I'm going to do when we get to the compound. I can probably count on Rigs to go along with whatever half-assed scheme I come up with—as long as it's legal. But his criminal defense attorney instincts will kick in if I step over the line. The less I tell him the better it will be for both of us.

As if reading my mind, Rigs asks, "What do you plan to do if we find the guy?"

"Good question," I say. "If he's not too mean looking, we can probably walk right up and take it. I've got the keys, after all."

"And if he *is* 'mean looking'?" Rigs says with obvious concern, then adds, "Or worse—if he's armed?"

"Well, then we get his plate, and call it in to the sheriff's office." This isn't really a plan, just some ad hoc crap I feed him while I try to figure out whether Papa Bear could be setting some kind of trap for me.

"Right," Rigs says with a cynical laugh. "You make it sound so easy."

Within twenty minutes, we're turning onto Elwood Road, as I suspected, retracing the route Tom and I took as we fled Papa Bear. The turnoff to the compound is only a mile ahead. What to do...

"Do you have a gun?" I ask Rigs.

"What—like on me?"

"Yeah. In the truck."

"No. Jesus, Nick. It's only a Jeep. Don't wack out on me, all right?"

"It was just an idea," I say. And it's the truth. I don't really know what I'd do with a gun anyway, other than brandish it as a bluff. Even with a scope I can barely hit an unarmed, stationary elk. I wouldn't stand a chance with an armed opponent.

"Yeah, well, your 'ideas' need a little dose of chill, dude."

"Wait," I tell Rigs when we reach the turnoff. "I recognize this place. I've been here before."

He looks at me. "Really? Like, with the Census, you mean?"

"Rigs, you know I can't tell you that."

Title 16

I CAN SEE THE JEEP AT THE BOTTOM of the drive, inside the compound, just where I expected it. Papa Bear's made no effort to hide it; it sits right beside the two white Econoline vans. It's like he's baiting me, daring me to come back for it.

"So?" Rigs asks as I climb back into the truck after taking a closer look.

"It's there all right. The bastard's displaying it like a trophy."

"Why do I get the feeling this guy isn't a total stranger to you?"

"Maybe," I say.

"And you're not on the best of terms, I'm guessing," Rigs says, to which I nod. "So are you going to ring the bell and confront him?"

I think about this for a minute. I can't figure how it would work in my favor. The guy's not going to say, "Oh, sorry—my bad," and step aside while I drive off in the Jeep. And I have no leverage over him, not even a gun to scare him with—as if he were the type to be scared by one. And Title 13 won't let me report him for the theft of the Jeep anymore than his abuse of the boy. My contact with him must remain entirely confidential.

Still, in the face of all rational thought, I can't just walk away and let him win.

"Yeah," I tell Rigs. "We're goin' in. I want my fuckin' Jeep."

"We?" Rigs asks with a skeptical look. "How about I just drop you off and wait to see what happens?"

"You sissy," I tell him. "Grow a pair and take me in there. C'mon, reach over and press the button. I'll do the talking."

"You bet your ass, you will," Rigs says. "In fact, I'm not even getting out of the truck. Just promise me I'm not going to be an accessory to anything that'll get me disbarred."

"Scout's honor," I say with a cheesy grin and a three finger salute. "Besides," I add with a wink, "I've got a good lawyer if things go bad."

He shoots daggers at me before turning to press the intercom button.

A moment later, a young male voice comes through the tinny speaker. "Who is it?"

"Let me talk to Father John," I say.

A minute of silence passes before a deeper, gruffer voice replies. "Can I help you?"

"Yeah," I say. "I'm here for my Jeep."

There's no reply, but the gates begin their slow inward journey. "Well," I say, looking at Rigs. "This is it."

He sighs and lets up on the clutch. "How do you get me into this shit, Prince?" he says as we roll through the gate. "I'll never learn, will I?"

Father John's waiting for us beside the Jeep. He's a tad over six feet, with a full head of salt-and-pepper hair and a barrel chest. He probably weighs 260 pounds to my 200. He reminds me of Brigham Young, with a beard and no mustache. But he's not looking very religious at the moment: he's armed with a scoped Remington rifle. It stands at his side, stock to the ground, so I'm guessing he's planning on talking before shooting.

Besides, what's he got to be so pissed about? He's the one who committed the crime here. All I did was give his stepson a lift into town. It's a free country, I tell myself, as I gin up some anger for what I've got to say.

I jump out of the truck before it rolls to a stop. "You've got my Jeep there," I say in my most confident tone, the one I use for all the would-be shooters I deal with. "You know that, right?" I walk right up to him, showing no fear, though I have plenty of it. I keep an eye on his gun arm. I don't know why; I've got no martial arts training. A smile is the only tool I've ever had to disarm someone with.

"What I know is you got my boy!" he bellows at me without flinching a muscle. In fact, his lips barely seem to move.

"From what I hear," I say, feeling more than a bit cocky, "he's not even yours."

Fire flares in the man's eyes and he moves as if to clock me, but checks himself as his nose reaches mine. "But he's my responsibility until he's eighteen!"

I flinch, the wind knocked out of me. He's lying, right? "What do you mean?" I say, less confident now. "He's nineteen. He told me."

The man regards me with slightly less hostility, if only for a moment. "Those are the words of the Devil. The boy ain't right, you know. Can't believe a word he tells you."

It occurs to me that this is just what an abusive parent would say in a he-said, he-said courtroom face-off. The first tactic the defense always uses is to impugn the character of the complainant. But it occurs to me that the kid could have just as easily lied to me. It certainly wouldn't be the first time a 17-year-old got me into trouble by being less than honest about age. Besides, no matter what the kid's age, I've seen what Father John does to him. I'm not about to trust the guy.

"Well, that might be," I say noncommittally. "That's none of my concern. I'm just going to take my Jeep and get out of your hair." I start toward the driver's side, but he moves to block my path.

"Not so fast. Every action has its recompense. Every sin its restitution."

Like I'm supposed to know what this means. "Sorry?" I say. I consider adding that I flunked out of Catholic Catechism classes, but decide against it.

"I have what you want. You have what I want. It will be an even exchange: your Jeep for my boy."

"I don't have your boy," I protest. "He's on his own now. Just give me my Jeep." I move again to the Jeep and open the door, this time without interference.

But Father John is now grasping the rifle with both hands. He's not aiming it yet, but he's only a split-second away from it. He doesn't say a word. Instead he lets the cocking of the hammer speak for him.

I stop and consider what this might look like to a jury. I'm a convicted sex offender who might now have walked off with another minor. And I'm in a face-off with his angry parent who can claim I kidnapped him. In court it won't matter what the kid told me; my character is already impugned. The prosecutor's job is already done. Basically, I'm fucked.

I step back from the Jeep and close the door. "Right," I say. "I see your point."

Title 17

IT'S JUST AFTER NOON WHEN RIGS DROPS me off at home, where once again I find "lost" hikers poking around in my garden. "Uh, yeah, the trailhead's about a hundred yards that way," I say, pointing toward the river.

"That's cool," the geek says, while his date rubs Meatloaf's belly on the picnic table. "What is this place anyway?"

"It's my home, dickwad."

"No way! Seriously?" he says, as though he's being given a tour rather than an eviction. "Dude, this place is awesome." His girlfriend has already disengaged the cat and is beating a retreat, throwing him pleading looks that he's oblivious to.

"Yeah, well it's *my* awesome, so get your scrawny ass back to the trail." I'm not always so blunt with the looky-loos—it's a kick to show people around once in a while—but I'm in no mood for it today.

"Sorry," the girlfriend mumbles as she tugs the doofus's arm and they make their exit.

Ever since Rigs and I left Father John's compound I've been trying to figure out how I can get the Jeep back. Every plan I envision involves the boy; that leaves me no choice but to go find him. First, however, I need to eat.

I head straight for the kitchen and fix myself a sandwich. I've just taken my first sip of Pabst when the phone rings. It's Angie. I let it go to voicemail and head out to the patio with my lunch. I've barely finished eating and am lying on the chaise lounge finishing my beer when she calls again. I may as well get it over with because I know she won't quit until we've talked.

"Hi, Angie. I just got in. I was just about to call you," I lie.

"Hey, Big Guy, you've been MIA for a couple of days. What's up?"

"Nothing, why?" I say defensively, wondering whether she's heard anything about the incident at the compound.

"You've had a new caseload sitting on the server for two days already," she says, annoyed, "and you haven't even downloaded it yet. You've got to plan your itinerary for the observation on Saturday."

"Oh, right. I guess I lost track of the date. I've been... well, I had something come up that I've been trying to take care of. Something personal."

"C'mon, Big Guy," she says in her most patronizing tone, "you know you've got to multitask in this job. We've all got personal lives to juggle. You just have to make time."

"Right," I say. There's never any point in offering a defense. The house could be on fire and it wouldn't impress her. "I'll pick up the new cases as soon as we hang up."

We end the call and I go back to my beer. Soon I'm dozing.

✳   ✳   ✳

It may be futile, but I've come into Portland's Old Town this evening to start looking for the kid. The obvious place to start is the Portland Rescue Mission. Of course, there's no telling where he might end up; if he's a minor, the mission would have to notify Child Protective Services. If the authorities already have him and my name comes up, I could be in for a world of hurt.

"Hi, I'm Nick Prince from the Census Bureau," I tell the outreach coordinator at the mission, handing him my card. I'm taking a risk using my Census ID for this, because I've actually interviewed here before, but I figure it's the only way I'm going to get the cooperation I need.

"David Collins," the coordinator says, offering his hand. He's an earnest-looking guy about my age. "Are we due for another count already?"

"No, no," I assure him. "I'm looking for a young man who might have been here two nights ago. He's just shy of six feet; curly blond hair, medium length; green eyes; clean shaven."

"To be honest," Collins says, "I see so many faces—seems like more every day—I rarely get a look at the color of their eyes. Even hair and skin color can be hard to judge, the grime is so thick on some of 'em."

"Right. I understand," I say. "But this was the kid's first night on the street; his clothes were clean: dungarees and a blue denim work shirt."

"I don't recall seeing him," Collins says, pursing his lips in thought. "How old did you say he was?"

"He's about 18; I'm not really sure."

"Come with me. There's someone we can ask." He leads me outside to the sidewalk, where men of all ages stand, sit, and shamble in the approximation of a queue that reaches around the block, all waiting for dinner to be served. I try not to wince at the collective scent of this mass of unfortunate humanity.

Collins leads me to a young man approximately the same age as Tom. "Hey, Georgie," he says to the kid, "How's it goin'?"

"S'awright, Brother C. Same soup, just reheated," the kid says with a laconic half-smile.

"You been in the neighborhood for the last couple of days?"

"Sure. Got nowhere else to go, do I?"

"I hear you," Collins says with an obvious empathy that makes me feel like a jerk for sending Tom into this situation in the first place. "Hey, you seen a new kid around—about your age—in the last day or two? Blond, about six feet, clean clothes, unfamiliar with the street scene?"

Georgie thinks for a minute, or pretends to, then asks, "Why? He in trouble?"

"Well, I don't think so," Collins says, turning to me. "Mr. Prince here is looking for him. Why don't I let him give you the details."

"Hey, Georgie," I say, extending my hand out of habit. The kid ignores it and waits for me to explain. "No, he's not in trouble. I sent him down here to ask for help, but I screwed up and I want to make things right with him. I'd like to give him a place to stay and get him some food and clothing, if I can find him."

Georgie sizes me up for ten or fifteen seconds before replying. "You like family or something?"

"No, just an acquaintance," I say. It doesn't seem to be enough information for Georgie, so I add, "He comes from an abusive home, and I'm trying to help him."

The kid's body language says that he believes me. "He a skinny kid with rosy cheeks, all in blue?"

"That's him," I say, my excitement evident. "You've seen him?"

"Dude was on the Sleep Train the other night, saying some weird-ass shit about 'iron rods' and big buildings and shit."

"The Sleep Train?" I ask.

"That's what the street folk call the MAX," Collins explains. "They ride the trains back and forth within the free-rail zone to steal some sleep before the system shuts down at midnight. Then they stay awake all night on the street, watching their backs, until the trains start running again at 6 a.m."

"When did you see him last?" I ask Georgie.

"Last night," he says. "He didn't want to get off the train that was going out of service, so the driver says he's callin' the Transit Police. Dude didn't wait; he obviously didn't wanna see no cops. He took off so fast he musta got some kinda record."

"And you don't know where he went?" I ask, my optimism fading.

"Naw. He tried to hang with us, but he just kept talkin' weird religious shit and nobody wanted to be around him. Last I saw, he was headed toward Union Station. But they don't let no one sleep there, so I don't know where he at now."

Shit. Did he jump a train? I know he didn't have any money. And I can't see a clueless kid like him knockin' over a food-cart vendor or mugging someone to get it. In any case, it seems that he's long gone. I can't just walk the streets looking for him.

As I head home, I'm wondering if I can bluff my way through negotiations with Father John. As long as he thinks I have the boy, maybe I can still get the Jeep.

Title 18

It's dusk by the time I get back to my place. The house sits deep enough under the forest canopy that once I turn off the road, the only light comes from the motion-sensor floods near the front and back doors. I roll the Ducati into the driveway, triggering the light in front. The one in back is already on. This isn't unusual; the lights are often on more than off during the night due to wildlife activity. Still, I like to know what kind it is. Bears are a distinct possibility this far out in the forest.

I lock the bike in the garage and tiptoe around the far end of the house. I detect no movement as I peek around the corner and scan the garden. The light is focused about twenty yards from the building; there are too many shadows to make anything out on the patio. It was probably just a raccoon anyway. I walk back to the front of the house and let myself in, where Meatloaf greets me with a rub on the leg.

Fifteen minutes later, the cat fed, we're both in bed. I don't know how long I've been asleep when I'm awakened by a sound. I'm too groggy to register what kind it is or where it came from; in fact, I might have dreamt it. Except that I see from the illumination in the living room that the back floodlight is on. Still muzzy with sleep, I slip out of bed. Meatloaf opens one disapproving eye and watches me grope for my slippers and fish my shotgun out of the closet. I grab a flashlight from the nightstand drawer, and go out to the living room. Just then the sensor light goes out; it's pitch black again.

Without making a sound, I press the lever down on one of the French doors, inch it open, and step outside. I'm too close to the house to trip the light, so with the flashlight in one hand and the gun in the other, I switch on the light and aim it across the patio. As I do so, the butt of the gun bangs the glass of the door behind me, causing me to jump. A sudden commotion erupts on the still-dark patio, not twenty feet away. Startled again, I drop the flashlight. As I grab for it, I inadvertently fire the rifle and the living room window shatters.

The clatter of patio furniture adds to the chaos and amps up my adrenaline. The sensor light comes on just in time for me to watch Tom go sprawling over an upended Adirondack chair onto the brick pavers. "Don't shoot me!" he screams. "Please! I didn't mean any harm!"

"Jesus Christ!" I scream back, my adrenaline pumping so hard I can feel my heartbeat in my ears. "You scared the holy shit out of me!" Then I realize that I've scared him a whole lot more than he scared me. The irony is inescapable: I've spent all day looking for this kid and here he is at my place. Then I almost shoot him. I can't do anything but stand there and laugh as the nervous tension peaks.

I put the gun down on the picnic table and walk over to give him a hand. "Jesus, Tom," I say, helping him to his feet. "I thought you were a bear." The kid's knees are still wobbling, and I start laughing all over again at the sight of him. A moment later, he's laughing too.

I upright the fallen chair and we both sit down to collect ourselves. After a few minutes he says, "May I please have something to eat?" He's looking at me like a neglected dog.

"Oh, man!" In all the commotion it hasn't dawned on me that he's been on the street for over 24 hours without any money. "Sure, dude. Let's see what I've got in the fridge." I jump up and head into the kitchen; he follows.

Twenty minutes later we're sitting at the kitchen table. The house smells like bratwurst and Hormel chili. There's no sign of Meatloaf, who's probably been under the bed since the gun went off.

"Where'd you sleep last night?" I ask the kid as he devours his food, barely pausing to breathe.

"Under a bridge, down by the river," he says between swallows.

"Why didn't you go to the mission? You could have had a bed, you know."

He shakes his head vigorously while he chews. "Too many people," he says. "Scary people." He pauses for the first time since he began eating and fixes his gaze on mine. "It was what I imagine Hell looks like, all those dirty people…" He trails off, returning to his meal.

He has a point, I realize. For someone who lives off the grid and has never been closer to the city than Estacada, the soup line can be pretty daunting. "So, what—you got back on the train this morning?" I ask.

He nods.

"How'd you pay for it?"

"I didn't," he says.

"And you didn't get ticket-checked?"

"I did," he says casually, chewing his bratwurst.

"Really?" I say, surprised. "So, what did they do, give you a citation?"

He shakes his head. "They asked me for identification. I told them my name, but they wanted something in writing, they said. A license or a card or something."

"And, of course, you don't have any ID," I say, stating the obvious.

"But I did have a card, so I gave it to them."

It's my turn to be confused. "Huh? What card?"

"The one you gave me," he says, finishing his sausage.

"What?" I say, processing this information. "Wait—you gave them my business card? The Census Bureau card?"

"Yeah," he says flatly. "They wanted contact information—an address or phone number."

"And you gave them mine?" I ask, nonplussed.

"Of course," he says. "They wanted to know where I lived." His eyes dart across the kitchen, then back to his empty bowl. "May I please have some more?"

I'm willing to give the kid all he can eat. This probably has something to do with the twinge of guilt I feel about what I'm about to tell him: he most certainly does not live here. While he eats his second and third helpings I describe my return visit to the compound earlier in the day. But I wait until he's finished before I get to the punch line.

"Listen, Tom," I say as he all but licks his plate clean. "I've got to take you back. I need that Jeep." I watch for a reaction, but he remains expressionless, licking his molars for any missed bits of chili. "I mean, I gotta have it—it's how I do my job, you know?" I hear the defensiveness in my own voice and it ticks me off. I'm not the one who started this mess, yet I'm feeling guilty again.

Tom continues to eat in silence. I have no clue what's going on in his head. At one moment he seems like an oblivious child; at other times I get the feeling he's way ahead of me. Like now, when he says, "I know how you can get your Jeep back."

Title 19

APPARENTLY I'VE BEEN MAKING PLANS in my sleep, only they have nothing to do with the Jeep, which is what I ought to be focused on. Instead, I've made up my mind that I have to see Beth. Now that I know she's just up the road, my irrational need to see her has destroyed any good sense I might have possessed a day earlier.

I'm under no illusion that we can simply pick up where we left off a decade ago, but I need closure, at least. We were madly in love the last time we saw each other, in that courtroom: she with her parents, me in shackles. That can't be the way the story ends.

Tom is dead to the world as I fix breakfast. Only when I've finished do I wake him. "Hey, kid. Help yourself to breakfast; pancakes and bacon are in the oven. Just be sure to turn it off when you take 'em out. I'll be back in a few hours."

It's a twenty-minute ride to Beth's parents' house. Despite the summer heat, I'm wearing my full racing leathers. The reason for this seems a bit silly, even to me, but I'm just going with my gut. I have no idea what her parents might do if they see me, but I'm prepared for a quick getaway. There's only one way in and out of the Royer Road neighborhood, so if I have to run, it will be at high speed on two-lane roads. A little extra protection may come in handy in a worst-case scenario..

My heart's pounding by the time the house comes into view. There's a car in the driveway, and one at the curb. The first is most likely her mother's. I'm guessing the latter, a red Toyota 4Runner, is hers. Which means her father's probably at work. Still, I can't just go up and knock on the door. I need to catch her alone, either when she goes out, or after her parents do.

My only option for now is to stake out the place. Not that this is anything unusual for me; I do it all the time for the Census Bureau. When someone who's obviously home refuses to answer the door time and time again, I just park myself outside until they come out. It's what they pay me for.

But I've never done this with a motorcycle before. Not only does this make me more obvious, but the seat is not designed for lounging about on. So, after a couple of passes by the house, I park the bike just around the corner and down the road beside an orchard. I unzip my leathers down to the crotch for some much-needed air circulation, and take up a position in the shade of a cherry tree, with a direct line of sight to Beth's front door.

I settle in for as long as it takes; I've got nowhere else to go. I take off the backpack in which I've got water, trail mix, and a book to read, although right now I'd rather just sit and think about Beth. Pathetic, sure, but it's how I spend most of my downtime anyway. What can I say?

I've been here just over an hour—during which time only one car has come up the dead-end road. Now a second approaches from my right, leaving the neighborhood. It slows as it passes, and the woman driving gawks at me with a concerned look. I wave and smile, but it does nothing to melt her icy stare. She drives to the end of the short block, then stops. I can see from her silhouette that she's got a cell to her ear. She's probably sounding the alarm to the Neighborhood Watch.

It doesn't take long to confirm this. Within minutes of the woman's departure, a pair of women is approaching me on foot. I make sure to zip the leathers at least nipple high as I stand up to greet them; these are probably churchgoing folk. "Good afternoon, Ladies," I say, giving them my most disarming smile.

"May we ask what your business is here?" the taller one says without acknowledging the greeting.

"I'm with the U.S. Census Bureau," I say, more out of habit than anything else, but it does provide a convenient cover.

"Census?" the other woman says. "I thought that was over long ago."

"Well, actually, here's how that works," I begin, launching into my standard explanation of the Census Bureau's program of ongoing surveys. As I do this, I'm trying to dig a couple of business cards out of my wallet. The problem is, the wallet's in the inner pocket of my leathers, which means I'm unzipping as I dig. I watch the shorter woman's eyes ride the zipper down. She's probably wondering if the kilt rule also applies to motorcycle suits. I spend a little more time digging than I need to, making sure the zipper slides all the way to my crotch, just so I can enjoy her trancelike focus.

"If you'd like to know more," I say, handing them each a card from my wallet, "you can call the 800-number for the regional office. The local number is mine in Sandy." I give the short one a wink, just to keep her happy. I can tell she already likes me.

She stops examining my zipper long enough to examine the card, but the tall one doesn't even look at the card she's holding. "You don't look like any Census worker I've ever seen," she says, giving me a jaundiced eye.

And you don't look like most pit bulls, I think, but I don't say it. Instead, my attention is drawn away by the vehicle that is now coming down the street: the red 4Runner. I've already forgotten about the busybodies as I strain to see who's driving. It takes me only a second to recognize the profile: the pixie nose and the full red lips. Just as Laura said, Beth's hair is barely shoulder length. And it's less curly than I remember, but still gorgeous.

She smiles and nods to the ladies without really looking at them, and continues down the street. If she noticed me at all, nothing registered. She's turning onto Walgren Road by the time I push past my interrogators and jump on the Ducati. I'm already chasing Beth down Royer Road before I realize that I've left my backpack behind. The Ladies' Club is probably already going through it for proof that I'm a terrorist. But fuck it. I've got Beth in my sights for the first time in ten years. I'm not about to go back.

Less than two miles later I'm off the bike and following her into the Damascus Safeway, at a discreet distance. Despite all my earlier rehearsals, I'm not sure what to say to her. For now it's enough just to look at her. Of course, I've gotten everything but a full frontal view of her—something I'm not likely to get by stalking her.

She enters the store without stopping for a basket, and heads directly to the peanut butter. I pause at the end of the aisle, taking her in as she searches the shelf. I'm still practicing what I want to say when she grabs a jar and turns back toward me. I freeze like a deer in headlights.

She stops in her tracks as well. "Nick," she gasps.

At least she remembers me. That's a start.

"I need to talk to you," I say without considering where the conversation might go. For all the time I spent imagining such a reunion, you'd think I would have rehearsed it.

"Now? Here?" Beth asks in a low voice. She looks up and down the aisle with an anxious expression. "You can't... I mean, everybody knows me here."

"OK. Out in your car then," I suggest, afraid to let the moment get away from me. The frustration and loss of ten years is welling up inside me; a sudden sense of desperation threatens to make me do something irrational.

"Nick, no," she says, her tone urgent. "This town is too small."

"Anywhere, then," I say. "Name the place." I can't take my eyes from hers for fear the moment isn't real.

She shifts nervously from foot to foot, thinking. "OK. Meet me Tuesday morning, eight o'clock, at the Starbucks in Clackamas Promenade.

Title 20

I'M WAKING UP SLOWLY; MY MIND IS STILL replaying the scene with Beth in Safeway. It's been on an endless loop all night. The phone rings. I push Meatloaf out of the way and grapple it off the nightstand. "Yeah."

"Hey there, Big Guy! You ready for our big day?"

Shit. Saturday: the observation.

"Uh, yeah," I lie, eyeing the clock. It's already ten after eight and I'm supposed to meet Angie at nine. There's no way I can make it on time. I don't bother to tell Angie this. I'll hear all about it when I get there; listening to her bitch about it now would only eat up more time.

"Well, I hope you've got an itinerary planned," she says. "You did remember to download your September cases, right?"

"Yeah, sure. I'm looking at 'em right now," I lie as I jump out of bed and switch on the computer. It takes a good three minutes just to bring up the initial start screen.

By the time I get Angie off the phone, I can finally begin logging in. I punch in enough IDs and passcodes to launch a nuke, then run to shave while my September caseload streams to my computer.

I run through the list. Nine cases up the mountain; six down around Estacada; six up in Gresham; and four over in Happy Valley. *Oh, shit.* One of the addresses is on Norwood Loop, directly across the street from Mrs. X; there's no way I want to take Angie anywhere near Mrs. X's lair. I throw together an itinerary that leaves out Happy Valley altogether. We'll start with the Mountain and wrap up with Estacada, where Angie can get some face-time with the shooter-types. That should be entertaining at least.

With less than thirty minutes to spare, I jump in the shower, throw on a dress shirt and a clean pair of jeans, and throw the computer bag over my shoulder. I'm ten minutes late when I pull up to Peet's in Happy Valley.

Angie's at an outside table, where she can squeeze three hours of smoking into one, just in case we get an interview and her next cigarette break is delayed. "Not a good way to start the day," she chides, looking conspicuously at her watch. "Punctuality is one of the eighty-two categories on the review."

Right. More bureaucratic brilliance from Washington. For all I know, they score my right hand separately from my left.

"And what's with that thing?" she asks with a nod toward the Ducati.

"Uh, yeah. Well, the Jeep's in the shop," I lie. *Yeah, if only it were.* "We'll have to take your car."

"That's not how it's supposed to work, you know," she scolds. "You'll still be doing the driving," she reminds me. "Your driving skills are part of the evaluation."

✳   ✳   ✳

"OK," she says when I return with my double-shot of espresso, "let's see your itinerary."

I turn my laptop toward her and explain my plan. She interrupts immediately.

"Wait, wait, wait," she says. "That's thirty miles one way! Why are you taking me all the way up there when you have four cases right here—they can't be more than, what, a mile or two up the road?"

Angie will have none of my lame excuses. "I don't want to be here all night. We'll do the closest ones first. Right here in Happy Valley," she declares with a finality I know better than to question.

Shit.

✳   ✳   ✳

Fifteen minutes and two cigarettes later, as we pull onto Norwood Loop, we're nearly clipped by a low-riding, black '67 Chevy Impala that is blowing through the stop sign. "Fuck!" I shout as I swerve out of the driver's path, though my voice is drowned out by the deafening rumble of the Chevy's glass packs. Wide-eyed, Angie turns to me and says, "Nice reflexes, Big Guy." I believe it's the first genuine compliment she's ever given me.

As I pull to a stop in front of the sample address, I steal a glance across the street, hoping maybe Mrs. X has moved away by now. But I recognize the bamboo wind chimes over the front steps—the ones I used to hit my head on. At least I'm not driving the Jeep; Mrs. X won't recognize Angie's Toyota if she happens to look out the window.

I keep my back to the street as Angie and I walk up to the front door at the sample address. Angie's scribbling in her notebook, probably rating my posture and the length of my stride. I'm thinking only about getting in the door or getting the hell out of here.

Dogs begin barking inside the house as soon as I ring the bell. I'm ready to leave my card and a brochure, and make my escape, when a woman calls from an open window. "Who is it?"

"U.S. Census Bureau," I reply, cursing my luck.

A moment later the woman speaks again through the barely open door. "I have to be careful my puppies don't get out. What is it?"

I show her my ID and introduce Angie and myself.

"Well, come on in then," she says, opening the door a little wider. "Mind the dogs."

I thank her and step quickly into the opening. I freeze in my tracks. It's one of those split-level houses, where the front door opens onto a landing, with one stair going up to the living room, the other down to the bedrooms. The woman's "puppies" are on the upward stairs in front of me, barking furiously. One is a terrier of some kind. The other is a pit bull.

"Oh, don't mind her," the woman says of the pit bull as she slips past the dogs and reaches the top of the stairs. "She's fine."

"Uh, she may be fine," I say, "but I'm not sure I am." Pit bulls are the only thing about this job that I'm more afraid of than Angie.

"No, no," the woman says, "really. Don't worry." She calls to the dog. "Pepper. Come." The dog ignores her, never once breaking eye contact with me.

"Just go on," Angie says from behind me, impatient. "She says the dog won't bite."

I don't budge. The woman is calling, "Treats, Pepper! Come!" and again tells me that it's fine to proceed. Angie can wait no longer. She pushes past me and heads up the stairs, right past Pepper. The dog gives her a brief glance then continues to stare me down.

Seeing Angie's success, I reconsider my reluctance. Maybe I am being overly cautious. Angie says so in less flattering terms. "C'mon. Don't wimp out on me, Big Guy."

My masculinity now questioned, I start up the stairs. In an instant Pepper is airborne. I dodge to the right, barely saving my face. But my left bicep is now lodged in Pepper's jaws as I fall back into the storm door, which is not fully latched. As Pepper and I sail onto the porch, I let out a scream so bloodcurdling that it scares me even more. My worst nightmare has become reality.

Pepper loses her grip as we thud onto the concrete stoop. I'm already back on my feet by the time she hits the iron railing with a yelp. I've still got my computer bag slung across my chest. Somewhere within it is a can of pepper spray—appropriately named, I note, in spite of my panic. I'm groping for it as I flee across the yard.

I reach Angie's car, but the door is locked. There's no time to go around it, so I clamber over the hood and into the street. Snarling furiously, Pepper first tries to leap over the hood after me, then decides to go around. This gains me an extra second on her and I'm finally able to pull out the spray. Just as Pepper opens up for another mouthful of me, I let 'er rip.

She squeals like a stuck hog as I catch my heel on the opposite curb and I sail backwards across the sidewalk onto the lawn. Pepper lies on the sidewalk, shrieking and pawing furiously at her face. She's still too close for comfort, so I waste no time in crab-walking backwards up the lawn away from her.

I hear her owner, shrieking in tones similar to the dog's. "Pepper! Oh, Pepper! Come! Come, Baby!" The next thing I hear is the guttural rumble of what can only be the '67 Impala. A split second later it blows around the bend at a healthy clip. It does not prove so healthy for Pepper who, temporarily blinded by the spray, is now making her way back across the street toward the sound of her owner's voice. With a wail of finality she sails about thirty feet farther down the block.

The dog is beyond saving, but someone has rushed to help me. The last thing I remember before I pass out is staring up into Mrs. X's worried eyes.

$$* \quad * \quad *$$

I'm lucky. If I'd been "Peppered" on my own time, I'd be paying out of pocket for these just-shoot-me-now rabies vaccinations. But since it was an on-the-job injury, Workers' Comp has it covered. I even get some time off now. Not official paid leave, mind you, since I have no benefits, but a week to recuperate.

I also get the chance to file a "CA-7 Claim for Compensation," which must be accompanied by a "CA-7a Time Analysis Form," so some bureaucrat who gets paid twice what I do can decide if I should get paid for hours I might have worked, had I trusted my instincts and sprayed Pepper on sight. Then, the Census Bureau will fill out their portion of said forms and send them on to the Office of What-the-Fuck, or whatever it's called, where my claim will languish under scrutiny until such time as I either die from my wounds or move to a Third World country to afford the medical treatment that the government has denied me. At least I have Angie as a witness to the attack, so some dickwad can't claim that the wounds were self-inflicted for the purpose of taking a paid vacation.

Of course, the dog bite isn't the only thing Angie witnessed yesterday. She's still wanting to know why she found me lying unconscious in the arms of a tearful woman who had me in a lip-lock. She didn't buy my explanation that it was probably just a Good Samaritan trying to perform CPR. "Don't ask me," I told her. "I was unconscious."

In any case, with a week off I'm now free to focus on a more pressing matter: the boy and the Jeep. I use the word "focus" loosely; it's a relative concept in my oxycodone-induced Nirvana. My grasp of the world at the moment has been reduced to two states: pain free, in which case I probably shouldn't be riding the Ducati; or wincing and cussing, which means I'm no greater menace on the road than usual.

In one of these two states—I can't remember which one at the moment—I grab the phone, scroll down to Laura's number, and press the Call button.

"Laura? Nick. Hey, how's it goin'?" I get straight to the point. "Your restaurant's closed on Sunday, right?"

She confirms this and I lay out Tom's plan for getting my Jeep back. "How would you feel about impersonating a Child Protective Services worker tomorrow?"

"What exactly would that entail?" she asks cautiously.

"Here's the deal," I explain. I omit the fact that my involvement in this scenario stems from Census business, saying only that Father John took my Jeep hostage because he was pissed that I gave his runaway stepson a ride. "So, I make a call to Father John and offer to exchange Tom for my Jeep."

"Jesus, Nick," she says, "you'd really be that callous?"

"No, no," I assure her. "That'll just get us in. Then you'll point to Tom's shiner and tell the old man that the kid stays in protective custody until your investigation is complete."

"What makes you think it'll work?" Laura asks.

"Tom thinks it will. The last thing the guy wants is the government poking around his property. But if he gives you any shit, you can have Tom lift his shirt and show off his other bruises; then you bring up criminal charges."

After probing the plan further, Laura finally agrees to help. "All right, but I have to go to Costco for supplies in the morning. The soonest I can pick you up is eleven."

Title 21

TOM'S RIGHT BEHIND ME AS I STUMBLE into the passenger side of Laura's rig in a medicated haze. I let him ride shotgun this time; my grasp on reality feels rather elusive at the moment and I'd rather not be so close to the door.

"Hey. You ready for this?" Laura asks me. "How's that arm?"

"What arm?" I say. "I think they removed it back in the ER."

"Good drugs, I take it?" she says.

"The best that taxpayer dollars can buy," I say with a giddiness that sounds foreign, even to me. "How about you? You all set?"

"Got my wig and fake mustache in the back," she says with a laugh. "And I even wore my mother's pantsuit. What do you think?"

"Works for me," I say as I check out her costume. "I'd swear you're the real thing, an honest-to-God bureaucrat."

"Hey, I'm not sure how to take that," she says as she backs out into the road. "So, Tom," she says, leaning around me to address the kid. "Your stepfather knows we're coming, right?"

"I called him," Tom says. "But I didn't mention you; I only told him about me and Nick."

"I thought—" Laura says, then changes her mind. "Well, it doesn't matter now; he'll know soon enough." She looks at Tom again. "So, how do you think he'll react?"

"He'll be none too happy, that's for sure," Tom says with a certainty born of hard-won experience. "But he doesn't want no trouble with the law, so he'll do whatever he's got to do to get you off his back."

"Including letting you leave with me?"

"Yes, ma'am, if he's convinced that stopping me will bring the law down on him."

✳   ✳   ✳

We arrive at the gates just before noon. Laura leans out to push the button, but the gates are already swinging into action. Then I see why. Tom is pointing the clicker at them. I'd forgotten he brought it along during his escape.

"Oh, shit. I almost forgot," I say to Laura as I reach into my pocket. "Here's my old badge. Just hang it around your neck and don't let him look at it too close."

Laura takes it and puts it on. "OK, now I'm official. Time to rock and roll."

Unlike on my previous visits, the grassy area in front of the main house is full of people today. It looks like a community picnic, only I realize that what I'm seeing is one big, extended family. I don't bother trying to count them, but I'm sure all twenty-four of Father John's other children must be present, as well as the various wives. They're scattered about the lawn, sitting in small groups. All of them stop and take notice of our arrival.

"What's with the welcoming committee, Tom?" I ask, nodding toward the gathering. "Is that good news or bad?"

"It doesn't mean anything," Tom says. "In the summer the family always gathers outdoors for worship and the Sabbath meal. The women prepare a picnic on Saturday so they won't need to cook on Sunday."

"Well, maybe having an audience will keep Father John on good behavior," I say.

"That's why I chose to come today," Tom says.

Shit. The kid thinks of everything.

Father John emerges from the heart of the gathering to meet us as we pull to a stop next to the Jeep. Tom is first to step out of the truck. He faces off with the old man, head held high, defiant in his stance. His stepfather remains impassive, not giving away the rage I figure is just below the surface. The kid has not only defied him, he's humiliated him as well. And now he's brought the law within his walls. This isn't the kind of guy who can tolerate that behavior. I have no doubt that it would be suicide for Tom to stay behind now.

I get out and grab the gas can from the bed of the truck. I don't make eye contact with Father John. My job is to worry about the Jeep; Laura will do all the talking. This is for two reasons: one, it will establish her authority, and two, it will put a "softer" face on the confrontation—not that this guy's got a great track record on women's rights. But Laura can hold her own. When she wants to, she can be more intimidating than most guys I know.

She gets out of the truck and walks straight up to Father John. "Mr. Allred, I'm Laura Jacobsen from Clackamas County Department of Human Services."

"And what is your concern with my family?" he says. His expression reveals nothing of what he might be thinking.

"Your stepson, Thomas, has requested that we remove him from the household and place him in protective custody."

Father John appears to stifle a response, but his muscles tighten.

"Of course," Laura continues, "this is neither your decision nor his."

"Are you suggesting, Miss Jacobsen, that such family matters are the prerogative of the government?"

"Not at all, Mr. Allred," Laura says. "The decision is his mother's— she is his sole legal guardian." I'm impressed by her ability to adlib.

Father John puffs up his chest and purses his lips, but says nothing.

"If you don't mind, I'll just have a word with her," Laura says.

The old man steps aside as Laura walks past him to where Tom has already gone to speak to his mother. Father John now eyes Laura with the same contempt he's been throwing my way since we arrived.

Laura, Tom, and Rebecca—Tom's mother—are out of earshot of Father John, which means I can't hear them either as I fuel the Jeep. The plan is for me to keep my distance—we don't want to turn this into a pissing match between me and the old man. But I know pretty much how the conversation is supposed to go.

Contrary to what Laura has told Father John, she tells Rebecca that no one can stop Tom from leaving the compound; that he has filed for emancipated minor status in court. Fighting this would bring unwanted public scrutiny to the clan's unconventional marriage arrangement. Laura urges Rebecca to give her consent, however, and to persuade her husband to comply in everyone's best interest. Tom is convinced his mother will agree.

I've got the Jeep fueled now. As expected, a peek underneath confirms that it is still leaking fuel. But it's coming out faster than I had expected, so I'm anxious to get going.

Title 22

LAURA'S WALKING OVER TO ME NOW; I'm hoping the news is good.

"Tom's straying a bit from the script, it seems," she says.

"What's that supposed to mean?"

"He's says his mother is coming with us, and his brother too," she says, giving me a look that tells me she considers this a viable option.

"No fucking way," I say. "I'm in deep enough shit here already. Let's just stick to the plan." But she's having other thoughts. I see it in her eyes. "Don't even go there," I say louder than I intended. "Look. I know she's got a real problem on her hands—he's one fucked-up dude—but we're not fucking UNICEF here. There's only so much we can do."

Laura shrugs and returns to Tom and his mother. After a moment the three of them separate. Laura's walking back to the truck, but Tom's heading back toward the houses and Rebecca is calling the other wives to her.

I don't know what the hell is going on, but if Tom's not in the Jeep by the time I pull out, he's going to have to depend on Laura. I fire up the engine and pull up alongside Laura's truck. "Hey!"

She ignores me. I rev the engine in frustration. Finally she looks at me. "Are we getting out of here or what?" I ask.

"Cool your jets, cowboy," she says, unfazed by my irritation. "We're going to leave a little something behind in exchange for Tom-Boy."

"What the hell are you—"

She points to the bed of her truck. "I've agreed to donate some of my food supply to sweeten the deal."

"What? Is the asshole demanding a payoff?"

"No. It was Tom's idea."

"And you can afford this?"

"I can write it off on my taxes," she says with a shrug. "It's a charitable contribution to a 501(c)(3) religious organization."

Just then Tom pulls one of the vans to a stop beside the truck. Atop the van are six mountain bikes in a detachable rack, making it look like one of those escort shuttles that accompany bike-a-thons. Moments later Tom, his twin brother, and a pack of six or seven younger boys are transferring supplies from the truck to the van. Meanwhile, the girls and their mothers have gathered around to watch this new form of entertainment.

Laura waits in the truck while the exchange is made. She's making faces at me that I'm guessing are meant to placate me, but it doesn't help. As relieved as I am to have my Jeep back—one hole shy of complete—I just want this whole drama to be over. The oxycodone has begun to wear off and my arm is starting to feel like it's in a slowly closing vice. I'd take another dose, but I've still got an hour's worth of driving ahead of me.

"Over here, now! C'mon, hurry." Tom's suddenly shouting orders. *What the hell?* I turn to look, as does Laura. The truck bed is still about a quarter full of boxes, but Tom is herding the other boys up into the bed. I'm puzzling over this when I turn back to see that the women are simultaneously herding the girls into the van.

"No!" I shout, jumping out of the Jeep. But no one's listening. I run to Tom and grab him roughly by one arm. "You can't do this, Tom! You're just making the situation worse." He shakes free with surprising force; his expression is one of pure menace. I'm taken aback. For a moment I'm caught in indecision. Do I go after him or start pulling boys out of Laura's truck? Or do I make my case with the mothers, who now have all the girls in the van? Before I can make up my mind, the van doors slam shut, with Tom behind the wheel. The women pile into the Jeep—one sandwiched between the rear seats—as Tom fires up the van and shoots up the road.

"No, goddammit!" I shout, to no effect. "Now listen, ladies," I say, but Tom is already gunning for the gate. *Fuck!*

I look to Laura, who just throws her hands in the air. Then her expression turns to one of alarm. "Nick," she yells, pointing over my shoulder. "Go!" She jerks her head toward the house as she fires up the truck. Before I can respond she jams it into gear and guns it.

I turn to see what spooked her. Father John, who has apparently run to the barn for his rifle, is now sprinting toward us. He hasn't started firing yet, but he'll be within range in a matter of seconds. I've got no choice but to run. I jump back into the Jeep and slam it into first. "Hold on, ladies. It could get a little bumpy!"

I fly up the driveway behind Laura and Tom, making for the gate. I check the mirror. Father John's veered off toward a second Econoline. I glance over my shoulder at the surplus wives. They're terrified, but stoic, not uttering a peep. The boys in the back of Laura's truck are a different story. The younger ones, about eight or nine years old maybe, are bawling; the older ones are hanging onto them so they don't go flying as Laura bumps up the washboard road. I can only imagine what's going on in the van, where Tom has more than a dozen girls and toddlers packed in among the boxes like sardines.

I keep waiting for the gate to open as the van draws near, but it doesn't. Did Tom lose the remote back at the house? What's the holdup? I look back over my shoulder, but there's no sign of the old man yet. I turn back to see that Tom has jumped out of the van and is messing with what looks to be a utility panel in the wall. He's trying to open it. I can only assume it's the manual trip for the gate.

The pungent smell of the leaking gas fills my nostrils as I throw the Jeep into neutral and set the brake. I jump out and grab the tire iron from the back. A minute later I'm beside Tom, prying the panel open with the crowbar-end of the iron. "He shut down the power to the gate," Tom tells me as he trips the release. A moment later we're pulling the gates inward. When I return to the Jeep, I see terror in the ladies' faces. Then I see the cause; Father John is closing the distance in a flatbed truck.

As I pop the Jeep into gear, Tom is already through the gate. But Laura has stalled the truck. The gas smell is nearly overwhelming now, as I yell, "C'mon! Move!" I don't have to turn around to gauge Father John's distance. I hear the bullets begin to strike, ricocheting off the Jeep's bumper and kicking up jets of dust from where they're hitting the ground. He's trying to shoot the tires out.

Finally, the truck bolts forward through the gate. I pop the clutch and follow. Then I hear it: the zing of a ricochet followed by a resonating *whoosh*, like a giant gas-fueled barbecue grill igniting. *Shit!* The flames are just a few feet from the Jeep. I yell to the ladies to jump as I hit the brakes hard and throw the Jeep into a 180-degree spin, putting as much distance between the gas tank and the approaching flame as possible.

I grab the wife directly behind me, and the one between the seats as well, and dive for cover into the pine-needle duff beside the gate. I can only hope the remaining wives have the presence of mind to do the same. Seconds later the Jeep is engulfed in flame. I press the women's faces mercilessly into the duff and brace for it. Then it explodes. The heat is scorching and I hear chunks of debris flying overhead. Several instantaneous fires erupt all around us in the pine-needle tinder.

I jump up and yank the ladies to their feet. They're in shock as I prop one against each shoulder and hustle through the gate. I see beyond the flaming carcass of the Jeep, which now blocks the entire gap between the walls, that the other two wives are scrambling to safety as well. I hurry my two wards to Laura's truck, which has stopped just yards ahead. All the boys are screaming now, even the older ones.

Tom has already jumped out of the van to help his mother and the fourth wife.

"C'mon," I yell. "We can't stop yet." The August-dry forest is already erupting in flame. I don't know what Father John's disposition is; he's somewhere beyond the Jeep, armed and dangerous. "Load up and let's get moving."

Then it dawns on me. Laura's got ten kids in the truck—three in the cab and seven in the bed, along with boxes of supplies. Tom's got fifteen, including himself, in a van designed for twelve, plus the remaining boxes of food. Where are we going to fit five more adults? I could ride the truck's bumper, but the women—who've already gone to comfort the screaming children in the van—are another story. I barely have time to consider this when the gunshots begin again. Father John, still held back by the flames, is now aiming for the truck's tires.

"Go! Just go!" I scream to Laura as she jumps back into the truck. She pops it into gear and spits dirt and gravel as she swings around the commotion at the van. That's when I see Tom's proposed solution to the transportation crisis: he's detached the bicycle rack from the top of the van, and all six bikes come crashing to the ground. He shoves a bike into his mother's hands and is urging the other wives to follow suit.

"Come! Hurry!" he says, holding a bike for me. It's preposterous, but there's no time to debate, and no other immediate solution comes to mind. I grab a bike and join the women already peddling furiously down the road. I hear the van get underway, just as shots ring out again.

Title 23

THE SCENE IS SURREAL: I'M JACK-HAMMERING down an unpaved forest road with the Four Merry Wives of Elwood, all of us on bicycles, led by a truckload of terrified adolescent boys, and followed by a van full of screaming children of all ages. Somewhere behind us is an angry polygamist in hot pursuit, armed with a rifle. Just another day with the Census Bureau.

And to think, this was supposed to be my week off to recuperate from the pit bull impression in my arm, which at the moment is screaming louder than the children behind me. I managed to extract a couple of oxycodone from my pocket and dry-swallow them before mounting the bike; now I'm just waiting for them to kick in.

We're traveling about ten miles per hour, barely faster than a jog, but it feels a lot faster on the rough road. The percussion of the tires on gravel, transmitted through the handlebars, sends staccato stabs of pain in a steady rhythm up my arms and into my skull.

The truck ahead and the van behind look like they're moving in slow motion. The ladies are doing better on their bikes than I expected but, despite the steady downgrade, we're not going to be able to pick up the pace until we reach the pavement some distance ahead. I look back over my shoulder yet again. There's no sign of Father John yet, but if he manages to get around what's left of my Jeep, it'll take him only seconds to catch up in the van. And since he's armed, we need to reduce the possible number of targets for him to shoot at. Starting with the kids.

I speed up and roll alongside Laura's open window. "Go on ahead to Elwood," I tell her. "We'll regroup at the school. Pull in behind it and wait for us."

"What about Father John?" she asks.

"I think we can handle him," I tell her with more certainty than I'm entitled to. "He's not going to be shooting at his wives. It's me he wants. And maybe you," I add. "We can probably get him to negotiate if we use the kids for leverage."

"How's that?"

"If he wants to see them again, he'll have to agree to the ladies' terms."

"And those are?" Laura asks.

"Hell if I know. It's not like I planned this."

Laura does as I tell her. I fall back and tell Tom the same. Both vehicles go on ahead and disappear from view as I rejoin the Four Wives-a-Cycling. The five of us are now hurrying far too slowly down the mountain. I'm still clinging to the faint hope that the flaming carcass of my Jeep will prevent Father John from getting the van around it. Then we can count our little bicycle outing as nothing more than a day's exercise.

The kids are out of immediate danger now, but I still haven't figured out where we go from here. I don't know what the ladies' intent is, or if they've thought that far ahead. I know there's a shelter for battered women in Portland—and probably others in Clackamas County I'm not aware of—but chances are near zero that any single shelter can accommodate four mothers with twenty-five kids among them. What does one do with extra wives? Donate them to Goodwill?

Finally we hit the paved road and begin to pick up speed. It's all downhill and—except for the occasional blind curve—there's nothing to slow us down now. I look over my shoulder yet again; that's when I see him—and laugh so hard I almost fall off the bike.

Just when I thought our predicament couldn't get any more bizarre, Father John is rounding a curve about a hundred yards behind us. But instead of driving one of the Econolines, he's on the sixth bicycle, clutching the rifle across the top of the handlebars. I know this isn't exactly a laughing matter, but the oxycodone is kicking in now, and I can't help myself.

Father John is moments from the blacktop, where he'll pick up speed as well, so we need to get a larger lead on him. "C'mon, ladies," I tell the sister-wives as I pull out ahead. "Let's pick up the pace."

The next time I check, Father John is still close behind, but no longer gaining. Finally able to breathe a sigh of relief, I reassess our situation. That's when, still peddling furiously alongside my gingham-clad posse, I have an oxycodone-induced flashback to The Sound of Music, where Julie Andrews leads the Von Trapp children in song while cycling a country road. I burst into giggles again.

Then I hear the sirens. It's hard to tell where they're coming from or going to; in this terrain the Doppler waves play funny tricks. So does the oxycodone. Belatedly it dawns on me that we probably set the entire forest ablaze back at the compound. By now the spotters in the Forest Service lookout towers will have called in the fire teams.

Sure enough, I see the first of the fire rigs farther down the road ahead of us. "Get in single file and stick to the right shoulder," I tell the wives as I pull into the lead. "The trucks will be passing by any minute now. We'll pull off the pavement right up there." I point to a turnout on the uphill side of the road, well before the next blind curve.

Less than sixty seconds later two rigs from the Elwood Station scream into view as we move to the side. The narrow road, the tight turns, and the steep grade combine to keep the fire trucks moving at a less-than-urgent pace, so the fire team has plenty of time to give us the once-over as they pass by. I can only imagine what the fire crews must be thinking at the sight of us. I'm hit with oxy-giggles once again as they breeze by, staring. I can't help but wave with a shit-eating grin.

Just as the last of the rigs sails past us, I hear the blast of an air horn to the rear, followed by screeching brakes and squealing tires. I turn just in time to see Father John rounding the last bend, wobbling precariously as he attempts to brake and move aside. But it's too late. He loses control and clips the front bumper of the lead truck. I watch in numb detachment as he floats over the embankment toward the ravine eighty feet below. His crumpled bike rebounds off the fire rig and clatters into a heap on the road shoulder; then, as if in slow motion, it tips out of sight and follows him off the precipice.

I hear a collective gasp from the women as I try to focus on what this development means for our impromptu adventure party. It's apparent to me that Father John's fall is not a survivable one, especially when you lead with your head as he did. I'm not sure if his wives have come to the same conclusion, but three of the four are now pedaling toward the scene of the accident, emitting shrieks of grief.

Only Rebecca stays behind. I try on an empathetic expression as I turn to look at her, but it doesn't fit quite right. I'm not sure if she wants my condolences. Her stone-faced expression reveals nothing of how she feels about her husband's probable demise. What I do know is that a moment ago she was fleeing him. And it speaks volumes that she has not joined the other women in running to inquire after his condition.

For a long moment we stand there astride our bikes in silence, me looking at her, she looking into the distance. I get the feeling that she is calculating, rather than observing the scene unfolding before us.

"This changes nothing," she declares at length.

I can't tell if she's talking to me or reminding herself. Then she turns and looks me in the eye. "You will still help us?"

"Uh, well, yeah. Sure," I manage to say at last. "What do you—"

"Then we must be going." Before I can respond, she lets out a shrill whistle and waves to the sister-wives, who are now being approached by one of the firemen.

Without hesitation or any further communication, all three turn back and start pedaling toward us. Rebecca falls in with them as they reach us. Wordlessly the four of them continue down the hill. As I mount my bike to follow, I see the fireman, now waving his arms in the air, calling after them. As they recede down the hill he looks to me. I give him a shrug and hurry to catch up.

Title 24

THE MOTHERS HAVE REUNITED WITH THE children in the Elwood school-yard. I have no idea what they're telling the kids about Father John. I'm not sure why Rebecca has shown no interest in inquiring of the firefighters as to his status. Maybe she hopes he's dead, glad to be rid of him. Of course, there would undoubtedly be some uncomfortable questions; maybe she doesn't want to have to explain the polygamy thing. But still, you'd think she'd want to know. If the other wives are curious, they'll have to wait for someone else to fill them in; they never speak to "outsiders."

Me? I've got no desire to stick my nose any further into this fucking mess. I'm already up to my eyeballs. Father John's almost certainly dead, which means there'll be an investigation. And the fire at the compound makes the whole thing a lot more suspicious. Once arson investigators run the tags on the Jeep, I'm going to have my own set of uncomfortable questions to deal with.

Laura and I stay with the vehicles and discuss our next move.

"Look," I say, "they're safe now. Let's just wait for the teams to knock down the fire, then take them back home—"

"And what if they don't get it under control today," Laura says. "Or worse, what if—"

Her thought is cut short by the appearance of Tom, who's just stepped out of the van, where he has apparently been listening to our conversation.

"We can't go back there," Tom says, as though he's been a part of our conversation all along. "Not while the authorities are there."

"Sure you can," I tell him. "You're not required to talk to them. They're just firefighters."

"Oh, come on, Nick," Laura says in Tom's defense. "You know they can't go back there now; we don't know how big that fire's going to get. Besides, they're probably going to enforce a mandatory evacuation."

Tom's eyes dart from me to Laura, then back to me again.

What I want to ask is how this is my problem, but I know she's right. My conscience reminds me that I'm at least partly responsible for their predicament. "So what are you suggesting?" I ask Laura.

"I've got a truckload of food," she says. "You all can have a picnic while I head back up the mountain and scope things out. If it doesn't look like the crews will have this thing knocked down today, we can figure out where to put this gang for the night."

Tom starts to object, but stops midsentence, seeming to have a change of heart. "Good idea," he says, already turning to go. "I'll get the boys to start unloading the food."

✳   ✳   ✳

It's over an hour before Laura returns. The kids are in the midst of cleaning up the picnic with the same organizational efficiency they employed to set it up. It's as though they've been training for disaster relief operations all along.

Laura's expression tells me more than I want to hear. "It doesn't look good," she says shaking her head.

"The fire?" I ask.

"Father John," she says with a grim expression.

"Dead?"

"I can't be sure," she says. "They wouldn't confirm it to me. But a couple of firefighters had rappelled down to the bottom of the ravine, and from what I could see, they didn't seem to be working on him. An ambulance pulled up on the highway side of the creek and the EMTs were scrambling a litter down to him when I left. I'm guessing it's a recovery operation at this point."

This is what I'd expected to hear. "And the compound?" I ask.

"They've got a pretty good fire line established between the front gate and the houses, but the forest on both sides of the road is fully involved, and it's moving down-slope into the ravine, where it'll be harder to fight. There's no way they're going to have it beat down tonight."

"Fuck." It's not the most helpful response, but it's the only one that comes immediately to mind.

"So we're going to have to get a roof over their heads for tonight, at least," Laura says with the serenity of someone who sees the glass half full. It's not that I see it half empty—I just want to know what's in it.

"A roof over twenty-nine heads? How do you plan to accomplish that?" I ask.

Before she can answer, Tom is back, again interjecting himself into our conversation. "Your house," he says, looking to me for a response. But there's no question in his tone. It's like he's got it all figured out already.

"My house? No, no," I tell him, shaking my head. "There's no way I'm going to squeeze thirty people in there."

Tom stares at me with unnerving conviction. I can feel victory already slipping through my fingers. How does this kid always get to me like this?

"No," I say again, looking away. My relief from his scrutiny is short-lived; when I turn back Laura is giving me a look similar to Tom's. "Oh, come on," I say, already knowing I'm losing the battle. "I'm not the fucking Red Cross."

✳   ✳   ✳

By the time we've gotten the Von Trapp Family tucked in at my house, the scene looks like a refugee camp. The four mothers are sleeping in my queen-size bed; Tom is on the couch, his brother Luke on the chaise lounge outside. The remaining thirteen kids are arranged head to toe on the brick floor of the gazebo like so many Africans on a slave ship. Furniture cushions and air mattresses serve as makeshift beds for most, while the rest make do with flattened cardboard boxes. Three opened sleeping bags and half a dozen blankets provide covers. Clothing is wadded up for use as pillows. Meatloaf, who has finally emerged from under my bed, tiptoes among the children, wondering whether this development bodes well or ill for his daily routine.

Despite their makeshift quarters, none of them complains as I retreat to an air mattress on the floor of the garage, next to the Ducati. It's after ten o'clock. "What a fucking nightmare," I say to no one as I lie staring at the century-old rafters. The smell of gasoline permeates my Oxycodone haze for only a few minutes before I'm dreaming of Beth.

Title 25

"GOD, IT'S GOOD TO SEE YOU," I BLURT when Beth gets within earshot. I want to pick her up in my arms and squeeze her, but I'm still rational enough to realize that this might be a little premature. Besides, I've been sleeping in a garage and haven't showered since yesterday morning. I let my eyes slide a little lower; her breasts are fuller, more round than before. In fact, she's put on a few pounds all around, though it's nothing to complain about. She's clearly no longer the schoolgirl I fell in love with; she's a mature woman now and a mother. But still beautiful.

"You too," Beth says. But it's tentative, without enthusiasm. "How did you know where to find me?"

"Laura Jacobsen told me you were back in town."

"Laura?" she says, surprised. "I didn't know you two stayed in touch."

"We didn't. I happened to run into her the other day. It's a long story." I don't want to talk about Laura, or anyone else. I just want to hear about Beth. Or even just listen to her, regardless of the subject. As the barista takes her order, I fixate on her soft, pink lips—her perfect, round little mouth—older now, but no less inviting.

"How long will you be at your parents'?" I ask her after placing my order.

"I don't know," she says, rolling her eyes. "I'm looking for a place…" She trails off, reluctant, it seems, to finish the thought.

I consider offering to share mine with her, but apart from being premature and entirely impulsive, the offer would be complicated by the fact that I'm currently running a homeless shelter for abused polygamists. Besides, I don't even know what her situation is. "Are you seeing anyone?" An indelicate question, but I don't see a ring and I have to know.

"Not exactly," she says with a smirk and a downcast glance. "I spend so much time with the lawyers there's no time left for anyone else, including me."

My heart skips a beat. If there's not another guy in the picture...

"I've got two boys, Nick." She says this as if apologizing, or perhaps warning me off.

"Hey, I love kids," I say, perhaps a little too enthusiastically. Then, like an idiot, I add, "In fact, I've got a houseful right now myself."

Her expression registers what: Surprise? Disappointment? "Oh. So you're married?"

"No. No," I say quickly. "They're not mine. It's just temporary. Another long story." I laugh nervously. "In fact, it's the same long story."

"Oh," she says again, her expression now unreadable.

We pick up our coffee and seat ourselves at the only indoor table. "So where do you live?" she asks.

"You won't believe this," I say, wondering how she'll react. "Remember that little old lady out on Waterworks Road? The one with the little house at the Bull Run trailhead?"

"Yeah?" A twinkle in her eye says she's already guessed what I'm about to say.

"She died last year and I bought the house."

"Oh, Nick," she says, in what is probably her first unguarded response. "You didn't."

"Yeah," I admit. I can't help but grin at the memories I know are filling both our heads right now. "I just had to."

"I'd love to see it again," Beth says, relaxing further. "Is the gazebo still there?"

"Of course. I haven't changed anything. The stream, the bridges, the yard art—it's all still there. I just made some improvements on the inside. I mean, the place is ninety years old."

Beth falls silent. I'm not sure if she's lost in some sort of reverie about the good times we had, or whether she's reluctant to express what she's feeling. In any case, I'm content to sit back and stare at her shoulder-length red hair as she absentmindedly brushes it back from her face.

After a moment, she comes out of her trance and interrupts mine. "Is there any chance I could come up and see it?"

"Absolute—" I begin to say before I again remember the current occupants. "Oh, well yeah, but—"

Beth cuts me off. "No, I'm sorry," she says. "I shouldn't have—"

"No, no, no," I rush to assure her. "That's OK, really. It's just that I'm sort of loaning out the place at the moment."

"Oh." She seems disappointed. I'm wondering if her request is a pretext to be alone with me, or is it just the house she's still got the hots for?

"But, hey, they should be gone by this weekend. Why don't you come up on Saturday?"

"Really? I'd love to," she says with a childlike glee that reminds me of the college girl I fell in love with.

We talk for another few minutes—me not asking about her marriage, she not asking about my relationship history—before she looks at her watch and says, "Look, Nick. I've got to get back to the boys. My mom's got an appointment."

"Sure. Sure," I say, barely hiding my desire to wrap her in my arms. "So, are we on for Saturday then?"

"Sure. Mom will be home to watch the kids in the afternoon. Would two o'clock work?"

"Absolutely," I say, my heart already racing at the thought of it.

We get up from the table and stand around for a long moment looking awkwardly at each other, like teenagers at the end of a first date. Does she want me to kiss her? I start forward; she turns to go. I pull away; she turns back. Our eyes lock and I go for it—a quick kiss on the lips. I pull back. She stands frozen in place. I'm not sure what to make of it. Then she lunges at me and we go at it full bore for at least thirty seconds.

I do my best to ignore the implications of the song that's playing in the background: Evanescence's "Everybody's Fool."

Title 26

LATER THAT AFTERNOON I'M STANDING IN THE office of Child Protective Services in Oregon City with Laura, trying to wash my hands of the Gang That Couldn't Marry Straight.

"What do you mean they don't qualify?" I shout at the woman behind the counter. It's the first thing I've said in five minutes while Laura laid out the facts of the case. Our plan called for Laura to be the voice and I her silent spokesmodel, but the red-tape runaround she was getting finally scrambled my brain and I couldn't help but vent.

The practiced bureaucrat ignores me. "You said that the abusive parent has left the household; is that right?" she asks, still addressing Laura—who is obviously the more well-behaved of her two guests.

"Well, yes," Laura says. "But, like I said, we can't be sure of his status. He disappeared during the fire evacuation; he might turn up again at any moment."

I'm quietly impressed by how easily Laura is able to manipulate the facts with half-truths. She'd be perfect for government work.

"If he does come back, then you can contact us again and we'll open an investigation. However, as long as the children are with a legal parent or guardian who presents no threat to their welfare, the agency can't intervene. The children must be in imminent danger."

"Well, until two days ago they were in plenty of danger," I blurt, again unable to stifle my contempt. "And now there's been a forest fire. They might be homeless. Can't you investigate that much at least?"

"That's a different matter entirely, sir," she says with an oozing of-ficiousness. "If their home has suffered damage, I suggest you contact the Red Cross."

"Well, that's really fucking helpful," I say, turning away from the counter in disgust. I head out to the parking lot before I have to hear any more of the ritual idiocy the woman's going to spout.

$$* \quad * \quad *$$

"There is some good news," Laura says in an upbeat tone when she joins me in the truck a few minutes later. "They do qualify for food stamps."

"Thank God for small favors," I say with dripping sarcasm. I'm feel-ing nowhere near as charitable toward my unwanted houseguests as I was when I left the house this morning. I only got involved because Father John was an abusive jerk, but now that he's been dispatched, I want out. I just want to focus on Beth.

"However," Laura continues, ignoring my tone, "at least one of the women will have to go into town to apply." She looks at me as though she's fearful of my reaction.

But I've managed to cool down since my outburst. "That would have to be Rebecca," I say, looking at my watch. It's already going on five o'clock. "Would you be able to bring her down here later in the week to do that?"

"Can you handle it, Nick?" Laura says. "I've really got to get back to the café. Bruce is complaining that I've been MIA lately."

"I suppose," I say, not relishing the thought. "I don't go back to work until next week."

"OK, then," Laura says as she starts the truck. "But there's one more thing to take care of first."

"Oh," I say, wary.

"Yeah. In order to get the food stamps, she's going to need to establish an address, so you may want to figure out where they're going to be staying before she applies. If they stay with you, your income will be figured into the eligibility equation."

*   *   *

By the time Laura deposits me at the Clackamas Promenade where I've left the Ducati, I've decided that my house is not where the carnival is going to be staying. With Beth back in the picture, I can think of much better uses for my romantic cabin in the woods.

The easiest solution, I tell myself on the ride home, is to take the lot of them back to Elwood. I'm trying to convince myself that there will be enough of the compound left to make that possible, but the only way to know for sure is to go back and see what's what. With any luck, I can move them back in before the weekend. Then Beth and I can have the place to ourselves. I don't want to consider the alternative.

Title 27

THE AROMA OF FRESH-BAKED BREAD DISTRACTS me from my purpose as I walk through the front door. Deborah and Marilee—or is it Marilee and Julie—are busy with the baking operation, assisted by three of the children. There are so many people running around the house they don't even notice me.

Everywhere I look the house buzzes with activity. Two girls are knitting or crocheting—or whatever it's called—on the couch; two more are washing the windows overlooking the backyard, where a three-year-old is chasing a miffed Meatloaf into the gazebo. The patio sounds like a construction site; hammers compete with the whine of a circular saw—mine, I assume—as Tom, Luke and two of the younger boys appear to be erecting a permanent roof over the brick patio.

"Whoa, hey, what the hell..." I sputter as I head out back to interrupt them. "Guys! Guys!" I yell over the sound of the saw. I make a throat-cutting motion to get Luke to turn the thing off. "What the fuh... uh, *heck*, are you doing?" I ask, remembering my underage audience at the last minute. I direct the question at Tom, who's up on a ladder nailing a roof joist.

"Hey, you like it?" He beams back at me with obvious pride. Clearly he's misreading my expression at the moment.

"No, I don't like it," I shout back. "What makes you think you—" Tom's crestfallen expression is pathetic enough to keep me from finishing the thought. I pause to reconsider my approach.

"Hello, Mr. Prince." Rebecca has taken advantage of the lull to in-sert herself into the conversation. Despite my agitation—or perhaps because of it—I suddenly wonder if she has instinctually moved to pro-tect her children because I've raised my voice with them. Is this what it's like to live with an abusive husband?

"Hello, Rebecca," I say, softening my tone and turning to greet her. "And you can call me Nick, OK?" I force a smile that I'm sure is less than convincing.

"Yes, Nick," Rebecca says, moving closer and fixing me in the eye with a quiet intensity that is both warm and resolute. I'm reminded of my seventh-grade World Civilization teacher (on whom I had my first adolescent crush). "The boys have been busy repaying your generosity with some minor improvements. I do hope you're pleased with their work."

Somehow Rebecca's presence has taken the edge off the angry out-burst I had planned; now I'm struggling for words. She holds me in her gaze as easily as a Klingon tractor beam does the Starship Enterprise, immobilized by an unseen force. It calms me and makes me feel like a dick at the same time.

"Come, Nick," Rebecca says barely, but noticeably, touching my arm, "let me show you what else the children have done to show their gratitude." I follow mutely, as she leads me back into the house. I manage to nod and smile an apology to Tom as we leave the patio. A moment later the saw is whining again.

Rebecca leads me into the bedroom. "The girls have been making curtains," she says, waving toward the window that used to offer an unobstructed view of the forest. "I'm sure you don't mind," she offers by way of explanation, "that they used some of the bedsheets from the linen closet. You had far more than were necessary for the one bed in the house."

I find myself nodding, as though such a conclusion were obvious. I'm mesmerized now, as much by the speed with which they work as I am by whatever superpowers that Rebecca might possess. The previously ordinary gray sheets-now-curtains are now embroidered with bouquets of tiny flowers.

In the bathroom she points out a bowl of soaps in half-egg shapes. These, she explains, were made by Julia and the older girls.

"But how... I mean, with what?" I stammer, amazed at the resourcefulness of these people who have completely taken over my home. "Really? You made soap?"

"Certainly," Rebecca says, as though people do this all the time. "We made lye from the ash in the woodstove; we used cooking oil for fat; and scented it with pine sap. Here," she adds, lifting a bar to my nose, "see? Isn't that refreshing?"

"Well, I'm impressed," I say, without pretense. "You guys have really been busy."

"Oh, that's not all," Rebecca says. "Come. Let me show you what the girls have been up to in the kitchen." She's already leading the way.

I realize that I have misjudged this woman. I had thought her a demure and helpless soul, held captive by a domineering husband; a poor waif too dependent on her man to take care of herself. But she's running my house with an efficiency and air of command that would put any military operation to shame. In just one day she's accomplished more than I could in a month.

The kitchen is no less astounding. There are jars of salmonberry and blackberry jam. "And some huckleberry compote to put on potato pancakes," Rebecca explains as one of the sister-wives and her young assistants beam with pride. The refrigerator also holds several bags of freshly harvested salad greens, including watercress, dandelion, red clover, miner's lettuce, and others I don't recognize. Rebecca opens a paper bag to reveal a gob of chanterelle mushrooms that would cost a fortune in the market.

"You gathered all these yourselves?" I ask, still incredulous. I know these things are plentiful around here, but I had no idea they could be found in such quantities just by walking out my back door.

"Of course we did," Rebecca says. "The children know where to look. They've been doing this since they were old enough to walk."

Only moments ago I had been ready to read this woman the riot act, scolding her for taking liberties in my home. I was prepared to tell her that she would have to make other arrangements as soon as possible. Now the wind is gone from my sails and all I can do is stand in slackjawed wonder. I really could use a woman around the place, I realize. Just not so many of them.

Title 28

MY FACE IS TINGLING FROM THE COOL morning wind as I downshift the Ducati and veer onto Elwood Road. Tom does a better job leaning into the turns than he did on his first ride, though he still holds me too tight. If he's scared, he's not letting on.

As his clan's eldest male, he says he's now the "Patriarch" and the one to "take charge of temporal matters." He's a little young for such grandiosity, it seems to me, but I'm not about to argue the point; just as long as somebody takes responsibility for the entourage and gets them out of my house.

We pass the spot where Father John met his demise just two days ago. I can't help but wonder if, while Tom is taking responsibility, he feels any guilt at having set in motion the death of his stepfather. I know the guy abused him but, hell, Tom ought to feel at least as guilty as I do. Not for his stepfather's sake, but for the other kids at least; the guy was their father, after all.

The extent of the fire is evident long before we reach the turnoff to the compound. Only the blackened remains of the forest are visible for the last half mile. But wildfires tend to be fickle, so here and there a few islands of unscathed trees still punctuate the view. All in all, it looks like the firefighters got a lucky break; the damage appears limited to a couple hundred acres. A wildfire in August could have turned out much worse.

Despite the dry summer conditions, the road in is pretty chewed up from the firefighting efforts and the repeated passage of heavy equipment. Large amounts of water have been dumped in the vicinity of the gate. We fishtail in the mud several times before we finally reach it. Tom's grip, already energetic, feels more like the Heimlich maneuver each time the tires slip; we're both relieved when we finally ooze to a stop.

The air is tainted with the odor of charred wood as we dismount and inspect the damage. Yellow crime tape, fluttering in a slight breeze, adorns what's left of the entrance to the compound. It also surrounds the remains of the Jeep: the blackened shell of the cab sits twisted atop the chassis; the wheels lie beside the wreckage, tires since liquefied by the heat of the blaze.

As I consider the significance of the crime tape, I can't help but wonder what conclusions the arson investigators will have drawn from the scene. I note that they have left the Jeep's carcass exactly where I abandoned it, blocking the main entrance. Instead, they've bulldozed a section of the adjacent wall to gain access to the compound. This has to mean that the Jeep is deemed evidence; otherwise they would've moved it out of the way.

With all that's happened in the last forty-eight hours, I had been feeling lucky just to have survived—not only the gunfire and explosion, but the pit bull attack as well. What I need to consider now is how I'm going to explain the Jeep's presence here when it leads back to me, as it inevitably will. I haven't reported it to the insurance company yet, not just because I've had my hands full with a houseful of women and children, but because I haven't yet worked out the story I need to tell them. Saying that I was being shot at by an angry polygamist for running off with his stepson sounds pretty wacked out, even to me. Not to mention the problem with Title 13.

Tom and I make our way down the driveway to get a better look at the structures. "Well, they're still standing, at least," I say, nodding toward the houses at the bottom of the hill.

"Yeah, but look at the maple," he says, pointing at the huge tree at the center of a blackened lawn. The tree is now leafless and charred, with nothing but the trunk and principle branches remaining. Standing as it does at the edge of the burn, it looks as though it died defending the house behind it. The house, still coated in a Chinook-hued frosting of aerial-dispersed retardant, appears unscathed.

"I helped plant that tree when I was six," Tom says, more wistful than I have yet seen him. "That was the year we came here and built the first house."

I can't help but note that he seems more upset about the death of the tree than that of his stepfather. I can't say I blame him; I'm not exactly crying over the guy either. "So what happened to your biological father?" I ask as we walk around behind the main house to get a look at the rest of the buildings. I've been curious as to how his mother, who seems like a perfectly capable and rational woman, ended up with a badass polygamist.

"I don't remember my dad very well," Tom says, eyes to the ground in front of him. "I was only five when we left him."

"So your parents divorced, then?"

"I don't think so. I'm not sure," he says without emotion. "I think we just left."

"Huh," I say, wondering what Rebecca's version of the story might be. "Do you know where he is now?" I ask, not without a little selfishness. I'm wondering if I might be able to turn this whole mess over to Tom's real father to sort out.

"He's dead."

"Oh, sorry to hear that." I pause before asking, "Did he have other wives too?"

"No, no," he says, shaking his head vigorously. "He was a Salt Lake Mormon. I mean, I guess we all were then."

"Wait," I say, taken aback by this revelation. "You mean your mother wasn't raised in a polygamist cult... uh, culture?" I say, recovering from the near insult.

"No way," Tom says. "The Salt Lake church doesn't approve of it. She only converted to the Principle when she married Father John."

"And she knew he already had other wives at the time?"

"Yeah," Tom says, still sounding wistful. This time I don't think it's because of the tree. This might not be what he wants to talk about, but I feel a sudden need to get some answers while I have a chance.

"What on earth persuaded her to marry a man with three wives?" My voice is unintentionally shrill. "I'm sorry," I say, cranking it back a notch, "but if she wasn't indoctrinated in that kind of life, it's hard to understand how she could suddenly accept it."

Tom shrugs. "We lived with the sister-wives for three years before she actually married him. We were already a family then, so it didn't really change all that much. Except..." He turns to look out the window as he trails off.

"Except?" I prod.

"Except, he started getting meaner after they were married."

"Abusive, you mean?" I ask. "Is that when he started hitting you?"

"No. Not right away. He was just hateful—not just with me and Luke, but with Mom." Tom sighs before continuing. "I mean, before they were married he was always being sweet to her—and to us— trying to win her over. But afterward he just started giving her orders."

I can tell he's not really comfortable talking about this, so I let it go as we continue our tour of the grounds. We move from the houses to the barn. Only now does it occur to me that they must have abandoned some livestock here. Tom confirms this: six cows, ten horses, a dozen sheep and goats, and several dozen chickens are among the now missing residents of the barn. He's visibly upset.

"I don't get it," he says, once again becoming the innocent 17-year-old. "The barn wasn't touched by the fire. What happened to them? Did somebody steal them?"

"Relax," I tell him. "The authorities probably called in an animal rescue team to take them to safety."

Tom looks at me, hopeful. "You think so?"

The kid baffles me. One minute he's the naïve, aw-shucks country bumpkin, the next he's a shrewd, headstrong schemer. At the moment he's all whimper and pout.

"Yeah, I'm sure of it," I tell him, though I'm not sure of anything.

Thirty minutes later we've completed our fact-finding mission. The net loss appears to be most of the orchard and the grain crops, as well as the storehouse, including the solar panels that once covered its roof. The remaining two Econolines are untouched. We've removed the rear seats from one of them, and loaded and secured the Ducati. We'll each drive one home.

I try to put a positive spin on the situation, not just for Tom's sake, but because I have to believe the place is still habitable. I need the circus at my house to end, pronto.

"Well, it looks like we can start moving your family back in," I tell Tom.

He looks at me with what is either disappointment or bewilderment; I'm not sure which. "But how?" he says. "There's no electricity; all the chilled food is lost. The dry foods are gone with the storehouse. The fruit trees and vegetable gardens are gone as well. And there are no animals, so we have no milk, eggs, or meat."

I'd forgotten how self-sufficient these people were until Tom says this. I'm certain that they have no insurance either. Then I remember. "What about the fire safe? The one you said Father John kept under his bed?" I expect this to be good news, but Tom's expression puzzles me. I seem to have caught him off guard. He's got a faraway look, as though he's trying to remember something.

After some hesitation, he finally returns to the moment. "Oh, yeah."

"Why don't you go see if you can find it," I suggest. "Maybe there's enough there to put this place back together."

Title 29

"THAT'S NOT NEARLY ENOUGH," REBECCA says in a rare moment of vulnerability. This rock of a woman who didn't so much as twitch when her husband plummeted to his death, or when a forest fire left her and twenty-eight other family members temporarily homeless, seems undone finally by the news that her husband hasn't left the family quite the sum of treasure he led her to believe he'd stashed away.

She looks at me as though I'm going to resolve her dilemma.

"Hey, it's not exactly chump change," I say, trying to sound upbeat. In spite of their plight, I need them out of my house by the weekend when Beth will be here. "With all the free labor at your disposal, fifteen thousand dollars will buy a lot of repairs."

Her distress turns to something more akin to impatience. "Mr. Prince—"

"Nick," I remind her.

"Nick, have you ever had to feed twenty-five children?"

The question is clearly rhetorical. I wait, rebuked, for her to make her point.

"Without our winter stores and fresh produce," she continues, "fifteen thousand dollars will barely keep us all fed for six months. And it's too late in the season to plant much of anything for this year's consumption, so we'll be buying food for at least that long."

The other wives gathered around the kitchen table nod in agreement. Tom remains silent, no longer trumpeting his "patriarchal duty"

as the eldest male in the household. Instead, his head is bowed in def-
erence to his mother as we discuss the family's immediate future. I
decide he's either bipolar or a master of manipulation.

"And while we could grow many of the vegetables faster if we rebuild the greenhouses," Rebecca goes on, "we would deplete our funds
in doing so." Again she's looking at me like I can somehow change this
equation.

"Hey, I'm sorry," I say. "Really, I am. But we can get you food
stamps, at least."

"Nick," Rebecca says. "That's just not possible. In order to apply we
would have to answer questions that would bring government scrutiny." Her expression chides me for overlooking the obvious.

"Well, I'm happy to help you get resettled up there," I say, not
wanting to lose the momentum that will get them out by the weekend.
"And you can even help yourselves to my tools and scrap lumber, and
whatever else you can find out in the garage." When no one responds, I
add, "Staying here is not going to help you. If you're going to rebuild,
you need to be living onsite."

The reaction around the table is less than enthusiastic, but no one
refutes my point. Rebecca glances around at the sister-wives, then fo-
cuses on Tom. It's almost as if she's telepathically extracting a response from him. Her gaze is intense, but strangely beautiful. It's as if
I'm noticing for the first time how attractive she is. Maybe it's because
when she fixes that kind of gaze on me I'm powerless to make such
observations.

After a pause, Tom finally speaks. "All right. Then we'll take an inventory of the garage tonight and make up a list of what we'll need to
get started. You and I," he says to me, as though he's been appointed
foreman on this job and I'm just a union grunt, "will go into town for
building supplies in the morning"—before I can respond he continues,
turning to address the threesome I've come to think of as "the lesser
wives"—"while you prepare lunch provisions."

The women nod silently, as though they're accustomed to being dictated to, even if it is by a 17-year-old boy. I'm certain now that every nuance of Tom's interactions with the adults around him is a carefully considered strategy. Like they say—it's the quiet ones you've got to watch out for.

Tom goes on planning tomorrow's itinerary and making assignments, including to me. My first instinct is to take him down a notch, let him know he can't take those kinds of liberties. Fortunately I have an illuminating thought before I open my mouth: it's in my best interest to give their project all the help I can; the sooner it gets underway, the sooner Beth and I can have this place to ourselves.

With the planning session concluded, the lesser wives begin buzzing around the kitchen in anticipation of the dinner that will need cooking. As always, they're accompanied by a pit crew of young girls who seem to pop out of the furniture whenever there is women's work to be done. And around my place, I'm sure the need is endless.

I consider asking if there's something I should be doing to help—though I can't imagine how I could add anything to their Swiss-clock efficiency—when Rebecca tells the clan, "Mr. Prince and I are going into town for groceries. Have you prepared the list?"

Julie grabs a tablet of paper off the kitchen counter and hands it to her. "Is this everything, then?" Rebecca asks, flipping through two or three sheets of scribbled items. Satisfied, she turns to me and smiles. "Shall we go, Nick?"

I've just pulled the van onto Bull Run Road when Rebecca says, "I want you to know how thorough our gratitude is for your assistance."

I give her a tentative smile, searching for the appropriate reply. She's got me unnerved again, but I don't know why. "Uh, yeah, sure," I

mumble finally, now uncomfortable with the look she's giving me—
something between appraisal and adoration.

"If we had more funds to draw on, I would gladly pay you for your
trouble," she says.

"That's OK," I tell her. "I'm glad to help." Glad isn't exactly the
right word. I'm not sure what is: Relieved? Desperate? Compelled?

"You know," she says, never taking her eyes off me, despite the
sharp curves in the road that cause her to brace herself on the armrest,
"you don't have to hold yourself responsible for what happened."

To some people, of course, this is a backhanded way of saying "I
hold you totally responsible." I glance at her while a half-dozen snarky
replies compete for a spot on my thick tongue. But for some reason my
innate snark is impaired by her presence. "Yeah, thanks," is the only
thought that finds its way into words.

"We did act rather hastily," she says, as though she's publishing
the result of some lengthy investigation into the matter. "But when the
Lord opens a door, there is often precious little time to walk through it
before it closes again." She smiles at me with an almost shy bat of the
eyelashes. From any other woman I would consider it flirtatious.

It occurs to me that she's not wearing any makeup—unusual for
the women I usually hang with. I find this strangely—and incredibly—
sexy; I can't help but turn back for a second helping. *Fuck!* What is
wrong with me?

Title 30

I WAKE TO THE SOUND OF SOMEONE knocking on the front door. My watch tells me it's barely after six a.m. *What the fuck?* I get to my feet and push the garage door open just far enough to see Tom open the door of the house to a Clackamas County Sheriff's deputy. I'm pretty sure he's here about the Jeep. I've decided that all I've got to do is tell him it was stolen—Rigs is a witness to that—and I won't be liable for whatever happened with it.

Right now, however, I'm more concerned with what Tom might be telling the deputy. The kid's a wily little bastard, even if he means well. In any case, I'm not comfortable with the idea that the first impression the law will get of the current situation is going to come from Tom.

I grapple for my pants and throw on a shirt as I push out into the driveway, buttoning as I go. "Good morning!" I say to the deputy in my best Wal-Mart greeter voice. "What brings you all the way out here so early in the day?"

The deputy regards me with more than a little apprehension. I'm pretty sure his right hand moves toward his weapon. I guess I could have been a little more subtle than to burst into his peripheral vision without warning. Instinctively I throw my hands out to my side and give him a goofy shrug. "Sorry. Didn't mean to startle you."

"Deputy Tucker Denton," he says, letting his weapon arm relax. He doesn't return my smile, however. "Are you Nicholas J. Prince?"

"Yessir."

"And you're the registered owner of a 2010 Jeep Wrangler with the Oregon tag 174 WNX?"

"Uh, yeah," I say, as casually as I can. "Have you found it?"

The deputy looks at me with a jaundiced eye. I recognize this look from the faces of the bartenders down at the Safari Club during happy hour. It's the one they give the poor drunk bastards pleading for just one more drink after they've been cut off. "Can you tell me when you last saw your vehicle, Mr. Prince?"

This is a question I'm prepared for. "It was stolen last week," I say, carefully evading the question of when I actually saw it last. "Let's see, that would have been Thursday."

"And you reported the theft to law enforcement?" the deputy asks, his eyes still narrowed in skepticism. He doesn't seem to have detected my evasive answer; that's because he's a patrolman, not a detective.

"I've been recovering from a job-related injury," I say, showing off my bandaged arm, "and dealing with a houseful of guests for the last week." I nod in Tom's direction, as if to offer him as evidence. I'm winging it, but technically, I still haven't lied yet. So far, so good. I wonder how long I can keep this up.

"And your insurance company?" Deputy Denton asks.

"Not yet," I say with a smile and a wave of my bandage, as if this will reiterate my excuse. It's a stupid, nervous gesture that a detective would be sure to pick up on. Not this guy though. They don't pay him to be that clever.

"Mr. Prince," the deputy says, shifting his weight to the other foot. "Did you tell anybody of the purported vehicle theft, either at the time of the event, or since?"

His use of the word "purported" doesn't escape me; it tells me that my song's a little "pitchy"; I might yet be voted off this little stage I'm dancing on at the moment. "Uh, yeah. I sure did," I say with a tad too much enthusiasm. "I had a buddy drive me back to where it broke down. That's when we discovered it was gone."

"And you can give me the name of this buddy?"

"Sure. Rigs... I mean, Jerry Thomas," I say. "He's a criminal defense attorney up in Boring." This last part I add in an unconsidered effort to shore up the fact that Rigs actually exists. It's not until after I say it that I realize that cops and defense attorneys are about as friendly with each other as lions and zebras. So those probably weren't the best credentials to offer in this instance. Deputy Denton's next question immediately underscores my regret.

"And you've discussed this with your lawyer since then?"

"No. I mean, he's not *my* lawyer," I say, knowing I've just stepped in it. "He's just a friend who happens to be a defense attorney."

"Right," Denton says. "So, you wouldn't mind if I had a chat with him, seeing as how he doesn't represent you?"

This guy's smarter than I gave him credit for. If I say I don't want him talking to Rigs, then it either looks like I'm lying or that I've got something to hide. If I say, sure, go ahead, I'm consenting to let the deputy get another version of the events, one that includes my going to confront Father John at the compound. Not that Rigs wouldn't have my best interests in mind, it's just that I know he's not about to risk disbarment by lying to protect me.

"Sure," I say, not really having a viable option. "I'm sure he'd be happy to confirm what I've told you." Maybe I can get to him in time to get our stories in synch.

Buoyed by his progress, Deputy Denton squares his shoulders and hones his focus. "Have you ever been to a residence at 27450 South Elwood Road, Mr. Prince?"

Fuck. I was hoping it wouldn't get this specific. "I'm not really sure where that is," I say, dodging.

"How about this: have you been to Elwood in the past week?" Denton asks. "You do know where Elwood is, don't you?"

"Yeah, sure. I mean, of course I know where it is."

Denton just stares at me, waiting. Finally he says, "And? Have you been there in the past week?"

"Uh, yeah," I say, glancing at Tom, wondering if the deputy is going to question him as well.

"And did you visit a residence approximately fifteen miles up from the main highway, at the address in question?"

Suddenly Tom jumps into the conversation. "No, he didn't," Tom says in an authoritative voice. "He just picked me up at the school, down by the highway."

"Tom, no," I say instinctively, not wanting him to dig a hole neither of us can get out of. If he lies now, his credibility will be shot if we have to put the real story forward later. If only I'd thought to coach him beforehand.

"Hold on, young man," Deputy Denton tells him. To me he says, "Just answer the question, Mr. Prince."

I think about this for a minute. A respondent's address is "PII"—"personally identifiable information"; it's explicitly covered by Title 13. I risk five years and $250,000 if I say I was there; I don't see any way around that. "I'm afraid I can't answer that," I say.

"Then you won't mind coming with me," Denton says, grabbing my arm and twisting it behind my back before I'm even aware of it. In an instant he's got the second arm and slaps the cuffs on. "And *you* might want to be the one to call your lawyer friend before we ask you any more questions."

Title 31

IT'S NOT THE BENSON HOTEL, BUT I've got to admit that the bed in the holding cell at the Clackamas County Jail is more comfortable than my damp dirt garage floor. Not that I wouldn't rather be at home in any case. It's Saturday. Rebecca and her clan will be working up at the compound all day, and Beth is supposed to show up at the house at two. If I'm not out of here by then, she'll probably think I changed my mind and blew her off. Even if she gives me the benefit of the doubt, her favorable view of me is bound to evaporate when I explain that I was late because I was in jail, *again*—right where I was when she last saw me ten years ago.

It's going on ten o'clock and I've just completed another fruitless round of interrogation with Deputy Denton's colleagues, Detective Steve Priebus and his partner, Jonathan Segal. I'm sure I didn't help my case by referring to the latter as "Livingston," but after two hours of playing Good Cop, Bad Cop with the two of them, I got a little punchy and it slipped out.

The circular conversation went something like this—at least this is what I remember from the third iteration of it:

Priebus: So you admit to being in Elwood on Monday of this week, is that right?
Me: Yeah.
Priebus: And what was your purpose there?

Me: I was a tourist.

Priebus: Being a smartass, Mr. Prince, will not help your situation.

Me: Sorry. Born that way, I guess.

Priebus: How did you get to Elwood?

Me: I rode with my friend Laura.

Priebus: Laura Jacobsen?

Me: No—Laura Scudder.

Priebus: Were you in your own vehicle?

Me: No, we took Laura's rig.

Priebus: Which you say was—he checks his notes—a 90's-model blue Ford pickup with a canopy?

Me: Unless I'm color-blind.

Priebus: And where was your Jeep at the time?

Me: I told you—it was stolen on Thursday.

Priebus: And yet you didn't report that to anybody.

Me: Not the cops. Just—

Priebus: Yeah, I know—your attorney.

Me: Right.

By that point I had decided to stop asserting that Rigs was "just a friend" and go with the story that he was "my lawyer"; I figured this would prevent them from questioning him. But this hasty decision led the conversation down a different path altogether—one I hadn't considered.

Priebus: And why did you feel it necessary to discuss your missing Jeep with legal counsel, rather than with law enforcement or your own insurance company, Mr. Prince? Did you need to build a defense for something you'd done?

I tried to recover. *I've already told you—Jerry Thomas is a personal friend; he was with me when I discovered the Jeep was gone. We*

*thought maybe we'd find it somewhere in Elwood, so we went on ahead
to take a look around.*

> *Priebus: And did your little "look around" take you to the address in
> question?*
> *Me: I can't say.*
> *Priebus: Can't or won't?*

When I remained silent, as I had the first two times this question
came up, Priebus laid out his full hand.

> *This is more than just an arson investigation, Mr. Prince. A man's
> life is in the balance here. And we have witnesses that put you at the
> scene at approximately the time the fire was set. You ever been to prison,
> Mr. Prince? Oh, wait—I believe you plea-bargained your way to proba-
> tion, didn't you? Well, you may not be so lucky this time.*

After that, good ol' Livingston gave me the pep talk about how my
cooperation would leave me in a much better position than I currently
found myself. I realized by then that I probably should have had a
lawyer present. I'd been stupid to think I could get away with claiming
the Jeep had been stolen and leave out the Title 13 confidential data.

In the end, they learned nothing more from me after two-plus hours
than they had in the first thirty minutes. I, on the other hand, learned
a lot from them. First, I learned that Father John is *not* dead; not yet
anyway. He's in a medically induced coma at Providence Medical Center, in critical condition.

As I lie in my cell contemplating how the dude could possibly have
survived that fall, a Nickelback song keeps going through my head:

> *And you can leave me there for days*
> *And I'll stay alive*

Just to follow you home
And I will survive

I finally conclude that Father John doesn't present any immediate threat to me in his current condition, and he may not survive anyway, so it's too early to worry about it. But if he does come around, he's not gonna be too happy about Tom's pilfering of his strongbox and Rebecca's spending of the funds. Neither of them is legally related to him—Marilee, his first wife, is the only one the law recognizes. So if Father John wanted revenge against Tom, he could make a case for grand larceny. But if the old man dies, probate will leave it all in Marilee's hands anyway, and she's a willing accomplice, so everyone's likely off the hook. His death might be the best outcome for everybody. Except him, of course.

One other piece of information that Priebus and Segal left me with is that I'm being held as a material witness, not a suspect. That, according to Livingston, means they can hold me up to 72 hours without charges. But since today's Saturday, and that clock only runs on weekdays, it won't start ticking until Monday morning. It could be midnight on Wednesday before they decide to let me go—or charge me with something. That's why I've asked for my phone call this morning; I've got to bring Rigs in on this before it gets out of hand. If it hasn't already.

✳   ✳   ✳

"Why am I not surprised, Prince?" Rigs is speaking to me from the other side of the bullet-proof glass by means of the blue, unmonitored, "attorney-privilege" phone in the visitor's booth. "You have this way of turning a simple fire drill into a mass evacuation."

"Hey, I can't be awesome all the time; sometimes I've got to be an idiot."

"And this has to involve me, why?" Rigs isn't complaining; he's just giving me shit like he always does.

"Because you're the one with the JD. It's your job, remember?"

"Sorry, Pal. A job is something you get paid for. And unless you've just won the lottery, I'm guessing these aren't billable hours."

"What can I say? You oughta be more careful about who you choose to hang with."

Twenty minutes later I've told Rigs the whole sorry story, including the Title 13 stuff. I figure the attorney-client privilege prevents anyone from knowing that I told him. Rigs has confirmed my analysis.

"So what happens next?" I ask him.

"I petition the court for a bail hearing."

"Will that be a problem? I mean, other than eating up your Saturday morning."

Rigs grimaces. "Well, yes and no," he says. "Getting the hearing today won't be a problem. But arson is now classified as an act of 'terrorism,' so you're going to have to come up with some cash; there'll be no recognizance release."

"Me? A terrorist? Just 'cause I ate all those falafels in college…"

"I'm afraid this part's not going to be that funny, Nick. Even though you're only a material witness at this point, the Patriot Act lets the Feds hold you indefinitely without bail if they want."

"Fuck. You think that's a possibility?"

"Well, it's not likely, but you *are* considered a hostile witness because you've refused to answer their questions. My guess is that the judge will make you post a high bond, and he'll give extra scrutiny to your character witnesses."

"Shit. Character witnesses? Like who?"

"We need to talk about that. I know you don't have any local family, so let's start with longtime friends. Who have you got here besides me and Jerry?"

"No one, really. Unless you count Beth." I say this without think-ing. I left the part about finding Beth out of my story to Rigs; it didn't seem germane to why I'm in this fucking cell.

"Beth?" Rigs says with predictable surprise. "You mean you've stayed in touch?"

"No, no. I just ran into her the other day and... and we went for cof-fee, that's all."

"Are you fucking kidding me, Nick?" That right there can get you locked up for five years—forget the arson charge."

It's a harsh reality that I'm already aware of, despite living in denial for the past week. "Well, nobody knows but me and her," I say. "And now you, but that doesn't count, Counselor."

"Well you'd better hope it stays that way," Rigs says. "Now, who else have you got?"

"Hey, there's Laura," I say, remembering.

"I don't know, Nick," Rigs says with a slow shake of his head. "You knew her ten years ago and, except for a few days this week, she knows nothing about your life since. Besides, she's connected with Beth. It wouldn't be good to remind the court of those associations, even though your record will already be laid out before the judge."

"Well, except for the guys down at the Safari Club, I'm afraid I'm fresh out of recent friends," I say, realizing the shit I'm in is looking a lot deeper.

"How about coworkers, business contacts, professional relation-ships—that sort of thing? You've got to have someone there you could call on."

"Dude, I'm a field rep; I'm either driving around all day or making phone calls from home. It's not like I have an office full of cubicle-mates."

"Yeah, but you have to check in once in a while. You report to somebody, don't you?"

The laugh that rips from me is so loud that Rigs has to pull the handset away from his ear. It's not intentional, and it's not as though my situation isn't serious. But I just had a vision of Angie standing in a courtroom speaking in my defense. If anything boggles the mind, it is that.

"Care to fill me in?" Rigs asks with obvious annoyance.

"Sorry, dude. It's just that, well, my boss is not someone you want to ask to say nice things about me."

"Listen, Nick. You're not in a position to be picky. Give me a name and number and I'll look into it."

By the time Rigs leaves I'm certain of one thing: I won't be getting out of here any time soon. In fact, I imagine that if Angie gets a chance to give the judge an earful, I may never get out at all.

Title 32

"WOW." FOR A MOMENT I CAN THINK of nothing else to say.

"I was afraid of that," Rigs says, pursing his lips and heaving a sigh. "Your sex-offender status tainted the judge's opinion."

"Yeah, but ten grand? That's a little steep for playing with matches, even with my history."

"Hey, you're lucky he didn't declare you an 'enemy combatant.' You'd have been turned over to the feds and there wouldn't be any bail at all."

"Well, shit. If my options are to raise ten grand or rot in jail, maybe I should just say to hell with Title 13 and tell 'em what they want to know. At least I could clear my name and get out of here."

"Don't get too worked up about it," Rigs says. "You'll get most of the bail back. And you're still better off going up against the county than you would be in federal court. The feds don't get to try many Title 13 cases, and with so much Tea Party focus on what the government does with Census data, they'd likely want to make an example of you. You know, lock someone up just to prove to all those anti-government types that their privacy is being defended."

"So, how am I supposed to come up with that kind of money? A bail bondsman?"

Rigs shakes his head. "You know, Rebecca called me this morning after they hauled you off; she offered a thousand dollars for a bail bond, but I had to explain to her that Oregon doesn't use a bondsman system. Here you need cold, hard cash—no credit, debit, checks, or food stamps.

"That's brutal," I say. I'm touched that Rebecca offered money on my behalf, especially since she's already said that the fifteen thousand she has isn't enough for her own family. "So where do you suggest I get the money?" I say, looking at the clock, thinking of Beth.

"How about a cash advance?"

"Can't," I say. "Don't have the limit for it. But, hey, if you could loan me the diff—"

Rigs cuts me off with a shake of the head. "Don't even," he says. "Conflict of interest. I can't take any financial liability for you."

"What about the pro bono you're doing for me?"

"That's different. All I stand to lose is a case if you jump bail, no tangible assets."

"Well, fuck." It's obvious I'm not going to get to see Beth today. Or ever again, maybe.

"Listen," Rigs says as the bailiff comes to collect me from the anteroom and take me back to my weekend suite, "let me see what I can do. I bet we can have you out of here by tomorrow at the latest."

"Right. OK," I say, feeling fucking sorry for myself as I turn to go with the bailiff. "I appreciate it."

✳   ✳   ✳

I've been in my cell less than an hour when a guard's unlocking it again. "Prince? Come on," he says, holding the door open.

"What? Where we goin', lunch?" I ask. I know Rigs can't have raised the money already; he's barely had time to drive home.

"You made bail," the guard says tersely, guiding me down the stark, whitewashed cinderblock corridor—the same corridor, I now remember, that I first saw over three years ago when I came here to do a census survey. I want to believe what the guard's telling me, but how the hell can it be true?

Yet it is, apparently, because I'm now in the processing area, and they've just given me a basket containing my wallet, phone, watch, and pocket litter. I put the watch on; it's going on one-thirty. I might still be able to catch Beth, depending on how I'm getting home. I'm contemplating the possible alternatives when the electronic door lock buzzes, signaling that I'm free to leave. I push it open and emerge into the lobby.

"Hey," Tom says, with the biggest smile I've yet seen on him. And if that's not enough of a surprise, he strides over and throws his gangly arms around me in a bear hug. "Are you all right?"

"Yeah, sure," I tell him, still off balance from his sudden assault. "I'm fine, really," I add, prying myself from his grip.

"I'm so glad," he says, backing off.

Gimme a break. Are those tears?

"I... uh, we were so worried about you," Tom effuses. "It's not fair what they did to you."

"Yeah, well, it's OK now," I say, looking around the lobby to see who else might have accompanied him. "So, Tom, how'd you get here?"

"I drove," he says.

"Alone?"

"Yes."

"Well then who paid my bail?"

The shit-eating grin returns to his bony face.

"You?" I say, perplexed. "Where'd you get ten thou... No! Tell me you didn't use Father John's stash to bail me out."

His smile fades into the lost-puppy look I've seen so many times before, as though I just took his chew-toy away.

"Jesus, Tom. Your family needs that money to rebuild," I say, wondering—selfishly, I know—whether this will delay their departure from my house. "Does your mother know you took it?"

His face answers before he does. "It's my money," he says with a defiant jut of his lower lip. In an instant the puppy has become a bulldog. "He had no right."

"Who? Father John?" I ask, leading him toward the front door. I've got to get back for Beth. "What are you saying?"

"Where do you think he got all that money?" Tom says, his voice rising as he trails me out to the parking lot. "He had no right!"

"So you keep saying, Tom," I say, more interested in finding the van than listening to him complain at the moment. I spot it in a handicapped parking spot just beyond a couple of patrol cars. "Mind if I drive?" I ask, extending my hand for the keys.

Tom hands them to me without speaking. His face is contorted into a mess of emotions I'd need to be a therapist to sort out.

Once we're on the main highway I'm ready to return to the question of the money. "Now what's this about Father John and 'your' money?"

"That was our insurance money," Tom says with all the bluster of an angry teenager. "Luke and I were supposed to go to college with it."

"You mean life insurance—from your dad?"

"Yessir," Tom says, nodding resolutely. "I told you, he had no right to it."

"How'd he get it?"

"What do you mean?" Tom says, looking confused. "He just took it."

"Well, what was your mother's response? Surely she didn't approve of that."

"She got no choice in it," he says. "He was the Patriarch." He spits the word. "But now I'm the Patriarch," he trumpets. "So I can do what I want with it."

As happy as I am to be sprung from the holding cell, I realize this kid's got issues, and that his using that money for my bail isn't the end of the story by a long shot. I'll have to talk to Rebecca about it. I wonder whether I might not have to surrender myself for a refund—after I see Beth, of course.

"Listen, Tom. I sincerely appreciate what you did for me," I tell him. "But I think we need to discuss this with your mother when she gets back." I look to see how he reacts to this suggestion.

"Back from where?" he asks, looking at me in response.

"From the compound."

"Naw, she didn't go."

"What do you mean? Today was the work party."

"We canceled it after you were arrested," Tom says.

"You what? No!"

"We couldn't go off and leave you in jail after—"

I cut him off. "Tom! Where are the women and children now?"

He cocks his head, as though he doesn't understand the question. "They're at home, of course."

"At *my* home?"

"Well, yes," he says tentatively.

"Oh, fuck!" I hit the gas harder as we fly eastbound onto the Clack-amas-Boring Highway, running two consecutive yellow lights—the latter of which might have been more red than yellow. I've got to head Beth off before she actually reaches the house.

Title 33

BY THE TIME WE TURN ONTO Waterworks Road, Tom is even more white knuckled than he was on his first motorcycle ride. But despite my NASCAR driving I'm not spared the sight of Beth's car parked at the end of the road. *Shit.* Maybe, just maybe, she's still in the car, and I can take her for a little hike along the river while the four Snow Whites and the Twenty-Four Dwarfs clear out.

Of course, I know this isn't likely, even as I'm thinking it, but I don't want to consider the alternative. How the hell am I going to explain this situation?

I pull the van in behind the other two in the driveway and kill the engine. Tom says nothing as he gets out and lets himself in the front door. I'm willing myself to stay in the van until I can think up a plausible story, but I'm not having any luck. Besides, I don't want to rekindle the flame with Beth by starting with lies. I'm just going to have to hope she'll cut me some slack when I tell her that I can't give her the details.

My stomach's doing flip-flops as I jump out of the van and head for the door. Before I reach it, it opens. The first face I see is Beth's, her coppery hair pulled up into a chignon, just like Rebecca's. Then Rebecca is at her side. The two are coming toward me arm in arm. And they're laughing. Laughing? What can be so funny? Then my heart skips a beat; is Beth laughing at *me*?

"Nick! Hey," Beth says, slipping her arm out of Rebecca's and half-skipping toward me with a Cheshire grin. For a moment I'm transported back to PSU, to the underage Beth who turned my life upside down. I stand rooted, unable to respond. *What the hell?*

"This is so cool," Beth says. "I can't believe what you're doing here."

"Uh, yeah," I say, stammering like a schoolboy. "But, you know, I really haven't changed the place that much. I kinda wanted to preserve it like I... like *we* remembered it."

"No, no," she says grasping my arm. Her perfume snags me in its heavenly scent and threatens to render me helpless. "I mean, the place is great, just like I remember it." She waves a hand toward the house. "But it's what you're doing with it that's so awesome."

"What I'm doing with it?"

"Yes," she enthuses, pointing at Rebecca, who is standing back. "Rebecca has been telling me all about it."

"Oh, you mean the curtains and the pergola and all that; well, I can't take the—"

"Come, now, Nick," Rebecca interrupts. "You must be hungry. Lunch is already on the table," she says, turning back toward the house before adding, "You haven't eaten yet, have you?" She looks back over her shoulder with a smile that speaks volumes, only I'm not sure in what language. I'm still too blown away by this unexpected reception. Completely off balance now, I have no choice but to follow the direction I'm being given. I could do worse, I'm sure. Because whatever Rebecca has said to Beth, it's got her loving me at the moment.

✳ ✳ ✳

The lunch conversation is inane—recipes and household hints and what the ladies have done with Beth's hair—but I'm not really listening to it. I'm still pinching myself to see if this is real. I'm sitting at my dining table beside Beth, which should be a dream come true. But the addition of four polygamous wives—the kids are eating out on the patio—has made it more of a nightmare. Not that they're disagreeable people—far from it. It's just not how I imagined this moment; bringing Beth back to this place was supposed to have been magical. Now, instead of reminiscing about the good times, we're sharing child-rearing tips.

Mercifully, when the meal ends, Beth is dissuaded by the other women from participating in the clean-up. "Absolutely not," says Marilee, who's been babbling—along with her sister-wives—like I've never heard before today. "You're a guest here. You go on and visit with Mr. Prince." Rebecca is the only one who calls me Nick. In fact, the others still speak to me as little as possible.

Beth finally stops offering to help. "Come on," I tell her. "Let's go for a walk. You know, up the trail."

She checks her watch. "Oh, Nick, I'd love to. But," she adds, with a pout, "I've got to get back to the kids."

"I thought your mom was watching them," I say, more insolently than I should.

"Well, yeah," Beth says. "But only for a couple of hours. She's got a church thing she's going to—a dinner she's got to set up."

I'm feeling desperate to keep her here, to have some private time to talk. But I can't see how that's possible now. I decide to punt. "Hey, if your parents are going to be at church, I could come to your place."

Her face goes ashen. "No! Nick, don't. I mean, don't ever come around my parents' place." She adds in a more conciliatory tone, "They haven't changed, Nick. They won't ever."

I can do nothing but sulk, reluctant as I move to see her out. I'm hoping for at least a few minutes alone outside.

"But, hey, I'll take a rain-check on the hike," she adds. "Maybe we could do that later in the week."

I brighten at this news. "Sure, just name the day and time," I say, masking my deeper disappointment. "I'm supposed to go back to work on Monday, but hey, that's the one nice thing about working for the Senseless Bureau: I get to set my own schedule."

Once we're outside, I stop and take Beth's hand. "Hey, I'm sorry about all this," I say, nodding toward the house.

"About what?" Beth says, looking for all the world like a kid who's just spent an afternoon at the playground.

"You know," I say, "the commotion, the women, the houseful of kids."

"Oh, Nick, no. I think it's wonderful what you're doing for those poor women."

"You do?"

"Oh, yes! I mean, to tell you the truth, I never thought of you as the kind of guy who'd open up his own home to domestic abuse victims. And sleeping in the garage even!"

"Domestic abuse..." I trail off, thinking better of refuting her. Is that what Rebecca told her? "Well, I mean, it's only temporary. You know, just a few more days maybe."

"A few days?" she says, looking at me funny. "But Rebecca says it will take weeks to get all those women and their kids resettled."

"Weeks? No," I assure her. "I'm just going to help them get the process started, then they're gone. I mean, they're lovely... uh, fine... I mean, they're good women, but I'm not equipped to handle that many bodies in this little place."

"It looks like they've taken care of that for you," Beth says. "Just look at all they've done and how effortlessly they work together. It's as if they've known each other for years instead of only a week."

"Uh, yeah," I say. "You'd think so, wouldn't you?"

Title 34

LAST NIGHT AFTER DINNER I DEBRIEFED Rebecca on the story she gave Beth, though I'd pretty much figured it out before I asked: she made me out to be a Good Samaritan who had opened up my home to four women, along with their kids, in order to rescue them from abusive men. Rebecca added that she had told Beth I came upon these women in the course of my Census work, and that my lawyer friend had helped with legal arrangements. That explanation would raise some eyebrows at the Census Bureau, without a doubt, but I guess it's not a problem for Beth to think that, if it works for her.

What I really wanted to know from Rebecca though, was whether she expected to be occupying my place for "weeks," as she had told Beth. Her answer was coy. "I don't intend to be here any longer than we are welcome, Nick." Damn her. Why does she have this way of turning everything around and laying it on me? What was I supposed to say to that: *You're only welcome through next Saturday?*

There are so many other things that I want to ask her now—about Tom, Father John, the bail money—I just don't know where to begin. But this is my chance to do it, while we're on our way to the compound. I'm driving and she's riding shotgun in one of the three vans; ours is loaded with tools and supplies. Our only other passengers are the two girls and one boy—about 4 to 6 years old—strapped in behind us. At the moment their noses are buried in books, and they're too young to understand in any case.

"Listen, Rebecca," I begin once we hit the Molalla Highway. "We need to talk," I say, glancing at her.

She says nothing, but turns to look at me with a question mark on her face.

"I need to ask you something." She remains silent, so I continue. "Did you pay my bail just so I'd help you with this rebuilding project?" It sounds harsh and accusatory, not exactly what I intended, so I backpedal. "I mean, you know, did you think I wouldn't help you if you hadn't...." I trail off, looking back at her.

"Nick, I don't understand what you're talking about," she says evenly. "First of all, I don't see how you could be here helping us if you were still in jail, so that would be a moot point. And secondly, I didn't pay your bail. What gave you that idea?"

"Tom," I say. "He paid the bail from your fifteen-thousand-dollar inheritance."

"He most certainly did not," Rebecca says. "I have that money put away for expenses—except what we just spent on supplies, of course."

"And you last saw it when?"

She throws me a look of disbelief; it's obvious she understands that I'm accusing Tom. "It's all there, Nick. I assure you. What are you trying to say?"

"Look, Rebecca. I like Tom, I really do. But I was there. The guard confirmed it. Tom paid my bail. In fact, he confirmed it himself when I asked him where he got the money." I watch her expression morph from imperious to concerned. "He said it was his father's insurance money."

Rebecca just stares at me for a moment. "But how can that be? I'm sure all fifteen..." she trails off. "Unless..." she begins. We both reach the same conclusion at once.

"...there was more than fifteen thousand to begin with," I say, completing her thought. We look at each other as if to confirm our conclusion. I instantly feel bad for having convicted her son this way.

Rebecca looks as though she could cry. We drive on in silence for nearly a minute before she speaks again. "He is a willful boy, I admit. And he has cause to be angry at his stepfather." I let her continue without comment. "But to withhold this from me—I would not have expected that from him."

"He seems like a good kid," I offer, attempting to soften the blow of her realization. "I think he means well."

When she speaks again the welling tears begin to spill. "I blame myself, you know."

"No, no, don't," I say instinctively. But it's a stupid thing to say. I have no idea what's gone on in this family prior to last week. For all I know it *is* Rebecca's fault that her son turned out to be a thief.

"Oh, Nick," she says with an air of defeat. "I have done a grave disservice to those boys. I should never have brought them into this lifestyle."

Her earnestness emboldens me to ask what I've been wondering for some time now. "How exactly did you end up with Father John? If you don't mind my asking." I keep my eyes on the road to give her some space. I don't want this to feel like a Priebus & Segal interrogation. Her story begins to unfold.

✳   ✳   ✳

"I met Merrill—the boys' father—when I was eighteen. We were both attending Dixie College in St. George, Utah at the time. Like any good Mormon girl I was anxious to find a husband and marry in the temple. Foolishly, I accepted the first proposal. Neither of us was ready, but no one would tell us that. He was just returned from a mission when we met, and by the time I finished my Freshman year and he his Sophomore, we were married."

She sighs and I make it a point not to interrupt. I think she needs to vent, probably more than I need the information. But I'm hanging on her every word, even so. After pulling an embroidered-flower hanky out of her pocket and dabbing at her eyes, she continues.

"Tom was born nine months later, and Luke a year after that. We were the model Mormon family, or so I thought. I was a teacher in the ladies' Relief Society, Merrill was a Webelos den leader in the Zion Cub Scout Pack and a Deacon's Quorum instructor. Our lives revolved around the Church. I worked part-time at Deseret Industries, a sort of Mormon Goodwill thrift shop.

"But after Merrill graduated we moved to Hurricane, twenty miles up the road and Merrill insisted that I stop working to raise the boys—and the other children we expected to be having soon. It didn't take me long to discover I wasn't cut out for small town life. I was born and raised in Scottsdale." She looks at me as if I should be granting her a pardon for this. I just smile and nod, trying not to let my surprise show. Somehow, I had not imagined her ever living in a big city.

"Anyway, the marriage started to deteriorate. Merrill spent more and more time on church business and with the Cub Scouts, and when he was home we would argue. I hated exposing the boys to that, so I started spending more time away from home as well. It didn't help that in a town like Hurricane everyone knows your business. They feast on the failings of others like vampires on blood." She looks at me for understanding.

"I know what you mean," I say. "Estacada's a bit like that; it's only about 2,500 people."

"Now imagine if they all went to the same church," she says with a laugh tinged with bitterness.

"Right. Good point."

"So one day Merrill doesn't come home at all. I was actually feeling a guilty relief at the freedom—until the bishop called. He said Merrill had been arrested and that he might be in jail for a few days."

"Well, I'm certainly not going to pass judgment there," I tell her, trying both to lighten the mood and to show some humility to this poor woman who's been through far more than I have.

"Oh, but Nick, this was altogether worse," Rebecca says fixing me in the eye. "He was a sex offender!"

My stomach jumps right out of the van. Even though she's not re-ferring to me, I feel indicted by her use of that term—and in such a hateful tone. How can I respond? Hey, I'm all for honesty, but there's no way I'm going to go that far. If the Census Bureau has taught me one thing, it's that there's such a thing as a "need-to-know basis." And that's one thing she doesn't need to know about me.

Title 35

THERE'S MUCH MORE TO REBECCA'S STORY, I'm sure, and I want to hear it, but we're already arriving at the compound, so it will have to wait. I'm thankful at least, that there won't be any more talk of sex offenders. Rebecca has fallen silent and is checking herself in the mirror, working at eliminating any telltale signs of her earlier tears.

"Are you going to confront him about the money?" I ask her as we roll to a stop. Somehow the intimacy of her own story makes me feel that I can be this direct with a woman I still barely know.

"I don't see how that would help anything at the moment," she says matter-of-factly, already sliding out of the van. "We need to get to work now. That can wait."

My first reaction is to defy her assessment. She's letting herself be manipulated and cowed by yet another "Patriarch." I'm thinking this needs to end—Tom needs to be called out. But I hold my tongue and reconsider. Rebecca is nothing if not pragmatic. She has a point; a clash with Tom now might imperil an entire day's worth of work. We need to focus on why we're here. But once we get home, he'll have some "splainin'" to do.

Within minutes of the arrival of the third van the lesser-wives have organized the children into now-familiar regiments based on age and ability. Tom and Rebecca begin doling out the assignments they drew up last night in a lengthy family conference. The youngest of those old enough to walk, with Julie's supervision, are tasked with salvaging any edible vegetables, then tilling the garden and planting fast-growing veggies such as spinach, lettuce, turnips, and scallions. Those a little older are assigned to salvage whatever can be salvaged from the damaged and destroyed buildings. This includes not only the contents, but the building materials as well; nothing will go to waste. If only half a plank or two-by-four is burned, the other half will still be used. This group is put under Deborah's watchful eye.

And while Marilee cares for the infants and toddlers, I join a work crew comprising myself, Tom, Luke, and Deborah's eldest, Mason, turned 14 this week. Our job is to transport the supplies to their various locations, then begin setting up the first two solar panels on the main house. With a combined output of 90 watts, they'll be enough to power one of the ultra–energy-efficient refrigerators, so Rebecca can start laying in stores of food.

I continue to be impressed by the efficiency of this polygamist army; by the time we break for lunch the salvage is complete and the cataloging has begun, several boxes have been filled with edible vegetables, and the gardens are tilled and ready for seeding. Our team hasn't been lagging either; the panels are installed and ready to be hooked up. Rebecca and Marilee have already left for town to buy groceries.

I was tempted to offer to go in Marilee's place so I could hear the rest of Rebecca's story; I've really started to enjoy her company. But I dismissed the thought immediately; it would have been contrived and awkward for the only adult male in this work party to run off and do the grocery shopping.

So instead of talking to Rebecca during our lunch break, I decide to chat up Tom instead. I so want to confront him about the money he kept from his mother—even if it was used on my behalf—but I figure it's best to let Rebecca broach the subject first. I can have my say later. Still, that doesn't keep me from beating around the proverbial bush a bit.

"If you don't my asking, how'd your dad die?"

Tom stares off toward the charred orchard as he chews on the question and his watercress sandwich. I don't pressure him. Maybe I should skip the interrogation; there's still work to be done and I really shouldn't put him off his game right now.

"That's OK," I say. "It's really none of my business."

Tom swallows and scratches his chin, then turns to me. "He was murdered."

"Man, I'm sorry." I really am sorry. "That's gotta be hard to handle."

"In prison," he adds, still meeting my gaze, as though he's measuring my response.

I shake my head. "Wow. Doubly hard to handle."

"Know what he was in for?" he asks, appearing to wince at the thought of it.

"Yeah. Your mom told me he was a sex offender." I don't push for any further explanation, but he apparently wants to talk about it.

"Molesting Cub Scouts," he says. "Ten-year-olds."

He wants a response from me, I can tell, but I'm not sure what kind of one. Does he want me to be disgusted? Or does he want me to excuse his father somehow? Maybe he just wants me to feel his pain. Unsure, I shake my head. What is it I *do* feel? I'm not sure of that either.

"So I can't really claim him, can I?" Tom says, clearly in a rhetorical sense.

"But you *can* claim his insurance payout." I'm as surprised by my statement as Tom is. It was a kneejerk response that even I didn't see coming. I don't know why; maybe it's just that this whole twisted story has gotten under my skin.

Tom's response is swift and intense. "Damn right, I can!" he spits, jumping to his feet. "He owes me that much. Look what he's done to our lives. Look at my mother, left to the evil designs of that... that monster. I've got to take care of her now. Why shouldn't it be with that money? He's worth more dead than alive." He turns and strides off toward the back of the main house.

I sit where I am, trying to figure out what my role is in this fucking Greek tragedy. What the hell does he want from me? And what does Rebecca want? Hell, what the fuck do *I* want?

Title 36

EVERYONE'S EXHAUSTED BY THE TIME WE pile into the vans for the ride back to my place. Tom accepted my apology with a shrug and we left it at that. I thought of filling Rebecca in on the conversation, but now doesn't seem the right time. Our conversation is sparse and limited to pedestrian topics.

Dinner is a relatively quiet affair due to the universal exhaustion, but everyone has a healthy appetite, including me. I'd love a second helping of shepherd's pie, but I can't help but feel I'd be taking food from the mouths of children if I asked for more. As usual, the lesser-wives refuse my offer of help with the dishes, so I retreat to my desk to prepare myself for the return to work tomorrow that I'd rather not think about.

I notice there's a message on the answering machine. I'm not sure when it was left; I haven't even thought to check messages since getting sprung from jail. My friends all have my cell number; the house phone is reserved for Census and nuisance calls—if that's not redundant. I press the Play button and cringe when Angie's voice squawks back at me.

"Hey, Big Guy, what the hell is going on? Jail? Really?" I'd completely forgotten that Rigs had contacted her for a character reference for the bail hearing. "Some paralegal from your lawyer's office called and asked me to vouch for you. She wouldn't tell me what you were arrested for, but I said only nice things about you, of course." If this had been a live conversation, this is where Angie would wait for me to thank her profusely for the undeserved favor she'd done me. Instead, her message continues, "But I'm afraid Seattle isn't as magnanimous about these things. They've had to suspend you until you're cleared of any charges, so your workload has been transferred to Mary. Anyway, call me. We need to talk."

No, we don't. The last thing I want to do is get Angie involved in this any further than she already is. Her penchant for gossip would turn my suspension into a firing within 24 hours. The irony of my situation is hard to escape: in my effort to defend the Bureau's sacrosanct Title 13, I get arrested and am summarily suspended from my job. Well, fuck it. Yeah, I need the money, but right now I've got too many other things to sort out. I can use an extended vacation.

I take a hot shower to think things through, but before I know it the day's labor catches up with me and my mind goes all muzzy. I close my eyes and start to relax, but immediately remember that two dozen other filthy bodies need washing before bed, so I'd better spare the hot water. I dress and head for the garage, where I intend to be asleep before my head hits the air mattress. As I'm saying my good-nights on my way to the door, Rebecca stops me.

"Can we talk?"

"Sure."

She pulls aside the open door and I follow her out into the driveway.

"Let's walk," she says, already leading the way toward the Bull Run trailhead. When we're a good distance from the house, she says, "I've had a talk with Tom."

"Listen, I'm sorry about what I said—" I begin, but she stops me.

"No, you don't need to apologize. He's sorry for his angry outburst. I'm sure he'll tell you so himself when he gets the chance."

"Well, I shouldn't have been so judgmental," I say. "You and your family have been through more than I can possibly understand. Tom's got a right to be angry."

"Oh, but he so looks up to you," Rebecca says, turning to look me in the eye.

"Me? But why?"

Rebecca sighs. "Tom is a complex boy, Nick. A man-boy now. He's trying to define himself, not only as an adult, but as the new Patriarch of this extended family."

"Is he though?" I ask.

"Is he what?"

"The Patriarch."

"Well, yes. In John's absence, Tom, as the eldest male in the household, bears responsibility. That's the way the Order works."

"The Order?" I say, pulling aside a vine maple branch that's grown over the trail. "You mean, like, the religious order?"

"Kind of," she says. "But it's not like a monastic order, if that's what you're thinking. It's the Patriarchal Order, the basic organizational principle of the celestial family—it's our form of government, really."

"So, your religion dictates that Tom has to take charge, despite his age?"

"Yes, when he turns eighteen next week."

"And if he's not ready?"

"It's my job to see that he's ready," Rebecca says solemnly. "And where he has flaws, it is my duty to shore them up, to help him improve."

"Even if that means being subservient to him, just because he's male?" I'm struggling to keep my knee-jerk annoyance in check this time. I'm never going to understand this situation if I keep flying off the handle like I usually do.

"Nick," Rebecca says, stopping and turning to face me. "I have spent my whole life in a patriarchal society. It does not mean to me what it means to you. I have my strengths, yes, and I'm content to pursue them for the good of everyone concerned. But I don't need to be in charge. I'm happy to leave that to others, so that they may grow too."

I can see her point, but only so far. "But if you, a mature woman, are better suited than an eighteen-year-old kid to make an important decision, shouldn't you assert your right to do so?"

I'm surprised when Rebecca laughs. I'm struck again by her simple beauty—her dimples and naturally rosy cheeks, her green eyes full of mysticism—accented now by the green and orange light of the evening sun through the forest canopy.

"You've never been married, have you, Nick?" she says with a gentle, knowing smile.

"No."

"A man may be the mouthpiece, but an experienced woman is often responsible for what it utters."

I can't help but laugh at this, because I know she's right. "I know a lot of men," I say, "myself included, who tie themselves in knots trying to say what a woman expects him to."

"True," Rebecca agrees. "But it goes far beyond the courtship ritual. When God commanded a woman to be the man's 'help-meet,' he meant for her to be his counselor. Her job is to advise him."

"And the more wives a man has, the more advice he gets?" I say this only half-joking.

Rebecca takes it in stride. "You can say that," she agrees. "But some men are impervious to advice, no matter how many women he has to offer it." Her mood darkens with this observation.

"Which reminds me," I say, brought back to one of my earlier concerns. "What do you plan to do if Father John recovers and returns to the compound?"

"That's a difficult question to answer, Nick." She throws me a look that screams doubt and worry. "If he returns after Tom's birthday, we have the right to hold a patriarchal council. We can try him for his abuses and banish him from the community."

"And if he returns before?" I say, wondering at the complexity of the microcosm these people live in, right under the clueless noses of the rest of us.

"Without another Patriarch to preside," she says, her worry still evident, "he will still be in charge."

"Surely you don't intend to submit to him again," I say, my voice rising in spite of my vow of self-control. "Not after that escape you pulled off. He'd..." I hesitate to complete my thought, because even I don't want to contemplate it. "Well, he'd make you pay, I have no doubt of that. Tom especially."

"I'm all too aware of that, Nick," she says, as we turn back toward the house. "We won't put ourselves in that position, no matter how this plays out."

I'm about to respond when she takes me by the arm. "Nick, now you understand why we need a place to stay until Tom turns eighteen."

I'm completely at the mercy of her compelling green eyes and the electricity of her touch. Unlike the erotic response that is more familiar to me, the power she seems to have over me is something entirely— well, maybe not entirely—but it's different. I feel as though I would be helpless to resist anything she might ask of me.

"You don't need to worry," I tell her in a comforting voice I barely recognize as my own. "I'd never let that jerk lay a hand on you again."

She smiles and releases my arm. "Thank you, Nick. Your kindness will not go unappreciated. You'll see."

Title 37

OVER THE LAST THREE DAYS WE'VE MADE a lot of progress at the compound. The full array of solar panels on the main house now provides power for all three houses, including a deep-freezer, where the sister-wives have begun laying in bread and baked goods for months to come. The newly planted garden is set to yield its first vegetables in about six weeks. And we've pre-assembled the outer walls for the new store-house. It feels good to have something to show for a week's work other than the empty six-packs and take-out food wrappers I'm used to. I could get to like this farm life.

Yesterday we stopped by Eagle Creek Farm and Feed on our way to Elwood and inquired about making some livestock purchases. Though this isn't the season for calves and kids, we've been put in touch with someone who can sell us the animals we'll need in a couple of weeks, as well as a few roosters and a couple dozen hens. This will be another phase of my rural education; the closest I've come to a personal relationship with cows and goats was at the 4H booth at the county fair when I was a kid.

We've already gone through nearly half of Rebecca's original fifteen thousand dollars for the solar supplies and lumber, though we now know that Tom also has five thousand remaining from the fifteen he kept to himself. When I asked Rebecca why she didn't press the issue of the money with him, she told me that Tom needed independence to be able to assume the mantle of Patriarch. Independence to rip off the family? I didn't say this of course. Rebecca insisted that accusations would be counterproductive, saying she preferred to give him "guidance" instead. This, I presume, refers to the manipulation she described so succinctly on our walk the other day. If it works for her, what can I say?

I'm thinking about just such feminine wiles as I wind the Ducati down Ten Eyck Road toward my date with Beth at Dodge Park. As much as she seems to get along with the sister-wives, I intend to have her all to myself for today's picnic. I don't need her picking up any tips from Rebecca on how to get me to do her bidding, though I have to admit, in my current state of mind I'm already willing to do whatever Beth wants.

I turn into the park's entrance and make my way toward the peninsula where the Sandy and Bull Run Rivers converge, to the picnic area where I'm to meet Beth. I don't see her anywhere, so I pick a table at the far end that is likely to offer the most privacy. Not that there's much of a crowd on a Thursday afternoon, even at the end of August. The few visitors in the park are mostly congregated along the beach near the Sandy River bridge at the park's entrance.

I spot her red 4Runner coming around the park loop just before three-thirty, over an hour late. I've got a once-chilled bottle of Pinot Grigio and two Solo cups laid out, along with a sliced apple and a hunk of smelly cheese, the kind we used to share all those years ago. By the time she pulls to a stop beside the Ducati, I've poured the wine, ready to toast our reunion.

My heart sinks when she emerges from the car along with two boys, about seven and ten years old—her kids, no doubt. They weren't supposed to be part of today's equation. I'm seriously disappointed, but I do my best to hide it. "Hey there," I say with a smile. "Glad you made it. I was beginning to worry."

Beth rolls her eyes as she guides the boys ahead of her. "Don't even start," she says with exasperation. "I'm lucky we made it at all. Mom forgot she was watching the boys today and scheduled a Bible study, so I had to pick them up at the last minute." She puts a hand on each of their shoulders. "This is Josiah," she says, introducing the older, dark-haired boy. "And this is Micah. Boys, this is Nick."

"Hey," Josiah says with little enthusiasm. His brother just mumbles and squirms out of his mother's grasp. "Can we go play on the swings?"

"OK. But don't—you hear me?—*don't* go near the river without me. We'll all go down together in a little while. Josiah, look after your brother," she adds as the boys are already trotting off to the playground.

"Hey," she says to me once they're gone. "I'm so sorry. Some days I can't seem to make it all work the way it should."

"Hey, no problem," I say, handing her a cup of wine. "I'm just happy you're here."

"No," she says, holding up her hand. "I can't drink with the kids here, Nick."

"It's not much. Are you sure?"

"Really. I'd love to, but…" she trails off with a demure smile.

Impulsively I give her a peck on her little upturned nose. "OK. OK. How about some cheese then," I say exchanging her cup for an apple slice spread with brie.

"Aw, Nick," she says, averting her eyes, then looking back to me. "I'm a vegan now."

I can't catch a break. I'm oh-for-two. "Your loss," I say in an effort to keep things light as I pop the hors d'oeuvre into my own mouth instead and swallow it along with my disappointment. But it's all worth it when she responds with a laugh, one of her best qualities.

"But I will take some apple slices," she says, looking to the picnic table, where I've laid out the food on a paper towel. She purses her lips and adds, "If you have any without cheese, that is."

I reach into my backpack and pull out a plastic baggie with a few brownish slices of apple. "Will this do?" I ask sheepishly. Then we both burst out laughing.

She grabs the bag from me and gives me a hug. "You haven't changed a bit, Jughead," she says, invoking a nickname that she gave me back in college. It's one that only she ever used. Hearing it now makes me want this moment to go on indefinitely.

"I've got an idea," I say, locking my hands at the small of her back, remembering the dimple there, where I used to love to plant kisses.

"Oh," she says warily, pulling back to look me in the eye.

"Why don't we pick up where we left off—pretend that nothing ever came between us." I don't mean this, of course, but the fantasy is an irresistible one.

Beth laughs. "Oh, sure," she says. "And I'm twenty pounds lighter and have no stretch marks."

"Hey, I won't notice."

"Right. And in case you also failed to notice," she says waving toward the playground, "I have children now."

"I can pretend they're mine," I say, keeping it playful, but wondering at the same time whether I could actually do such a thing. I've never felt mature enough for kids of my own.

Beth tenses and pulls away. After checking on the boys she turns back to me. "I'm afraid our days of 'pretend' are long behind us, Nick."

"Can't fault a guy for dreaming."

"That's your problem, Nick. You're a dreamer who never wakes up to do anything about it."

"Ouch." I smile to disguise my awareness that she's right. Then, unable to refrain from being defensive, I add, "Is that your father's assessment?"

"Oh, Nick," she says, with more melancholy than accusation, "we lead different lives now. We're not college kids anymore. You don't even know me."

"OK, fair enough," I say. "So let me get to know you all over again. Let's take a walk down by the water and you can tell me everything that's happened since we last saw each other."

"See, there's a perfect example," she says.

"Of what?"

"How clueless you are. I'm a mother; I've got to watch my boys. I can't go off on a stroll by the river just because you think it's romantic."

"Dammit, Beth! Gimme a break here, will you? I'm trying to say the right thing."

"That's just it, Nick. For you it's all about finessing the situation to your advantage. What about me? Do you even care what I'm dealing with?" The fire in her eyes is one I remember, but it's not a warm, fuzzy kind of recollection.

"Fine," I say, failing to hide my annoyance with her condescending tone. "Let's just sit here and talk." I sit and pat the bench for her to do the same.

She does so wordlessly, though her body language is guarded, another sign I recognize from all those years ago.

"Thank you," I say with more than a little condescension of my own. "Now, as long as we're airing our hurt feelings, I need to ask you something."

She gives me a sidelong glance, the flame diminished but the anger still smoldering.

"Why didn't you stick up for me at the trial?"

"Oh come on, Nick," she says with irritation. "Did you forget what it was like back then? The photos, my parents—"

I cut her off. "But why did you never stand up to your parents?" I feel the heat rising into my face as I struggle to keep it under control.

"Think about it, Nick. I was seventeen! I had no money. They were paying for my education. They were still my legal guardians. What choice did I have?"

She continues to make her case for the next fifteen minutes while I brood, wondering who I can blame for my misfortune, if not Beth. As her story unfolds we both calm down and the tension eases. I'm surprised and more than a little hurt to learn that just three months after my plea bargain, the day after her eighteenth birthday, she married a dweeb named Eric Swenson from her parents' congregation.

"It sounds to me like an arranged marriage. You couldn't really have loved him, not like you loved me." My statement is really a question; I'm hoping the answer is no.

"We were young, Nick. What did any of us know about love?"

"I loved *you*," I say, sounding to myself more like a pouting child than a grown man. But I can't help it. "Look at me and tell me you didn't love me too."

She looks at me. "I thought I did, Nick. I don't know. We were so young—*I* was, at least."

"Yeah, I don't think you need to remind me of that," I say, with more than a little bitterness. "You could have started by being honest about your age."

"Look, I'm sorry, Nick. That was a long time ago. It's not something I'm proud of, OK?"

I look away and try to stuff my anger. If there's anything to salvage here—and I hope to God there is, because without realizing it, I've been waiting ten years to try—I've got to put it behind me. "So, did you love Eric?"

"Not at first, but we made it work—after a while."

"But were you happy?"

"Kind of," she says with a shrug, then reconsiders. "Well, not really. I mean, we had a house in Happy Valley, and we lived well. Josiah was born the first year, and Micah came along two years later. They were happy and healthy..." She trails off, but I don't interrupt. "The thing is, Eric and I didn't have anything in common. He was a straight-arrow Christian who'd never gone to college, and never been more than fifty miles from home. Me, I'm—or I used to be, anyway—the curious cat, always questioning things, never accepting the status quo. I got restless and he just didn't understand."

I'm just about to ask her why she stopped questioning, when our conversation is cut short by the arrival of the boys. Chased by his younger brother, Josiah runs past us to the opposite side of the table, where he turns to face Micah, hanging back on our side. The two then skitter back and forth around the table in a game of cat and mouse.

"Boys!" Beth says, but makes no move to interfere with their game.

I'm drawn to Josiah, who's now using us as a shield from Micah, who's climbed up onto the picnic table behind us. Josiah's thick, curly hair reminds me of my own at that age. His dark eyes scream mischief, and his heavy eyebrows evoke Groucho Marx...the despised nickname I was given in grade school. Then there's his thick, stocky build... *Oh, fuck! I'm looking at myself.*

Title 38

THE QUESTION OF FATHER JOHN AND HIS possible return has been nagging at me for days now, but I keep pushing it aside to deal with more immediate issues that keep arising. Today however, the matter has come to the forefront. In fact, I'm accompanying Rebecca, Marilee, and Tom to Providence Hospital to see him.

Not that I plan to do any visiting. The guy's still in intensive care in any case. I'm only along at Rebecca's request. I'm not sure why; it's not like he's going to fly out of bed and attack her. But whatever her fears are, it seems Tom shares them; he insisted that she not visit Father John without him. Probably just a show of bravado to emphasize his new role as her protector—something a "Patriarch" does, I guess.

Our trip was set in motion when the sister-wives held a caucus last night and decided that someone needed to inquire as to Father John's condition. Rebecca tried calling the hospital this morning, but was refused information because she could not prove that she was an immediate family member. According to the hospital staffer she spoke with, she would need to come to the hospital in person and present identification.

Marilee, of course, is the only one with the requisite ID; she has a marriage certificate issued in Washington County, Utah that we found in Father John's fire safe. But Marilee is not experienced in "the world of the Gentiles," as the women have told me on more than one occasion, so Rebecca must accompany her to do the talking.

We've made our way to the nurse's station and Marilee has pro-
duced the required identification. But the charge nurse, instead of telling us what the man's prognosis is, has insisted on calling the doctor.
So now we're sitting in the waiting room fidgeting. No one has said it,
but it's rather obvious to me that all four of us have more than enough
reason to hope the guy isn't going to survive. That's what I'm thinking,
anyway. It's certainly what Tom wants; I have no doubt of that. The
women, who have the kids to think about as well, are harder to read.

A short, balding man with a round face interrupts our collective silence. "Excuse me. Which one of you is Mrs. Allred?"

Marilee raises her hand tentatively.

"And I'm her sister," Rebecca says, standing. "Rebecca Olsen."

Tom is also on his feet, but says nothing.

"I'm Dr. Savage. I'm happy to meet you folks," the unfortunately
named doctor says, seating himself next to me, across from the three of
them as Rebecca and Tom return to their seats. "We've been trying to
identify the patient's—your husband's—next of kin since he arrived
here." He directs this to Marilee.

"We live what you might call 'off the grid,'" Rebecca says.

"Yes, apparently," Savage says. "I'm told the accident occurred in a
very remote location." He turns back to Marilee. "Your husband's ex-
tremely lucky the fire team was able to respond so quickly and stabil-
ize him."

Marilee only smiles weakly. Rebecca jumps in once again. "Does
that mean he's going to make it?"

"It's too early to be certain of anything. He's in stable condition,
but—I don't know if anyone's told you yet—he's in an induced coma.
Do you understand what that means?"

Marilee nods. Rebecca says, "Yes."

"He's suffered massive internal injuries; most of his organs sustained some degree of damage," the doctor says in his best bedside

manner. "But all of his surgeries have gone well, and we have reason to hope that he'll continue to improve."

Marilee and Rebecca smile. Tom remains expressionless.

"Thank you, doctor. I'm sure you're doing everything you can," Rebecca says. "How long do you expect him to remain in this coma?"

"If there are no complications, I expect to bring him out within the week. But it's a day-to-day thing, you understand," the doctor says to Rebecca, then looks to Marilee. He's probably wondering by now if she's mute, as she hasn't uttered a word.

"Certainly," Rebecca says.

"Do you have any other questions for me?" Savage asks, again looking to both women.

"No," Rebecca says, looking to Marilee for confirmation. "I just wonder if we can see him before we go."

"Sure," the doctor says, getting to his feet. "However, hospital policy restricts ICU visits to immediate family only: parents, spouse, and children over sixteen." He looks at Rebecca apologetically. "His wife may see him," he says, "but I'm afraid the rest of you will not be able to just yet."

"I'm his son," Tom says, getting to his feet and towering over the doctor. "I can see him too."

"Why, yes, of course," Savage says. "Forgive me. We weren't introduced. I didn't realize who you were." He extends a hand, but Tom doesn't reciprocate.

"I'm Tom. I'm the eldest male in the family."

Savage smiles wanly at this awkward introduction. "Well, Tom. Feel free to accompany your mother, then."

No one corrects the doctor's misreading of the family tree. Tom helps Marilee to her feet and the doctor leads them to the nurses' station, where he bids them farewell. A moment later the nurse leads them down the hall to Father John. Rebecca and I are left to our own thoughts in the waiting area.

"I'd like to hear more of your story, if you're up for it," I say to Rebecca after a brief silence. "How did you end up with him?" I ask, nodding in the direction of the ICU.

"Oh, surely it would bore you," she says, smiling self-consciously. Something in her eyes tells me however, that she wants to share.

"Hardly," I say, encouraging her. "Is there anything more boring than sitting in a hospital waiting room?"

She laughs. Then her expression goes solemn; a memory flickers in her eyes. "I wouldn't know," she says with a pregnant sigh. "The last time I was in one was the night I met John."

I'm rapt as the story unfolds.

Title 39

"AT FIRST I REFUSED TO BELIEVE THE CHARGES against Merrill. He had always been good with the boys—not only ours, but the scouts as well. I just couldn't imagine him abusing them." A tiny shudder ripples through her as she speaks of the unthinkable crime. "But I was forced to confront the reality of it when the bishop called me in and told me it was my duty, as a wife and a mother, to forgive my husband."

"So the bishop believed your husband was guilty?" I ask.

"Oh, no," she says, shaking her head. "He *knew* he was guilty; Merrill had confessed to him!"

"And he expected you to just forgive and forget, like nothing happened?"

Rebecca nods. "What's more, he used his church influence to get the charges against Merrill dropped."

"How could he do that? Is the legal system in Utah so easily manipulated by the Mormon Church?"

"Not to that degree," she says. "But all he had to do was persuade the parents of the victims to keep their boys from testifying. They were all LDS, and they were all in the same stake—that's a jurisdictional unit in the Church. The stake president made sure that all the other bishops cooperated in silencing the boys' families."

"Shit," I say, then catch myself. "Sorry, but that's really messed up. You must have felt horrible."

"Worse than you can imagine. Merrill came home and expected things to go on as before. But that was impossible. I took the boys to a motel the very same night. I had intended to file for a divorce."

"But you didn't?"

"I didn't have the chance," she says, looking at her hands. She seems more fragile to me now than she did just a few minutes ago. "He came after us. When I refused to reconsider the divorce, he began to threaten me." She looks up sharply. "Not physically, mind you. But threats nonetheless."

"Such as?"

"He promised to use his priesthood position to make me a pariah. He would spread stories about my infidelity, my failure as a mother— all sorts of lies to turn the community against me."

"Is it that easy? Why would people believe him instead of you? Surely you had friends who knew better."

Rebecca laughs—a sad laugh. "Oh, Nick. You've never lived among small-town Mormons. The Church and the community are one and the same. If you go against church leaders, even your best friends won't risk being seen publicly with you, for fear of repercussions."

"So, what did you do?"

"I put the boys in the car and I drove south. It was the middle of the night and I didn't know where we were going."

"To Arizona, where you came from?" I guess aloud.

"Maybe," she says. "I wasn't sure. My family is LDS too. I had no as-surance that they would support me against the bishop and stake pres-ident. I just needed space to think."

I'm looking at her with a deep empathy—not the put-on kind you give when you feel it's the right thing to do—but a genuine compassion that I don't have a lot of experience with.

"But at some point I guess I fell asleep," she continues. "The next thing I was aware of was a man carrying me. A man I'd never seen before. It was John. I tried to ask about my children, but I kept fading in and out of consciousness. I remember angry voices, male voices. I thought Merrill was yelling, but I was delirious and in shock. I imagined many things that night.

"When I woke it was daylight. I immediately sat up to look for my boys, despite the pain. Though duller than the night before, it was still substantial. But a hand—a woman's hand—reached for me and settled me back into the bed. She said, 'Your boys are being cared for, as are you. There's no need to worry. Just rest, Sister.' It was Julie."

"Did you know her?"

"No. I hadn't met any of them until that day in the hospital when I awoke. John had already taken the boys into their home in Hildale."

"Where's that?"

"In Utah, on the Arizona border. It adjoins Colorado City on the Arizona side."

"Now that one I've heard of. That's where the guy—Jeffs, wasn't it?—went to jail for polygamy."

"Warren Jeffs," Rebecca confirms. "His crime wasn't polygamy, though. It was his coercion of underage girls into arranged marriages."

"Right," I say, suppressing my natural inclination to say how disgusting I find this shit. After all, I don't really know where she stands now on all the Mormon and polygamy garbage.

Our conversation is cut short by the return of Marilee. Her face reveals nothing of how she feels after visiting her husband. I have no idea whether she's saddened by his condition, or whether she wants him to recover or die. He is the father of her children, after all.

Rebecca stands and takes her by the hand and they sit down together in silence. I watch as Rebecca asks all she needs to with her eyes. No words are spoken. Marilee cocks her head with a shrug and returns a meager smile. Rebecca pats her hand and smiles back. And the exchange seems complete.

"So, where's Tom?" I say, feeling like an intruder on their shared silence.

"He was not ready to leave," Marilee says without inflection. "He will be here shortly, I'm sure."

Again I wonder at the many faces of that kid. One minute he's raging against his stepfather, calling him a monster, and stealing his mother and siblings from the guy's clutches. Now he's at the man's bedside paying his respects, thinking who-knows-what.

Our silence is broken by a shrill alarm from the nurses' station, followed by a flurry of activity. A blue strobe flashes from the wall nearby; a moment later two men fly by with a crash cart. "Code Blue, ICU" a soft recorded female voice repeats over the public address system.

None of us speaks, but I'm wondering if the wives are thinking what I'm thinking—*is it Father John?*

At that moment Tom comes around the corner beyond which the crash cart and the nurses have disappeared. His face is unreadable. Surely if the commotion had been for his stepfather he would be registering something. He ambles over to us in an almost Zen-like state of neutrality. "We can go now," he says, extending a hand to help his mother to her feet.

We all rise, and still no one speaks. We glide past the nurse's station and the hallway beyond, headed for the elevator to the parking lot. Just then, the head nurse appears out of nowhere and intercepts us.

"I'm sorry, Mrs. Allred," she says with a practiced look of condolence. "Your husband is gone."

We all stop dead—not the best word, perhaps—in our tracks. "I don't understand," Rebecca says. "She just saw him. The doctor said—"

"He simply stopped breathing," the nurse says, cutting the thought short. "It happens. Especially when a patient has suffered such massive internal injuries." She gives Marilee a sad smile. "If you'd like to wait to speak to the doctor..." She trails off as Marilee shakes her head.

"No, thank you," Marilee says with a quick smile. "There's no need."

"We do have counselors on duty if you'd care to meet with one," the nurse offers.

Marilee declines and the nurse takes her leave after confirming Marilee's contact information—my cell number—and saying someone will be in touch shortly about funeral home arrangements.

I'm not sure what I'm reading on Rebecca's face as we turn to go; it might be relief, but I don't ask as we amble toward the exit. No one speaks until Tom mutters softly, "It is better that one man should die than an entire family perish."

Rebecca shoots him a look; it seems for a second she's going to say something, but then thinks better of it and continues walking in silence.

Me, on the other hand, I'm flipping out. *Did Tom just kill Father John?*

Title 40

WHILE THE SISTER-WIVES ARE LEFT WITH the unenviable task of explaining to the children that their father is dead—even if he was a badass to their mothers, it will be difficult news—I'm off in pursuit of another father-son news blip that's been flashing incessantly across my radar for two days now: the question of Josiah's parentage. I've done all the math; that I might be his father seems even more likely now than when I stared into my own ten-year-old face at Dodge Park the other day.

Yes, Beth and I used condoms during our college romance. But there were at least a couple of occasions when one broke, as well as that one time we went a little too far before reaching for one. In fact, it was shortly before I was arrested. The kid's age is right. And why did Beth's parents rush her into a marriage to someone she barely knew?

The bigger question: why would Beth, with her fiery streak of rebellion, agree to it? Unless she was pregnant. Devotion to her religion certainly wasn't the reason; we'd had enough conversations about that. She didn't share her parents' enthusiasm for fundamentalist doctrine. I'm willing to bet it was a shotgun wedding with some Christian shmuck willing to save the poor wayward girl's honor. Hell, maybe he was even too stupid to do the math and thought the kid was his.

I'm going to get to the bottom of it. I've persuaded Beth to meet me at Laurelhurst Park in Portland, far enough from home that she doesn't need to worry about anyone she knows seeing us. And this time

I encouraged her to bring the boys. That'll give me another good look at Josiah; if I decide I'm way off base after all, I can still call off the accusation. With what I've been through in the last couple of weeks, I've considered the possibility that this is all a product of my oxycodone-addled head. Maybe the kid really looks nothing like me.

Beth's already at the playground when I get there. I give her a quick hug and turn to the swings, waving at the boys, who are having a competition to see who can swing the highest.

"Josiah! Micah! Slow it down," Beth shouts to them. "It's not safe to go that high."

I take the opportunity to go over and catch Josiah on the backswing, slowing him to a more moderate pace. "Hey, kiddo," I say. "Your mom doesn't want you to get hurt." I'm standing behind him as I grab, but the unwanted intervention—by a man he hardly knows—causes him to turn to me with an indignant scowl. My fears are confirmed: it really is my own pouting puss that's looking back at me. "That's better," I say, releasing him. "You two take it easy now."

Beth is now standing at my side.

"We need to talk," I say evenly. "How about over there in the shade?" I suggest, pointing to a stand of firs on the ridge above the appropriately named Firwood Lake.

"Boys," Beth says without answering me, "why don't we go feed the ducks now."

Micah is first on the ground, while Josiah makes a flying leap from the apex of his swing, landing on all fours about ten feet away. "Can I have the bread, Mom?" Micah says, grabbing at the plastic sack in her hand.

"OK," Beth says, ceding it to him. "But only two slices at a time, one for each of you."

He's already running toward the lake—a large pond, really—and Josiah's running to catch him. "Hey," Beth yells, "don't run near the water. Micah, do you hear me?" When he doesn't respond, she calls,

"Josiah, watch your brother, will you?" Josiah throws a hand in the air with the "hang-loose" sign, signaling his receipt of the message.

Beth is already moving after them and I'm right by her side. "Why don't we sit up here on the ridge where we can keep an eye on them," I offer. It's an unnecessary suggestion, as I'm sure she has no intention of doing otherwise. I'm just prefacing what I have to say with idle chatter because my stomach is doing somersaults. The question I'm about to ask is one of those where you don't want the answer to be either yes *or* no. I'm nearly certain I'm right, which has its own weighty implications. But to accuse her and be wrong could also mean that she'll get up and leave, blowing my chance to keep this reunion alive.

"So, what's up?" she says after we've settled onto the grass and she's confirmed the boys are where they should be.

I'm so keyed up that I plow in headfirst. "Am I Josiah's father?"

"Micah, be careful!" Beth yells without acknowledging my question.

"They're fine," I say, taking her hand and gently pulling her toward me. She tries to pull away, but then acquiesces. When she turns to look at me, her eyes are ringed with moisture. "Really?" I say, as everything but her face recedes to some distant unreality. "I am?"

"Nick," she starts, but a sob overcomes her. I put an arm around her shoulder and wait. Despite all my earlier calculations and conclusions, I'm as shook up as she is about this news.

"Does anyone else know?" I ask, wondering whether I'm the only one who's been left in the dark.

"Only my parents," she says, reining in her sobs. "And Pastor Jenkins, but he's retired now."

"And your ex?" I ask. I don't even know the guy, but I feel a visceral surge of animosity toward a guy who's been raising my own son behind my back. Is this what fatherhood means: insane jealousy of a kid I've known for two days, just because he shares my DNA?

"No," she says, shaking her head. "I mean, not for sure." She wipes her tears on the back of her sleeve. "I think he's always suspected though."

"What the fuck—and he never asked?"

She shakes her head.

How can a guy not want to know the answer to that question? Does he care that little about his family? Of course, Prince Charles probably never asked about Prince Harry either. Who would benefit? But still, a guy's got to be able to figure something like that out.

"Does he have visitation?"

"We have joint custody," she whispers, as though she's ashamed of what she's telling me. "He has them February through July; I have them the rest of the year."

"So he still lives around here?"

She nods. "He still attends Damascus Christian. He lives in an apartment about four miles from my parents."

This bothers me, but I'm not sure why. More of that genetically programmed response, I guess. I mean, it's not like I'm ready to start being a husband and father just like that. I should be grateful he's not a deadbeat dad. Right?

But I'm not. I want to go tell the guy he's not my son's father. Which would be stupid, of course, but that doesn't stop me from feeling like it.

I guess Beth can read this on my face, or something equally disturbing, because her expression is fearful as she says, "Nick. Promise me you're not going to say anything to anyone. Think of the boys."

I don't answer her right away. I'm still trying to figure out where I stand. I'm experiencing emotions that are completely foreign to me; it's like I'm on drugs, trying to ferret out reality from a mess of conflicting signals.

"Nick," Beth says again, with more intensity, staring into my far-away eyes. "*Promise* me."

"Yeah, yeah. Don't worry," I tell her. "It's just hard for me to process all this right now."

"I know," she says, eyes downward.

"Why couldn't you have told me?" I ask her. "I mean, this is something you don't keep from someone."

"When should I have told you, Nick?" she says, defensive. "While you were on trial? Or maybe when you were in jail, forbidden from seeing me? Or maybe I should have tracked you down later to tell you you had a son you couldn't see? And what purpose would it have served?"

"Purpose?" I say, my voice rising. "How about the purpose of being honest? We're talking about a kid, Beth. *My* kid."

"Yeah, and my kid too," she says, now defiant. "And I was the one with responsibility for him. Not you. Exactly how would bringing you into his life have been helpful to him back then? You weren't even allowed to see me, Nick. What was I supposed to do, send him over in a cab for you to look at? I didn't even know if you wanted a kid."

I'm just about to admit that I didn't know either when Micah scrambles up the grassy slope to where we're sitting. Beth hurriedly dabs at her eyes with the Kleenex she's pulled out of her purse. "Micah, go on back to your brother. Mommy's not quite finished visiting yet."

"Don't want to," Micah says.

"What do you mean, you don't want to?" Beth says, sounding like a typical mother. Like my mother, in fact. "Go on now and give us some peace and quiet."

"Aw, mom," Micah says, kicking at a molehill in the grass. "There's a weird guy over there."

"What?" Beth says with alarm, looking toward the lake. "Where?"

"In the bushes," Josiah says, coming up the slope to join us.

"The bushes?" Beth says, agitated. "What were you doing in the bushes?"

"We weren't," Josiah says. "The guy's in the bushes with a camera."

"A really long camera," Micah says, drawing out the word for emphasis.

"A telephoto lens?" I ask.

Josiah nods. "Yeah, I think so."

"Show me where," I tell him, my parental protectiveness surging from some well I didn't know I had.

He points to a patch of willow and dogwood near the far end of the lake, about sixty yards away. "Over there. On the other side of the lake."

I start making my way toward the lake, not seeing anyone, but picking up speed as I go.

"Nick," Beth calls, coming after me. "Be careful. You don't know wh...," but I lose the rest of what she's saying when I break into a jog.

I think I see some jostling of branches, but can't be sure if it's just a breeze, or—then he breaks out running toward the far side of the park. I adjust my angle of approach and begin to head him off. From what I can tell, he's at least twenty years my senior and no match for me in terms of speed.

Within seconds I'm tackling him and we both go skidding across the grass. I end up straddling him from behind. I grab for the camera, thinking that even if he gets away, we'll still be able to see what he was up to, the pervert. I snag the telephoto lens as he claws at the grass, trying to wriggle out from under me. The camera strap, still around his neck, snaps taut and the guy stops crawling. He's now clawing at his neck; it takes me a moment to notice through my adrenalin rush that I'm strangling the guy. I cut him some slack and adjust my weight. He rolls over on his back, panting, but he's still pinned to the ground.

He throws his arms upward toward me to fend off any blows that might be coming his way. But I'm not throwing any punches. Just questions. "What the fuck are you doing, huh?" I ask, moving my knee into his solar plexus. I notice Beth in my peripheral vision, about five yards away, a boy under each protective arm.

"Nothing," the guy grunts, squirming to no effect.

"Nothing? What the fuck? What's this?" I say, shaking the camera at him. "What are you, some kind of pervert who gets his kicks from young boys?"

He shoots daggers of indignation at me. "Boys? Absolutely not!"

"So what, then—are you going to tell me you were just shooting ducks with a fucking telephoto?" I say as I yank the camera free, almost taking his ear off with the strap.

"It's none of your business," he says impudently. He squirms partway onto his stomach and tries to get free again, but I dig my knee into his kidney. I grab his wallet while his butt's turned toward me. "Well let's see just who the fuck you are." I'm having trouble separating the wallet's Velcro with only one hand. "Here," I say, tossing it at Beth's feet. "See who this sonovabitch is."

But Beth doesn't pick up the wallet. Still clutching her boys, she says, "I don't need to look. I know who he is. let him up, Nick."

"What?" I say, rolling off the guy and looking at her for an explanation.

But she doesn't answer me. Instead, she speaks to him. "Tell me the truth, Brother Figley. My father sent you, didn't he?"

That's when I realize who he is: God's own sex police. The same sonovabitch who stalked us ten years ago.

Title 41

THE GUY LOOKS AWAY WITHOUT ANSWERING the question, which is all the confirmation she needs.

"How can you be so sweet to me and the boys at church, and such an asshole now?" Beth asks, surprising even me with her frankness. "You see, boys, this is what we call a hypocrite—someone who talks about the love of Jesus on Sunday, but disrespects people the rest of the week."

In spite of my anger at this Figley jerk, I can't help but admire Beth right now. I'm impressed with the way she's turning something really fucked up into an object lesson for her sons. *My son. God, how can that be?*

"Beth," Figley says in a treacly voice that's supposed to win her over. "Don't rush to judgment. Your father is only concerned for your safety," he adds, struggling to his feet and brushing at the grass stains on his khakis.

"The only thing I need to be kept safe from is stalkers like you. How'd you like me following your daughter around taking pictures? No wait, don't tell me—you probably hired someone to do just that."

"Now Beth," Figley says.

"Now, nothing," Beth spits at him. Then, to me, "Nick. Take the memory card out of that camera right now."

I do as she asks and hand the card to her.

Figley's eyes follow it. He's gone pale. "Now Beth, you don't want to steal that. Think of the example it sets for these boys."

"I'd keep the camera, too, Brother Figley, which *would* be stealing. But you've stolen my privacy—our privacy," she adds. "You'll get the card back once I've deleted the photos."

I take this as my cue and hand the emptied camera back to him with a threatening look. Beth has done such a great job of putting him in his place that I can think of nothing to add.

Figley looks from me to Beth. "Really, I must insist, Beth. I promise you I will delete the photos. No one will ever see them."

"Insist?" Beth says in a quietly manic voice. "Insist, Brother Figley? You're in no position to insist on anything. Just get the hell out of here and leave us alone," she says, waving her arm, "before I call the police."

"There's no need..." he begins, but I charge him menacingly and he stumbles backward. Getting the hint, he retreats without further protest.

As he does, Beth shouts, "And Brother Figley, if you breathe a word of this, or anything about Nick, to my father, I will stand up in Sunday School and make sure everyone knows just what a scumbag you really are. You know I will."

Figley stomps off without replying.

"Jesus, Beth. Do you think he'll rat me out?"

"No way. I've known the guy my whole life. He's all bluster. Besides, he values his reputation too much. He'd lose his precious Sunday School teacher job if I outed him as Peeping Tom," she says without any hint of relish. "And I'm sure I've got all I need right here"—she waves the memory card—"to do just that."

"You're not going to show anyone those photos, are you?" I say with alarm. After all, she's not the one who risks jail time for being here.

"Only if he blabs it first. Which he won't. Don't worry, I've got this covered."

"Well, it's my ass, you know," I say, just in case she's overlooking that detail. "In any case, I want to know what he's got on us. Do you have a way to read that card?"

"No, but I know where we can," she says.

✳   ✳   ✳

Twenty minutes later we're in Kinko's following the instructions on the Sony picture kiosk. I insert my credit card, followed by the memory card. A moment later when the first pictures come up, we're both glad we chose the self-service method.

"Jesus," I say, as Beth gasps and jumps in front of the machine, blocking the image from view.

"Josiah, take your brother outside and wait for us on that bench," Beth says, pointing just beyond the glass doors. "Don't go out into the parking lot."

The boys do as she says, but she remains frozen in place, even after they're outside. When she doesn't move, I say, "Are we going to see what else the motherfucker has on here?"

"Not until you turn around," Beth says, shaken.

"Beth, I've seen it all before, in case you've forgotten."

"Not for ten years," she says, too loud by several decibels. She resorts to a hoarse whisper. "It's not the same now. This is... is... it's obscene! I've been violated."

"You're not obscene—you're in your own bedroom," I say, hoping she's not blaming herself for the pictures. "It's Figley who's obscene for photographing you."

"Just turn around, Nick. I'm not going to look at any more of these with you leering over my shoulder," she says, not budging. "In fact, why don't you go out and take the boys for an ice cream at that Baskin Robbins over there." She starts digging in her purse for the money.

"All right, all right," I say. "But keep your money. I'll get this."

She stops digging. "Thank you, Nick. You understand, don't you?"

"Of course I do. It's just that you're not the only victim here. I'd really like to know what else is on that card. How long has this asshole been watching us—and you? Do you know when that shot was taken?"

"I don't know. I didn't look long enough," she says, her blush beginning to fade. "But I only leave the window open on those really warm nights, and we haven't had any for at least three weeks."

"Which means he was spying on you before I was even in the picture," I say.

We both reach the next conclusion simultaneously. "Which means..." Beth begins.

"That he wasn't hired by your father because of me," I finish. "That's a relief, at least."

"A relief?" Beth squeals. "Really?" She bugs her eyes out at me for emphasis. "Well those aren't your tits up there, are they?"

"You know what I mean, Beth," I say.

"Just go get the ice cream," she says.

I head for the door with a glance back at her. She waits until I'm out of sight of the screen before she turns around to look at it again.

When I get outside, the boys aren't on the bench. Typical. What boys of that age have ever been able to sit still and wait without something to occupy them? I'm surprised they don't both have a cell phone or some other electronic toy; then I remember that Beth clings to that hippie ethic that says TV is bad. She always said physical experience is the way to understand the world. That's about all we ever had, as a matter of fact: physical experience of the best kind. I wouldn't be surprised to learn that she shelters her kids from all electronic media.

I head further down the strip mall toward the ice cream shop; maybe they've got their noses pressed up against the glass there already. But no, they're not outside. I take a look through the windows; they aren't inside either. Maybe they went to wait in the car, if it's not locked. Beth told them to stay out of the parking lot, but I check the car anyway. Locked and empty. I think it's time to worry.

"Beth," I bark as soon as I walk through the door at Kinko's. "I can't find the boys."

"What do you mean?" she says, immediately wrenching herself away from the machine and running toward me. "Tell me you're joking, Nick," she adds with desperation in her voice.

"I'm not," I assure her. "I checked at Baskin-Robbins and at the car too. I didn't see them anywhere."

She pushes past me with the force and focus of a linebacker drawing a bead on the quarterback. She flies out the door, nearly ripping it off its hinges. "Josiah! Micah! Josiah!" she yells, running out into the parking lot. She turns a circle as she continues to shout. "Boys? Where are you? This isn't funny. Get back here right now!" When there's no response, she begins screaming their names again, still turning circles, scanning the parking lot and storefronts.

"Maybe they just went to use a restroom," I suggest. "I'll go check the taco place."

Beth doesn't respond. She's running toward the street, which is separated from the parking lot by a narrow strip of landscaping. As she makes her way through the bushes alongside the building, I check out the restrooms at both restaurants in the strip mall. No dice.

When I return to the parking lot, there's no sign of Beth. I hope to hell she's found the boys by now and maybe they've gone back to Kinko's. I head back to check. She's not there, but when I look at the photo kiosk, I realize Beth ran off and left the memory card in it. I'm greeted by an image of the two of us in a lip-lock at Starbuck's. *Shit.* The asshole has been shadowing our every moment together, right from day one.

I'm about to eject the card when a mischievous thought hits me. I'm not proud of it, but hey, we were in love once, and neither of us ever ended that. So it's not like I'm a perv for wanting a few mementos of better days. I scroll back to the first few pics on the card and hit the machine's Print button three times, once for each picture. I scoop up the prints from the output tray and stuff them in my pocket. Then I eject the card and race outside.

Still no sign of Beth or the boys. I'm starting toward her car when I hear voices coming from the bushes. I creep over to the corner of the building and peer through a large rhododendron. My heart stops.

Figley has Micah in a crooked-arm lariat and the boy's right arm twisted behind his back. Beth, clutching Josiah to herself with both arms, is pleading with Figley to let Micah go.

Title 42

FIGLEY IS DEMANDING THE MEMORY CARD.

"I told you. I don't have it," Beth says, in a hysterical voice. "It's in—"

"It's right here, Figley," I say, emerging from behind the bush.

All eyes are suddenly on me. "Oh, thank God," Beth whimpers, barely audible.

Figley, clutching a white-faced but silent Micah even harder, takes two steps back. "Stop where you are, Prince."

I stop, still holding the memory card where he can see it.

"Now, just toss it over here where I can reach it," Figley says, pointing with a nod of the head.

I look to Beth to see if she's OK with that. Wide-eyed and pale, she nods vigorously.

"OK, Figley," I say. "Have it your way. Just let the kid go and you can have the card."

"I wasn't born yesterday, Prince," he scoffs. "The card, then the boy. Now come on."

I hesitate a moment longer, trying to figure whether there's any other ploy I can try. I can rush him and call his bluff; he'd probably turn tail and run. But there's no telling what his state of mind is, being desperate to keep his ugly secret from being revealed. And if there's a chance he'll hurt Micah, whether out of spite or just plain fear, Beth wouldn't want me to risk it.

"Nick," Beth gasps, her voice cracking. "Just do it!"

I toss the card and it glances off Micah's shoe and lands nearby.

"Can you do me a favor, Micah?" Figley says in a Sunday School voice that makes me want to tackle him even more. "We're going to squat down slowly and I'd like you to pick up the memory card, OK?"

"Come on, Figley," I spit. "Let the kid go. We had a deal."

"Yes, we did," Figley says as he and Micah drop to snag the card. "And I'm keeping it." He snatches the card from Micah and gives him a nudge toward his mother. "Now that I've got my insurance." He waves the card victoriously. "You know they'll rescind your probation with what's on here."

"What you've got there can get us *both* sent away for longer than either of us wants, Figley," I say. "I'd destroy it, if I were you."

"Nice try, Prince," he says with a sneer. "I just have to erase everything but the pictures of you, and turn those over to the police."

"You'd be a damn fool, then," I tell him. "Computer forensics can easily find deleted data. Unless you reformat the whole card, the cops would be able to retrieve the deleted files. Enough of them to convict you, anyway." I'm not entirely sure this is the case, but I figure he's seen enough CSI episodes to consider it a viable threat.

"So I'll go home and reformat it then," Figley says, unsure of himself.

"Let's just destroy it right here, shall we? Then we can both walk away with the assurance we need. Look, if you want, we can go right over to Best Buy and I'll buy you a new one, OK?"

"Go on, Brother Figley," Beth prods him. "If you take care of it now, the story ends here. None of us will ever talk about it again."

Figley looks at her. "You promise?"

What I see in his eyes makes me sick. I know what it is because it's the same way I look at her. The pervert is in love with her. Probably for as long as I have been, since he goes to her family's church. Hell, who knows, maybe he's had his eye on her since she was a kid. It's all I can do not to react to this realization. But I've got to hold it together long enough to get that card destroyed. Then I'll have no problem beating the guy to a pulp.

"Absolutely," Beth says. "No one wants this unfortunate episode to be over more than I do. Let's just destroy that card and put it all behind us, OK?"

Figley swallows hard and looks at Beth.

"Go on," she coaxes.

"All right," he says. "If you promise, I'll do it." Then after a moment adds, looking back at me, "But how? How do I destroy it?"

"Well," I say, "Here's what we do."

✳   ✳   ✳

A half hour later we let Figley walk, much to my frustration. Beth was clear that no one was to get hurt, and I had to agree that it was best that way. Had the boys not been with us however, I probably would have gone all Rocky on his ass anyway.

After returning to Kinko's together—all five of us, like one happy family—I used the kiosk to delete the complete contents of the memory card. Since the machine didn't have an option to reformat it, we did the next best thing: we took it to the automatic hole punch machine and whacked it enough times that the casing split and the internal memory components were no longer viable. Lastly, we walked to the gas station next door and dropped it into a ten-gallon pail of used motor oil. Overkill maybe, but it gave us all the sense of finality we needed.

Now, as Figley drives off a free man, Beth nearly loses it. Her mask of stoicism crumbles into the face of a victim in shock. Still clinging to the boys—she hasn't let go throughout the entire episode—she fights the meltdown, as tears begin to slide down her face. I want to take her in my arms, but she has room only for her children at the moment—in more ways than one. And I'm OK with that.

"Come on, boys," she says, moving toward the 4Runner. "We need to talk about what just happened. I need to explain a few things to you."

"Beth," I say as gently as I can. "You and I also need to discuss this."

"Later, Nick," she says, not looking back. "Later, OK?"

As I watch her drive off in the same direction as Figley, I have a panicked thought: *What if he's waiting for her around the corner?*

But no. He's as relieved as she is to have this whole thing over with. He probably won't show his face again for a long time. Hell, if we're lucky, he'll pack up and leave town.

Unless I get him arrested, of course. And I can, I suddenly realize. I've still got those three prints in my pocket. But I'd have to rat myself out for making them in the first place. Am I willing to do that?

Title 43

AFTER THE FUCKING NIGHTMARE WITH FIGLEY yesterday, I decided the first person I needed to talk to was my lawyer. I've just finished laying out the whole ugly mess for Rigs, leaving out only one thing: that Josiah's my kid. It's taking me a while to get around to it.

"I shouldn't need to tell you, Nick," Rigs says, after a long draw on his beer. "There are so many reasons you don't want to keep those photos. First, never mind this Figley guy; you've got nude photos of the one person you're prohibited by law from getting within 500 yards of. Ever think how that might look?"

"Well, yeah. But I wanted to ask you," I say, changing the subject to the one that is still taking up the most real estate in my head. "That restraining order—it can't keep me from seeing my own kid, right?"

Rigs just looks at me for a minute, until it sinks in. "Shit, Nick. What the fuck? Are you gonna tell me... Jesus." Rigs rubs his eyes and sits upright. "OK, let's have it. The whole story."

Despite my promise to Beth, I have to tell someone about my newfound fatherhood. Besides, I've got an attorney-client relationship with Rigs now, so I know it'll go no further. He won't even tell his husband, who we both know can't keep a secret. So I spill my guts.

"I can still see my kid, right?" I ask when I'm done.

"Technically, yes. But get real, man" Rigs says, signaling the waitress with his empty bottle. "You're in no position to insist on anything. You're a convicted felon, you're out on bail for withholding evidence, and you've violated your probation by seeing Beth in the first place. And to top it off, you're carrying Peeping Tom photos of her."

"Hey," I say with a shrug. "That's why I hired the best lawyer in town. You're gonna fix all that, right?" I raise my beer to him and take a long suck on the bottle.

"Yeah, right," Rigs says with a huff. "You're as bad as Lindsay Lohan; you get deeper into legal trouble every time you leave home. Soon you're going to need an entire law firm just to juggle your court dates."

"Guess I'll settle for you in the meantime," I say. "So, where do we begin?"

"We start with the most immediate problem: the arson investigation," he says, pushing the empty bottle aside and opening up a file folder. "Once you give a deposition, that will go away and we can focus on the other stuff."

"Go away?" I say. "You make it sound so easy."

"It will be, as long as your friends cooperate."

"You mean Rebecca and Tom?"

"Them, yeah. And Laura," he says. "She's a material witness too; in fact, she's scheduled to be deposed this week. So we'll want to make sure she's aware of how you fit into the overall picture."

"You mean coach her?"

Rigs looks at me like I'm an idiot. "No. I'm not going to fucking get disbarred for you, Nick." He pauses while the waitress replaces his empty with a full one. When she's gone, he says, "She has to answer honestly, of course, but she doesn't have to volunteer any additional facts or opinions. We want to limit the amount of prejudicial information, if possible."

"So, what's the plan?" I ask.

"First of all," Rigs says after tipping back the new beer, "you're the only one who's prohibited from saying you were at the compound on Census business. Title 13 doesn't prevent Census respondents from acknowledging that. Rebecca and Tom can say as much as they want, then you're free to confirm or deny it. You have to be careful not to add any previously undisclosed details, but that shouldn't be a problem. You'll be able to explain how you came to be involved, and that's all they need."

"Yeah, but I wasn't there on Census business the day of the fire."

"No problem. This is the story we want to tell," he says as he begins writing on a yellow pad he's pulled out of his leather portfolio. "One. When you made your Census visit, Tom asked you for a ride into town. He'll confirm that, right?" He pauses and looks at me.

"Well, that's not exactly how it went down, but—"

"You're not listening, Nick. We tell the story we want them to hear—no extraneous details."

"Without lying?"

"Of course without lying," Rigs says, annoyed. "Tom wanted a ride with you. Isn't that true?" He doesn't wait for me to answer. "We have no obligation to tell anybody how he communicated this to you, or what his stepfather did about it."

"OK. It's not like Father John's here to contradict that, I guess."

"Now you're getting it," Rigs says with a smile. "As long as Tom corroborates it, we're good to go.

"OK, so Two," he continues. "Your Jeep breaks down and Laura rescues the two of you. Laura hears from Tom that his family needs food; she decides to donate some from her restaurant. You, she, and Tom return to deliver it."

"What about the trip I made with you?"

"Extraneous. TMI. Who's going to bring it up?" Rigs says with eyebrows raised. "I'm not being deposed; besides, I'm your lawyer, so they can't ask me. And Allred is dead."

"Right," I say, realizing he's got a point.

"Remember, the investigation is looking into the cause of the fire, not your entire relationship with these people. All we have to explain is why you were there—that's already covered—and how the fire started."

"Won't they wonder why he stole my Jeep, or why he was shooting at me?"

"Do you know why?"

"Well, it's obvious he—"

"Stop. No. Nothing under the law is obvious. Unless he told you why, you don't know. Even then it might not be true. Don't speculate. The investigators can speculate all they want, but unless they find evidence of a crime, there's nothing they can do about it. You and Allred could be the Hatfields and the McCoys, with a generation of bad blood between you. But until a crime is committed, it doesn't mean shit."

"Right. OK."

"Just remember, don't let them bait you into giving more information than is necessary. Always bring it back to the matter at hand: the cause of the fire. If you don't know something for a fact, don't give them your thoughts on the matter. You're only obligated to give them facts. And if you do get backed into a corner, just say you don't remember."

"And that'll satisfy them?"

"Hey, there's no guarantee of satisfaction here. Either you possess the facts or you don't. Ronald Reagan became famous during his Iran-Contra testimony in the eighties for answering everything with, 'I don't recall.' It's a classic dodge. How do you prove him wrong?"

"Only he was probably telling the truth. Didn't he have Alzheimer's?"

"Doesn't matter," Rigs says. "There's no proving what you do and don't remember. And unless you're an expert witness, your opinions and speculations are irrelevant."

"Right."

"So, number Three—the most important one," he says, adding it to the page. "Completely unrelated to your visit—and from what you've told me, this is absolutely true—the women decided to abandon Allred and leave the camp with all the supplies you'd brought. You started to object—true again—but when Allred became incensed and went for his gun, you had no choice but to flee along with the rest of the family. You did so in your Jeep—to which you have legal title, of course—so you weren't taking anything of his."

"Then he shot at the leaky gas tank and ignited the fire."

"Bingo. That's it. Fire explained, end of story."

"And they won't wonder what happened after that?"

"Only up until Allred's fall off the cliff. And you're not responsible there either. There are plenty of witnesses to that. In addition to you and the women, you've got the fire team, who've already given their testimony."

"And all I have to do is tell this story, and the contempt charge will go away?" I ask.

"As long as Rebecca and Tom tell the same story first," he says, peering over his beer bottle. "Can you count on them?"

"Rebecca, absolutely," I say, though I haven't asked her explicitly. "Tom is another story. The kid's passive-aggressive. I'm never sure just where he's coming from."

"Well, my advice is to sit them down together and explain what I've just told you—especially the importance of not veering off into extraneous details."

"You sure you don't want to do that yourself?"

"Can't," he says, shaking his head. "That would be a huge red flag. It would be seen as coaching the witnesses, even if I said nothing improper.

"You, on the other hand," he says with a crooked smile, "can say anything it takes to gain your friends' cooperation."

I don't respond. Instead I drain my beer and wonder if we can really get everyone on the same page and pull this off.

222 | Martin Bannon

Title 44

THE LAST THING I'M EXPECTING WHEN I roll the Ducati into my driveway is to see Beth's 4Runner, but there it is. My guess is that she needs to decompress as much as I do after the episode with Figley. Even with the threat of prison time hanging over my head, the stakes were even higher for Beth, watching a maniac holding her kid hostage like that.

Not that I believed Figley was prepared to hurt him. He's probably as much a stranger to violence as the pope is to pornography. But he might have run off with him, and for a mother that's got to be just as scary.

What I feel when I walk through the door to the sight of Beth and Rebecca together in the kitchen is probably like coming home and finding your ex-wife happily fixing dinner with your present wife. Somehow they just don't belong together in the same room, let alone engaged in domestic activity. Call me paranoid, but the idea that they're conspiring against me crosses my mind, if only for a second.

"Hey," I say to Beth, trying to gauge what is safe for conversation. There's no way she's told Rebecca about today's events, but I can't help but wonder what excuse she's given for being here.

"Hi, Nick," Beth says, as though everything's normal.

"Hello, Nick," Rebecca echoes.

I look around the house. Everything seems normal—the new normal anyway. The lesser wives and some of the children are out on the patio engaged in who-knows-what creative project. My house has taken on the air of an arts and crafts workshop for the creatively gifted. Handmade doodads, most with some very practical use, are everywhere. I'm sure the reality-TV producers can't be far behind to film an episode of "the Swiss Family Robinson meets Big Love."

Then I spot a face among the brood that don't belong: Josiah. *My kid.* What am I supposed to do with that? A pulse of anger surges through me as I remember that just hours earlier he was threatened by a gun-wielding pervert. But why is he here now? Why is Beth here?

I don't have to wait long to find out. "You let us finish that up," Rebecca tells Beth, who's been preparing a salad. "You and Nick go on and talk. We'll look after the boys. Dinner should be ready when you get back."

"I can't thank you enough," Beth tells Rebecca, removing her apron, "for letting me and the boys intrude on your dinner plans."

"Nonsense. There's no need to thank me," Rebecca says. "We're all beggars here. Nick has been more than patient with all of us."

She has no idea.

I wait until Beth and I are outside to ask, "Are you OK?"

Her face answers before she does. "Nick, I'm so scared," she says with a surge of emotion. "I keep thinking he's going to show up again. I can't erase the image of his arm around Micah's neck. I know it's silly, but I can't help it. I can't go back there."

"To Kinko's?" I say, wondering why that would be an issue.

"No," she says. "To my parents' house. I can't sleep in that room, knowing he watched me through that window. And with the boys in the next room—"

"Hold on, it's OK," I say, wrapping my arms around her. I don't know why, but I feel a twinge of guilt at the thought that Rebecca might be watching. "Let's take a walk," I say, leading her toward the trailhead. I can't help but note that not too many hours ago I was doing the same with Rebecca. And enjoying it more. With all the shit going down now, being with Beth has begun to feel more like duty than pleasure. It wasn't supposed to be this complicated.

"So," I begin, once we're on the path. "Where did you go when you left Kinko's?"

"I went home to pack some things," she says, making no effort to uncouple herself from me.

"Wait," I say with some alarm. "You packed? Where are you going?" I'm afraid she's going to say she's running off to join the circus—the one living in my house.

"I don't know, Nick," she says, almost pleading. "I just have to get away. Somewhere where the boys are safe and I don't have to look over my shoulder."

"What did you tell your parents?"

"I left a note and said we were going camping for a few days."

"I wish you could stay here with me," I tell her. Oddly, I'm not sure I mean it. I mean, I've fantasized for years about just such a possibility, but now it feels all wrong. What's really crazy is that I almost feel like I'm cheating on Rebecca by even considering it.

"I know, Nick. It's nice of you to say that," she says, squeezing my arm. "But you've got Rebecca now, and that—"

"What? Is that what you think this is?" I say, stopping to look her in the eye. "Why would you think that? Is that what she told you?"

"No," Beth says. "She didn't need to. I'm a woman. I can see it for myself."

"No, no, you've got it all wrong," I tell her, feeling defensive now. "She's... well, I mean, look... it's... it's just not like that," I say, trying to point out how obviously inappropriate her assumption is. But even as I'm fumbling to explain why this is, I'm panicking. What if Beth is right? Did her woman's intuition pick up on something I missed? Is that how Rebecca feels? Is that how I feel?

"OK, I'm sorry I jumped to conclusions," Beth says. "I didn't mean anything by it. Let's just forget it. What I really need right now is a place to chill while I figure out what I'm going to do."

Glad for a chance to change the subject, I ask, "Don't you have some friends who'd understand your situation? Not the thing with Figley, obviously, but that you're going through a divorce and you need to lie low for a while."

"All my friends are from church now," she says. "It would be too awkward. They'd expect me to be at Sunday School and Worship Service. I wouldn't know what to tell them."

A bright idea hits me. "Hey, I bet you could stay with Laura up in Brightwood."

"It crossed my mind," Beth says. "But she and I haven't been close for years. I wouldn't feel comfortable asking something like that."

"I'll ask her for you," I volunteer. I want to keep Beth at a distance from this place for now. The idea of her getting any more intimate with Rebecca and the gang gives me the willies.

Beth looks at me sideways. "I thought you and Laura didn't stay in touch. Didn't you say you just ran into her for the first time in years?"

"Well, yeah," I say. "But we've… I mean, she's… it's kind of…" With all the secrets I've been keeping lately, I can't seem to figure out what I *can* say, let alone what I *want* to say. "We've talked recently," I spit out finally. "She'd totally do it. I know she would."

Beth sighs. "Then you'll call her? I mean, I hate to ask you…"

"It's no problem, really," I say, taking her in my arms. "I'll do it as soon as we get back to the house. There's no cell reception out here."

As we turn and head back, arms around each other's waist, I'm thinking about those photos. I could put an end to Beth's fears by turning them over to police. Figley would be toast. But I can't get past what Beth would think of me for having printed them in the first place. Am I willing to find out?

The answer, I realize, is no. Sad, but true. I'm a coward. I tell myself it doesn't matter, that this will all blow over soon and be forgotten. I don't believe it for a minute, but I just keep repeating it.

Title 45

IT FEELS GOOD TO BE WORKING WITH MY hands. I didn't realize how many years I'd spent sitting on my ass until I started helping out here at the compound. After the first few days of this I was sore in muscles I didn't even know I had. I'd wake up stiff each morning in more than just the usual place. But I've finally loosened up now and I find the work invigorating. The summer sun, which never reaches my house because the forest canopy's so thick, brings out the familiar scents of the Cascades here: the fir, the damp soil, the char of the recent forest fire. All of them mingle in gratifying ways that conspire to make me want to live off the land like an Oregon Trail pioneer.

What I'm not so happy about is having Beth and the boys here. When Rebecca heard that they were planning to crash at Laura's—we both let her think that Beth was hiding out from her soon-to-be ex—Rebecca insisted that Beth come to the compound. "We have three empty houses up there and they're not being used," Rebecca had said. "There's no reason you shouldn't make yourself at home." When Beth asked why the families weren't living there themselves, Rebecca explained that more work was necessary before the place could sustain twenty-nine people fulltime. No mention was made of Father John or Tom's ascendance. It's like Rigs said, tell 'em only what you need 'em to know.

Today Rigs has taken Tom and Rebecca to Oregon City to give their depositions. I offered to drive them, but Rigs said it wouldn't look good

for them to be showing up with me, given my status as a hostile witness and unnamed suspect. My deposition is scheduled for tomorrow.
Rigs assured the investigators that I would be answering all their
questions regarding my involvement in the fire, as long as I was the
last to be interviewed. That, says Rigs, should clear me of suspicion
and get Rebecca's bail money back. I haven't asked her whether she's
reached an accord with Tom on the disposition of the funds.

A cool breeze dries the sweat on my neck and arms as Luke and I
nail siding onto the new storehouse. Keen-eyed hawks draw circles
against the blazing blue sky as they search for the rabbits hiding out
among what remains of the half-acre garden. The kids are spread out
among various projects, some at the new chicken coop scattering seed
and gathering eggs with Marilee, others helping Deborah repair the
fences, and the rest in the kitchen with Julie, laying out lunch.

I can't help but reflect on how nice it would be to live in such an
idyllic place. Lots of work, sure, but invigorating work with tangible
rewards. A far cry from the Census Bureau, where I chase down reluctant recluses and try to convince them to share their most personal
details with a government nobody trusts anymore. My only reward
there is to get chewed out, first by the angry respondents, then by Angie and her superiors for failing to extract the desired information. Not
to mention the occasional barrel of a gun in my face, just for laughs.

I'm lost in this reverie when Josiah and Micah come bounding
down from the house to announce lunch. The two of them seem to be
enjoying their new farm life, helping with the chores and playing with
the other kids. I wonder whether suburban kids like them could really
live out here long-term. Could I? I'd almost like to try.

Luke and I lay down our nail guns and head up to the house while
the boys continue their rounds to alert the others. "You're a fast worker," I say to Luke as we walk. "It's all I can do to keep up with you."

Luke gives me a crooked grin. "The sooner the work's done, the
sooner I get to rest," he says.

"Sounds like a plan," I say. "So what do you do for fun around here?"

"When I can, I like to go walking alone in the forest. But usually I just help with games for the younger children. Once a week, on Saturday night, we have storytime," Luke says. "And sometimes I write the stories."

"You're a storyteller, huh?"

"Yeah, kind of," he says with a self-effacing shrug.

"Maybe that's why you're so quiet—you're a man of letters."

"I guess," he says. "Nobody much wants to hear from me most of the time. Except when I read my stories."

"I'm sure that's not true," I tell him, trying to say what I think a kid his age needs to hear. "You seem like a good kid."

"Maybe," he says, kicking at the dirt as he walks. "But I'm not—or I wasn't—*his* kid. And I'm nobody's brother, except Tom's."

"Well, at least you two have each other."

Luke makes a sound somewhere between a cynical laugh and a scoff. "Yeah. We *all* have Tom."

"Should I ask what that's supposed to mean?"

"Nothing," he says, belying the contrary signals he's sending. "It's just that Tom always wants the spotlight. There's never any room for me—or anyone else."

"He does seem awfully protective of your mother. I suppose he's seeking her approval."

"That, and arousing Father John's ire."

"That probably wasn't hard to do, from what I've heard."

"Yeah. But it was like Tom was always *trying* to pick a fight. I never understood it. We'd all end up paying for Tom's mischief."

We walk on in silence for a minute before I say, "Well, maybe it'll be better now."

"That's not likely," Luke says, "with Tom as the new Patriarch. He's just so... I don't know... messed up lately."

"Messed up how?" I ask, not letting on that I'm inclined to agree with his assessment.

"I don't know. It's like, for the last year he has these sudden changes—Mom calls them mood swings—where he's all nice and sweet, then he's angry for no reason. Then he runs off and we don't see him until dinnertime."

"Maybe it's just puberty," I say, thinking aloud.

Luke doesn't say anything. When I look at him he's blushing. Maybe puberty's not a subject they talk about openly in this family. I restate my case. "You know, it's common for kids his—well, your age—to have difficulty becoming an adult."

"I don't know," Luke says, skeptical. "I'm doin' OK with it. I mean, I'm not being all crazy like he is. I don't scare people."

Title 46

SHORTLY AFTER WE ARRIVE AT THE HOUSE the rest of the battalion files in. It's the same regimented order they've displayed at my place. Everyone has their task and their place, and everything is accomplished with a minimum of instruction or confusion. Only Josiah and Micah seem out of place in the orderly functioning of the machine. Beth is seated next to me at the foot of the enormous dining table—Luke is seated at the head, flanked by Deborah and Julie. Though he's only 16, the family defers to him to assign the prayer to begin the meal.

"It's wonderful the way you've all come together here," Beth says to no one in particular after everyone's dug into their bowls of stew. "I mean, I can't believe you've done so much here with your own labor."

"It is nothing extraordinary, Beth," Deborah says. "We believe it is important to know how to take care of oneself. We simply do as our mothers and fathers have done before."

"Well," Beth says, "it's a lot more than my sisters and I could ever do. We couldn't even manage to live together in the first place," she adds with a laugh.

Conversation, as I've noted before, is limited during meals. I can't be sure whether this is a natural result of the appetites these kids work up with their flurry of activity the rest of the day, or whether it's a disciplinary code that's been instilled in them. After a few more futile attempts to start a dialogue, Beth finally resigns herself to the silence.

When the meal is over she walks outside with me. Men are never allowed to clean up in the kitchen, and Beth, having prepared the meal, is exempted from cleanup duty as well.

"It really is impressive how they can live off the land like they do," Beth says as we stroll down toward the storehouse. "And with so many kids."

"Hey, it's the kids that make it possible," I say. "They operate like a military outfit; everyone has specific tasks and they execute them with precision, even the little ones, though they sometimes need some help."

"I feel sorry for the kids though," Beth says.

"What do you mean?"

"Well, it's like child labor, you know?" she says. "Kids shouldn't have to work that hard, especially the young ones."

"It's not like they're abused," I protest. "The kids have household chores, like most kids. Everybody chips in to help."

"Oh, come on," Beth says, turning to look at me. "Cleaning chicken coops, building fences? That's a bit more work than taking out the garbage or washing the dishes."

"They enjoy it, though. There's a real spirit of cooperation. It all works somehow."

"Well, I'd never force my kids to do the heavy lifting; it's not right."

"They seemed to be enjoying themselves this morning, helping with the garden and the chickens," I say.

"Well yeah," she says with a cluck of the tongue. "This is like a vacation for them. It's a novelty. But can you imagine living like this, day after day, cut off from the real world?"

"I think I'd kind of enjoy it," I tell her, and I'm pretty sure I mean it.

"Really?" she says with wide-eyed exaggeration. "No TV. No Internet. Not even cell service? I'd go bat-shit crazy after a week."

"I'd be just as happy if my phone never rang again," I say, imagining the life that so unnerves Beth. "I mean, if I had enough people around, who else would I need to talk to? Not the guys at the pub. And sure as hell no one from the Census Bureau. My only real friends are the Jerrys; and they're close enough for an occasional visit. That's all I'd need."

"Yeah, but who are the people you'd want around?" Beth asks. "I think that would make all the difference in the world."

I don't respond immediately. The answer that springs to mind surprises even me: I'd want the very people who are now living with me—this well-oiled machine, unlikely as they are, who call themselves a family. It's nothing I would have dreamed up, but if I'm honest with myself, they are one of the happiest and most functional families I've ever encountered. And that's saying a lot, given the challenges they face.

"Yeah, you're right about that," I say at last, and let the subject drop. The fantasy in my head at the moment isn't one I'm ready to share with her.

We reach the storehouse and I show Beth the progress we've made, describing how things are laid out: the root cellar, the shelving for the canned goods, the bins for the dry goods. I explain how the solar power feeds the pump for the well and the temperature controls. Much of what I tell her I learned myself just this week from Tom or Rebecca. But I have no problem letting Beth think I'm well versed in such manly pursuits.

Luke's already on his way down from the house to continue with the siding work as Beth and I wrap up. "Speaking of going crazy after a week," I say, easing into the loaded question that's coming. "By this time next week they'll all be moving back here and my place will be free." The look on Beth's face tells me she knows what's coming, so I go for it. "Do you and the boys want to move in with me? I mean, for as long as you need to?"

"Oh, Nick," Beth says with apprehension. "I'd love to say yes—and thank you so much for the offer—but there's one big problem with that."

"The restraining order?" I ask, knowing this would come up.

"Well, yeah, there's that," she says offhandedly.

"We wouldn't have to tell anyone," I say.

"Yeah, but the problem is, there's already someone who knows," she says. "Brother Figley."

Title 47

EVER SINCE THAT DAY AT THE HOSPITAL, I've been wanting to ask Rebecca what Tom meant when he said "it's better for one man to die than"—whatever it was he said. But just what words do you use to suggest to a mother that her son may have murdered somebody—especially if it's her husband? And though I hate to admit it, Tom does have a point: things *are* better for the family with Father John out of the picture. The women no longer have to fear being beaten. Tom has no one to provoke into a rage that spills over onto the other kids. And the women won't be barefoot and pregnant anymore, resulting in who knows how many more mouths to feed. So maybe I'm better off not questioning it.

Whatever. I've got a date with another, more pressing matter at the moment. Today it's finally my turn to talk to the state arson investigators. Rigs assures me that the others' depositions were everything they needed to be for me to beat this rap. Rebecca and Tom have revealed that I first visited the compound on Census business, so I can go ahead and confirm it without violating Title 13.

When Rigs picked me up a half hour ago, Rebecca and the sister-wives were busy preparing for the move back to the compound this weekend—which means I finally get my house back. Sure, it'll be a little lonely there once the circus leaves town, but I've already worked out a remedy for that: Beth needs to move in with me. But to make that happen I've got to get Figley locked up—which means putting the

Peeping Tom photos in the hands of the authorities. I've toyed with ways to do this, looking for one with the fewest repercussions for me. Here goes plan number one.

"I've got a favor to ask you," I say to Rigs as he signals a lane change approaching our exit.

"Yeah," he says. "'Cause I haven't really done any for you lately, right?" he deadpans.

"Hey, I babysit Zeus and Ganymede, don't I?"

"They're a hell of lot less trouble than you are," he says with a cynical laugh. "So, what is it this time?"

"You know those photos of Beth, the ones Figley took?" I begin.

"The ones you snatched—sorry, bad choice of words—the ones you kept for yourself?"

"Yeah, those," I confirm. "Would you be willing to hand them over to the police?"

Rigs heaves a sigh. "And just where would I tell them they came from?"

"Tell 'em you got them in the mail—anonymously," I say. "Hell, I'll even mail 'em to you so you won't have to lie. And I'll include an anonymous note implicating Figley."

"You don't think anyone would find it suspicious that my client—and best friend—happens to have a history with her that includes a restraining order against him?"

"Well, like you said earlier, let them suspect whatever they want; without proof it means fuck-all, right?"

"Jesus, Nick. Sometimes you're a fucking idiot," he says, shaking his head. "It's one thing if you're already suspected of committing a crime. But you don't go around inviting suspicion where none exists."

"It was worth a try," I say with a shrug as we reach the Oregon City off-ramp. "Somehow I've got to get Figley off the street, preferably before this Saturday."

"Why Saturday?"

"The party's moving back to the compound and I'll get my house back. Beth won't move in because Figley knows where it is; she's afraid he'll spy on us, or worse, kidnap the boys."

"Nick, as your lawyer I have to advise you that moving in with Beth would be a really stupid thing to do."

"But no one besides Figley would have any cause to suspect she was there. If he's out of the picture, what do I have to worry about?"

"Yourself," Rigs says as we roll up to the Clackamas County Sheriff's Office. "You're your own worst enemy."

*　　*　　*

The deposition comes off without a hitch, just as Rigs promised. Before we leave the sheriff's office Rigs makes sure we get the paperwork that shows the contempt citation against me has been voided. The clerk says Tom, whose name is on the bail receipt, can expect to receive a check, minus a minor processing fee, within three weeks.

"Hell, Rigs," I say with genuine respect, "you're a genius."

He casts a sidelong glance at me, barely suppressing a smile, as he opens the truck door and slides into the driver's seat.

"I should keep you on retainer," I add, just to get his goat.

"How about you start by paying me for gas?" he says.

"Afraid cash is a problem, as usual," I say. "But tell you what: I'll do the next best thing and invite you to dinner."

He stops to look at me as he turns to back out of the parking space. "Remind me again why I'd want to eat your cooking?"

"Fair enough," I admit. "But you won't have to. We're having a big birthday bash for Tom's eighteenth, a week from Saturday. Rebecca has invited you. Come on up to the compound—bring Man. The sisterwives will be cooking, and there's always more than enough to go around."

*   *   *

I consider riding up to the compound after Rigs drops me off. There's still several hours of sunlight left, enough time to get a fair amount of work done—maybe put the finishing touches on the storehouse. It would also allow me to pursue plan number two: confessing to Beth and having her take the photos to the cops. It's the most honest thing to do; hell, it might even be noble. Sure, Beth will be pissed, but maybe my coming clean will make up for it.

But I know, before I even complete the thought, that it wouldn't go down that way. Even if she used the photos to nail Figley, she'd never forget that I printed them with other intentions. I don't want to risk the relationship if there's another way.

That brings me to plan number three.

Title 48

IT'S FRIDAY EVENING AND THE FINAL touches have been put on the compound in preparation for tomorrow's migration. The women and children are already on their way back to my place to fix the last dinner here. I've stayed behind with Beth and the boys, and I'm about to give her the news that I've been struggling to suppress all day.

"Rigs called me this morning before I left," I say as we walk out to the Ducati. I'm anticipating the relief we'll both share when I tell her. "He said that Figley is wanted for questioning in a Peeping Tom investigation."

Beth freezes, eyes wide with fear. "But how? Who knew about it?" she says, flailing for an explanation. "Do they have pictures of me? But we destroyed... Oh, fuck. There were more pictures..." she trails off at this assumption.

"Take it easy," I say, pulling her close to me. "Maybe it wasn't you. Maybe there were other victims. All that really matters is that he's going to be locked up and you'll be safe."

"But if they try him," she says, her face still creased with worry, "the pictures will have to be shown in court. God, the humiliation..." she trails off again, shaking her head in painful contemplation.

"Well, maybe they won't get to try him," I say. "According to Rigs, when the deputies showed up at Figley's place with a search warrant, he was nowhere to be found."

"So, he was out—" Beth begins, but I cut her off.

"No," I say, shaking my head. "He'd packed up and left. The neighbors confirmed he's been gone since last week, right after our little incident at Kinko's."

"So?" she says. "Maybe he's on a trip. They're still going to take this to court sooner or later."

"Well, that's out of our hands," I say. "But don't you see? With Figley gone, you and the boys can move into my place. There'd be no one to bother you there."

She fails to display the enthusiasm I was hoping for.

"Except me," I say with a grin, hoping a little self-deprecation might help.

"I can't, Nick."

"Why?"

"My divorce won't be final for another ninety days."

"Like that's ever stopped anybody?"

"You don't understand," she says with a plaintive look. "Eric's a Christian. If he thinks I'm 'living in sin,' he still might try to take the boys away."

"That'd be a cheap shot."

"What's worse, my parents would probably support him. As far as they're concerned he can do no wrong. They're always going on about how he's a better Christian than I am."

"Sacrament wine runs thicker than blood," I say, thinking aloud. "That really sucks. Shows how much they know about parenting." I stop myself before I really go off on them. We've had this conversation more than once before, ten years ago. Thinking on my feet, I try a new tack. "OK, so how's this: You and the boys move in at the cottage and I'll stay here at the compound until your divorce comes through. What do you say?"

"I couldn't do that, Nick. I can't throw you out of your own house."

"Hey, I bought it with you in mind," I tell her, which is true. "Besides, the clan can still use my help here. I'd actually welcome the chance to get out and do some more physical labor—we'd all benefit from the arrangement." I look at her, waiting.

She considers this. "Well, it would be nice…"

"Sure it would," I say. "The boys would love it. It'd be good for 'em to spend some time—" I almost say away from her parents "—out in nature for a change."

✳   ✳   ✳

By Sunday the great migration is complete. Beth and the boys are tucked in at the cottage and, for the time being, I'm the ranking male in Elwood. I don't make any pretense, of course, of being in charge of anything; I'm not going to step on Tom's toes. He seems to sense this and has welcomed me wholeheartedly into the clan. This is to be our arrangement for the next three months until Beth's divorce is final.

Tom insists that I sit with him and Rebecca at the head of the table during meals and family conferences, which are held at least weekly, or more often if issues arise. At the first such conference, held this afternoon, work schedules were drafted and voted on by every member of the household over the age of eight. Well, not voted, actually; Tom made the decision and they "sustained" him with a raise of the hand. According to Rebecca, dissenting votes, if any, would have been noted, but would not have changed the outcome. The word of the Patriarch is final.

Being here reminds me of those weeks back in high school when I served as a volunteer summer camp counselor. It's not unpleasant, but I try again to imagine this as a day-to-day lifestyle. Could I live like this full-time? The work is fulfilling, the company welcome, and the food is far better than I've ever prepared for myself. The only thing I'd have a problem with is submitting to the rule of an autocratic teenager, even if he's pleasant most of the time.

Beth and I have a standing date every Saturday; at her request, we'll start with once a week. I'm allowed to stay the night, but she's

244 | M a r t i n   B a n n o n

not promising any sex. "Let's just take it as it comes," she says. I'm strangely OK with that. The reality of Beth is so different from the memory of her, that I'm no longer sure what it is I want. I'm just as happy to play it by ear, as she's requested. My plan is to stay with Beth through Sunday afternoon, returning to the compound only after the clan is done with whatever religious mumbo-jumbo it is they practice. I can do without that shit. If Beth wants to, she and the boys have a standing invitation from Rebecca to join us for Sunday dinner.

As the week begins I throw myself into my new role at the compound, where Tom, Luke, and I are charged with the heavy-lifting projects. Our days are consumed with winching out the stumps of the dead and damaged trees in the orchard, in preparation for the replanting that will follow. It's backbreaking work, but I'm loving it. There's something viscerally rewarding about working with my hands and getting sweaty. The only drawback is that at the end of the day, I'm ready for a cold one, and there's no alcohol at the compound. This is a hard and fast rule. So I'm faced with the choice of driving down to the Safari Club, or settling for lemonade at home with the clan. It doesn't feel right to be ogling the dancers one minute, then coming back to Walton Mountain for evening prayers, so for now I'm foregoing the beer. But I've made no promises to anyone. Whatever the future holds, I've got no intention of becoming a teetotaler.

By Friday I'll be ready for my weekend with Beth and the brewski that goes along with it. There's a certain pressure here at the compound—self-imposed perhaps—to be a better person than I usually am and I feel like I'm ready to pop. I'm not sure if it's because I feel the need to prove to Rebecca that I've got it in me, or it's because I suddenly have two dozen kids looking up to me as a role model. Either way, I've taken it on as a personal challenge. Still, it takes its toll. I keep myself going with the knowledge that, come the weekend, I can let my hair down and be my usual slacker self. In any case, it sure beats the hell out of working for the Census Bureau. I don't miss that one bit.

Title 49

IT'S FRIDAY AND THE BOYS AND I HAVE just finished dragging the last of the stumps into a pile that will have to wait for the burn season. It's the last task of the day and I'm ready to get cleaned up for dinner. That's when I see an unexpected sight: Beth's 4Runner coming through the open gate. She's moving at a clip that suggests a woman on a mission. I sense she's not just coming for dinner.

"Go on and shower up, guys," I tell Tom and Luke as I head up toward the bottom of the driveway to intercept Beth. "I'll be in a little later." She's already out of the vehicle by the time I get there. I don't get a chance to even say hello, let alone ask a question before she's off and running.

"They have them, Nick!" she hyperventilates. "How did they get them? What am I going to do?"

"Hey, hey," I say, trying to grab her flailing arms, "Calm down." I've got her wrists now and they're trembling. "Start at the beginning: Who has what?"

"The cops. They have the naked pictures Figley took of me!"

"Who told you that?"

"*They* did!" she says, wresting her hands from mine. "They showed them to me!"

"What? When?" That the authorities have the pictures is, of course, my doing; I mailed them anonymously with a note implicating Figley.

But why they would show them to Beth, and how they found her so quickly, are both mysteries.

"They came to your place," she says. "They were looking for you."

"Me, why? What do I have to do with those pictures?" I left no fingerprints on the photos. I'm wondering if Figley has turned up to implicate me. Even if he did though, he has no more proof they came from me than I do that they came from him. They can't have any evidence against me.

"They think you took the photos," Beth says. "They had a warrant. They searched the house looking for you."

"Fuck. Are you sure you weren't followed?" I ask, scanning the ridge for any signs of a posse.

"I took precautions," she says. I can only hope she means it.

"What did you tell them?" I ask, trying to sort out just what went down.

"I told them you weren't living there, that I was renting for a few months."

"And? What did they say?"

"They didn't believe me!" Beth says, starting to hyperventilate again.

"OK. Take it easy. We'll figure this out," I tell her, leading her to sit on a nearby rock retaining wall. Just then the car door opens and Micah jumps out.

"Mom!" he yells.

"Micah, get back in the car."

"But I'm bored. Can we go up to the house?"

"No," Beth barks. "Do as I tell you!"

"You know, Beth. You ought to stay for dinner. You need to calm down before you drive back, and we need some time to sort this out."

She sighs, but remains on edge. "Yeah. You're right." Then to Micah: "All right. You and Josiah go on up to the house. I'll be up in a few minutes."

Car doors slam and the boys are off, racing each other.

"OK," I say, kneeling in the dirt. "Tell me exactly what happened. Step by step."

She takes a deep breath and begins. "When I answered the door there were two men, one in uniform, one in street clothes. They introduced themselves as Deputy Denton and Detective Priebus," she says. "They asked for you and I said you weren't there. They said they had a warrant for your arrest—they waved it at me—and then just barged in.

"I didn't know what was happening, but I didn't want the boys to be scared, so I rounded them up and took them out to the car to wait. When the deputies didn't find you, they came back to ask me questions. That's when I said I was renting from you and that you wouldn't be back for three months."

"And they didn't believe that?" I ask.

"Well, no, not really. I mean, they seemed confused. They asked me my name and how I came to be at your place. I lied and said that Laura arranged it; I told them she was a mutual friend."

"The detective asked me if I would be willing to look at some photos. I said, 'I guess so.' What else could I say? So he goes to the patrol car and comes back with a manila envelope. Then he pulled them out: the three photos of me undressing."

"What did you say?"

"I didn't know what to say," she says, still agitated. "I mean, I was as shocked to see the photos then as I was seeing them for the first time. I didn't have to pretend anything. The detective asked me if it was me in the pictures. I said it was."

"Did you mention Figley?"

"No. How could I? How would I explain?"

"And they said they thought I took the photos?"

"Well, no," Beth says, stopping to think. "No, the detective asked me if the pictures were taken with my permission. I said no, that I'd never seen them before." She looks pleadingly into my eyes. "Oh, Nick,

I was so scared. I didn't know what to say. I mean, here I am lying to the police, but I couldn't tell them that we made a deal with Figley, and I didn't know what would happen if I told them that you and I were involved. I mean, I thought maybe they already knew, and that's why they had a warrant for you. I didn't know..." Her rambling trails off toward hyperventilating again.

Even amid the crisis of the moment, I'm asking myself if she was always this fragile, or did that come with age and motherhood? "So, what makes you think they believe I took the photos?"

"He asked me if I'd been harassed or stalked by you in recent months. I said no. Then he asked if I was sure I hadn't seen you around anywhere. I said no. Then he said, 'Do you think it's possible that he took these photos without your knowledge?' I said, 'I don't know.' He kept looking at me like he didn't believe me. I thought I was going to cry."

"So he only asked you if I *could* have taken them, right?" I'm parsing her words carefully to see if she's just jumped to unwarranted conclusions. "I mean, he couldn't claim to know I did, because I *didn't* take them," I say, reasoning it out even as I was asking her.

"Not exactly," Beth says, regaining some composure now. "I asked him if he couldn't just let me have the photos—so I could destroy them—and I'd let him know if I saw anyone suspicious in the future. He said, no, they were evidence against you."

"Specifically against me? But how? Why?"

"That's what I asked."

"And?"

Beth takes a deep breath before she continues. "He said that forensic specialists had traced the photo paper to a brand distributed by Sony through their photo kiosks, the kind you find at Kinko's," she says, eyeing me in a way that's making me nervous. "And when they checked the nearest Kinko's stores, they found that one of the kiosks still had the images stored in memory." I'm beginning to sweat as she reels out the details in excruciating slow motion. "He said that the images are usually purged at the end of a transaction, but that this particular transaction had been aborted abruptly, creating an error file that retained the images."

"That sounds like a bunch of trumped up legalese to me. I wouldn't worry about it if I were you. They're just taking pot shots in the dark because of my history with you." I say, rambling like a guilty child. It pours straight from my addled brain, but doesn't sound very convincing, even to me.

"Nick," Beth says, fixing me squarely in the eye. "He says that the transaction was on your credit card."

Fuck. I'm nailed. I can think of nothing to say.

Beth turns away, then looks back. "Jesus, Nick. Tell me you didn't."

"Hey, I just wanted them to get that sonovabitch," I tell her. "I wanted some insurance."

"But, Nick, you printed those pictures while I was looking for the boys. Before you knew that Figley had come for the memory card."

I'm caught again. I grasp at anything that'll soften the blow, but all that comes out is a stuttering semi-denial.

"You meant to keep those pictures, didn't you?" Beth accuses.

"Beth, wait—"

"And you're the one who sent them to the police."

"Listen, Beth, if I—"

She doesn't let me finish. She turns and marches toward the house.

"Wait. Where are you going?"

"I'm getting the boys," she barks without turning to look at me. "We're going home."

Title 50

IT'S SATURDAY, JUST A WEEK UNTIL TOM'S eighteenth birthday, and the family has planned a suitably big party to welcome him officially into his new patriarchal role. After Luke's confirmation of my suspicions that all is not right with Tom, I'm more than a little concerned for what awaits the clan under Tom's leadership. But I keep these to myself. I'll be out of here soon enough, and it's not my place to raise such concerns. I'm sure Rebecca has it under control; she may be more staid and demure than Beth, but she doesn't shrink from a challenge. I have no doubt Tom will be well monitored.

Originally I had planned to miss the big bash because it fell on my weekend at the house with Beth. But after yesterday's confrontation, I'm thinking it might be better to give her some space to cool down. I'm definitely not going down there today, and I'm not sure I'd even be welcome as soon as next Saturday either—even if it is my house. So I told Tom I'd stick around for the party.

Turns out the event is more than just a rite of passage for Tom, according to what Rebecca's told me; the whole family will be shuffled as well. Tom, of course, is taking his stepfather's place as the master of the house—or *houses*, I should say. Accordingly, he'll take the master suite once occupied by Father John. Because they are Tom's blood relatives, Rebecca and Luke will occupy the main house with him. The rest of the family will share the two smaller houses. Despite being the largest of the three houses, the main house has the fewest bedrooms, due to the large kitchen and Olympic-size dining room, guest bedroom, and multiple work rooms. Rebecca and Luke will each have a bedroom upstairs on either side of Tom's, and I will continue to occupy the guest bedroom downstairs.

Other changes involve the financial oversight and the long-term planning for the clan. Monthly goals will be set by Tom, and daily work assignments made by him. All expenditures will have to be approved by him as well. Luke becomes his "counselor" and his stand-in whenever Tom is absent. The women remain subservient to the men in the Patriarchal Order, even if the men are mere boys, 16 in Luke's case. In fact, every male twelve and up—three besides Tom and Luke—is ordained to the priesthood and stands higher in authority than the women in their twenties and thirties. Fucked up, if you ask me, but nobody's asking me, so I keep this opinion to myself.

With most of the heavy lifting done around the place for the time being, I've taken to shadowing Tom, Luke, and Rebecca and learning the ropes of day-to-day maintenance at the compound. I feel like I'm at a vocational rehabilitation camp for wayward sex offenders. And after hearing from Beth last night that there's yet another warrant out for me, I'm just as glad to be living off the grid while I figure out how to wriggle out of the current mess. I need to talk to Rigs, and my cell is useless out here. But rather than show my face in town, I'll wait to talk to him at the party on Saturday.

It's somewhere in the neighborhood of four a.m. and Rebecca is teaching me to milk a cow. Four of them actually. She has milked the first one, and I'm about to try my hand on the second. I can't ignore the allure of Rebecca's scent as she hovers at my side, the two of us seated on handmade pine-log stools designed for the task at hand.

"OK," she says, "now take the cloth from the soapy water and wash each of the teats thoroughly."

It's adolescent of me, but I can't help but be embarrassed to have an attractive woman in very close proximity talking about 'teats.' I do as she tells me without looking at her, for fear of a physical reaction as well.

"Not too rough, now," she cautions me. "These are tender parts, even if she's only a cow. You've got to massage the flesh gently."

Yikes! I can't tell if she's being purposely suggestive, or if I'm just an idiot, but I can feel the heat throbbing in my face. I don't dare speak for fear that my voice will crack like an adolescent's.

"Good. Now dry your hands," she says, handing me a towel, "and apply some tallow from the pot there. The lubrication is important to keeping her happy; you don't want to chafe."

This is almost more than I can bear. Teats and lubrication and tender parts and chafing. In a classroom this might seem nothing more than innocuous instruction, but with Rebecca nestled into my side, smelling of soap and lavender, the terminology will not stay tethered to the cow in my sex-deprived head. It doesn't help that she keeps referring to the cow as "her," as though I'm learning the art of female massage. Yes, I know a cow is female, but I'm used to thinking of one as "it." "Her" just sounds too intimate.

Rebecca continues, oblivious I hope, to my mental meanderings, "Scoot forward a bit and secure the bucket firmly between your legs. You don't want your milk to spill if she gets upset and starts to fight you."

If she keeps talking like this I'm afraid my milk may spill regardless.

"Now wrap your thumb and forefinger around the teat, right at the base, and squeeze gently. You want to keep the pressure here so that the milk doesn't flow back up into the udder."

I manage to do this with my right hand.

"Good. Now do the same with your left hand on the second teat," she says. "Slowly wrap your remaining fingers around each teat, applying pressure in succession—like eking out the last of the toothpaste from a tube."

I do as she says. *Fuck*. Despite all of the suggestive images of a woman this process has etched into my brain, what I've got in my hands now feels more like a man than a woman. Not that I'd know, I mean, except for my own. But it creeps me out just the same. It only gets worse when the first squirts of milk shoot into the bucket. I am so out of my element here I almost want to cry, but I'm not about to wimp out in front of Rebecca.

I eventually manage to get the damn cow milked without spilling any milk, hers or mine. I'm thankful when Rebecca agrees to milk the remaining cows in the interest of time. I avoid watching now, because the motion of her hands on the dangling teats suggests something else entirely to me in my current state of mind. I can't help but think that with Beth, this would have been bawdy fun. But with Rebecca I'm just plain embarrassed at my juvenile thought processes.

Title 51

DESPITE MY WANTED STATUS AND SOME occasional awkward moments, such as the milking incident, I'm finding the days leading up to the big birthday bash to be some of the happiest I've had for a long, long time. The late summer weather is gorgeous, the work invigorating, and the strange band of religious misfits I've allied myself with have turned out to be the most genuine and uncomplicated people I've ever encountered. Sure, their doctrines are a bit obtuse, but on a personal level they exude a kindness and compassion that has always seemed missing from Beth's variety of Christian activists. These non-Mormon Mormons—I'm still not clear on the distinctions, despite the history lessons I've been given—care nothing for politics, and better still, they understand the meaning of "live and let live."

For as long as I've been resident at the compound, even Tom has seemed more stable than in the past. This isn't just my perception; I've confirmed it with Luke, who says Tom's happier than he's seen him in years. Luke speculates that it's Tom's impending official elevation to patriarch this week that's fueling his new attitude. He's probably right. Still, I finally had to ask Rebecca about that day in the hospital. She said Tom was paraphrasing a line from the Book of Mormon:

> *It is better that one man should perish than that an entire nation should dwindle and perish in unbelief.*

The statement, she explained, was made by a prophet who had just murdered a man to steal—and thus preserve—a record of his people for the sake of posterity. Hey, it may be scripture to these people, but if you ask me it's still a creepy justification of murder. And it does nothing to dispel the questions surrounding Father John's demise. Does Tom see himself as more than just a patriarch? Has he promoted himself to prophet as well? With a license to kill?

The more time I spend with Rebecca, the more I relish our time together. I can't help but compare her to Beth: both are loving mothers whose marriages have gone bad, struggling to make it on their own, with the assistance of family. But what sets them apart, I realize, has more to do with me than it does with them. The key difference is this: Beth makes me want to be a kid again. But Rebecca makes me want to be a man. And I figure it's about time I grew up.

It's the night before the party and everyone is dead tired, especially the girls who have been on baking duty all week. Much to my delight, Rebecca, despite her own exhaustion, has chosen to violate the strict ten-o'clock lights-out protocol to share a pot of peppermint tea with me on the front porch. Coyotes serenade us and various types of owls punctuate our dialogue with, no doubt, wiser interjections, as we discuss everything from Tom to religion to human nature. Now we've come back around to the rest of Rebecca's personal journey, a story I've been wanting her to finish for some time.

"John and the sister-wives let me and the boys stay with them, free of charge, for as long as it took to nurse us all back to health—nearly six months," she says with admiration. "It was the most generous thing anyone had ever done for me. I was ever so grateful."

"I have to admit," I say, "that seems to be a hallmark of your religion, from what I've seen."

"Not in every case," Rebecca says, "but, true, it's what we are taught. My time in Hildale to that point conferred another advantage:

no one knew where the boys and I were. And I needed that time to think. I believe our accident was Divine Providence, leading us there. What would the alternative have been? Running endlessly? Driving to where? I had no plan."

"Do you really believe in a God that would injure you to prevent you from making another choice?" I can't help but ask this. But our relationship has become so relaxed, that she doesn't take any offense from it. Nor did I mean any. It's an honest question, as my own belief in God is tenuous, at best.

"Sometimes He has no choice," she says with a smile. "Our egos are so big, it's the only way to get our attention." She takes a sip of her tea. "Just look at yourself," she continues. "Are you on the path you intended just a month ago, before your life began to go off the rails? Don't you think a higher power might have had a hand in that?"

"Ha!" I scoff. "You're assuming I think I'm better off now." She laughs at this, forcing me to abandon my attempt to appear serious. We both laugh. It feels good. My life has been too fucking serious.

"Well, you appear to be happy lately," she says." I've seen you out there, sweating with the boys and returning to the house with them, laughing and talking." I shrug my acknowledgement. "And best of all," she says, with that all-seeing motherly expression I've grown accustomed to, "I see you caring, Nick. Caring about someone and something. Something bigger than yourself."

Ouch. Talk about a backhanded compliment. "Faint praise, indeed," I say with a guarded chuckle. It in no way escapes me that her commendation of the recent me is also an indictment of the earlier version.

"Oh, Nick. I'm not being unkind. You know in your heart that you weren't a happy person when you showed up at our gate. Surely you have seen the change in yourself?"

"I have," I admit. "But there's still a warrant out for me, so it's not as simple as turning off one me and becoming another."

"All things in good time," she says, refilling both our cups.

"So," I say, removing myself from the uncomfortable spotlight, "how did you end up marrying John?"

"That, I'm afraid," she says with a sigh, "was an entirely pragmatic decision. Here I was in a beautiful, loving home, among women and children I adored—and with whom my boys got along famously—with no other place to go. When John proposed to me—with the consent of the sister-wives, of course—I had to ask myself whether there was any chance I could provide a better life for my children some other way."

"But didn't you think polygamy was a strange way to do that?"

"Not as much as you might think," she says. "I mean, being raised in an LDS home, it was always a part of my history. My own ancestors practiced polygamy before Salt Lake outlawed it to prevent the Federal Government from confiscating their temples. So it was a very familiar concept to me."

"But did you love him?"

"Nick," she says with an almost sad smile. "Romantic marriages are a Victorian creation. It wasn't until the Twentieth Century that they became the norm in the western world. Of course I didn't love him. But that's not the foremost consideration for a mother without means of providing for her children. You would understand that if you were a parent."

"Yeah, probably," I say as I contemplate the possible repercussions of telling her that, as a matter of fact, I am a father. But, no, I'll save that little revelation for later. "So, how'd you all end up in Oregon? Weren't you better off with other polygamists?"

"Normally, yes. It would have been much easier to live in the larger community," she says. "But, unbeknownst to me, John needed the Leader's permission to marry me. And he didn't get it."

"Why not?"

"He tried, but was refused because I hadn't converted and re-nounced the Salt Lake Church."

"Because you still believed?"

"Yes and no," Rebecca says with a wistful sigh. "I mean, it's a part of me—in ways I'm not even conscious of—so I don't think I could renounce it if I wanted to. There are things—administrative things—that I'm not always comfortable with, but that's no reason to throw the baby out with the bathwater."

"And the polygamy? If the Salt Lake Mormons call it sin, yet it's central to the beliefs of the version of the faith you practice, how do you reconcile that?"

"I don't," she says matter-of-factly. "That's not my job. All that's required of me is to live a Christian life. And that's what I try to do, no matter what everyone else is arguing about."

"Well," I say, reaching to squeeze her hand. "You're doing a much better job of it than most people I know."

Title 52

THE BIG DAY BEGINS AS ANY OTHER. If I've learned anything about this operation, it's that it relies heavily on routine. The children are conditioned—unlike any kids I've ever known—to get themselves out of bed and begin their daily chores with little or no prompting from adults. The livestock detail slips out of the house before dawn to feed, milk, and tend to the animals; by the time they get back to the kitchen with the milk and eggs for breakfast, the house is humming with activity. It's still a source of amazement to me. It also amuses me to see that, even with all their individual responsibilities, thirty people manage to sit down to every meal together, a feat that the average American family of 4.3 persons has trouble doing even once a week.

The blessing of the meal said, the food eaten, and the table cleared, the party set-up begins in earnest. The event is scheduled as a lunch, in order to accommodate our guests, Laura, Rigs, and Man, who'd be hard-pressed to navigate Elwood Road at night, what with its killer ruts and recently demonstrated perilous drop-offs. Beth and the boys were also invited, but the prevailing sentiment is that, in light of her recent hasty departure, she probably won't be in attendance.

My task at the moment is to help Luke rearrange the staggeringly heavy hardwood dining tables into a wedding party formation, with a head table and multiple satellites. No sooner do we have them in place than the girls are laying hand-embroidered tablecloths and napkins, and the youngest are bringing in fistfuls of wildflowers to be put into vases. Still others are hanging garlands of colored fabric crisscrossing the room. The rest are in the kitchen frosting cakes—it'll take more than one to feed this crowd—and doing who knows what else.

"Let's go get the extra chairs," Luke says after we move the last table into place.

We head down the hall to the first of the two workrooms.

"So, Luke," I say. "With Tom the new head honcho here, where does that leave you?"

"What do you mean?" he says.

"Well, unlike him, you can't just hang around and wait to inherit the job. You probably want your own family someday, don't you?"

"Yeah, I guess," he says. "Someday."

"Where will you find a wife?"

He looks at me as though he doesn't understand the question.

"Don't you need to go out into the re…uh, the outside world to meet a girl?" I say, catching myself. Rebecca has chastised me—kindly—for speaking of the "real world" outside. She says it invalidates the family's own experience—the only world the children have ever known. She's right, of course, but habits are hard to break.

"No," he says. "I'll take one of the sisters to wife."

"Your own sister? Wouldn't that be strange?"

"I don't see why," he says. "We're not related by blood, so it's permitted."

"Huh." I decide not to press the issue further. There are obviously some ideas around here that I still need some time to get used to.

✳   ✳   ✳

The final countdown to zero-hour is marked by the arrival of the guests. Laura is the first to arrive and I go out to meet her at the truck.

"Whatcha got there?" I ask, nodding toward the blue plastic tarp that covers the bed.

"Tom's gift," she says, slapping my hand as I try to lift the corner of the tarp.

"Another Costco run?"

"Yeah. What else could I get him?"

"Well, you'd better hurry in and get your apron on. The women work around here, you know," I say in my best Bubba.

"And who's gonna make me, cowboy, you?" Laura says.

"I wouldn't dream of trying," I say.

"Didn't think so," she says with a laugh. "Besides, I spend all week in a kitchen. Hell if I'm gonna offer. I'm a guest today."

"Well, good thing I've called in reinforcements," I say, as we both turn toward the gate, where Rigs's diesel is chugging down the road toward us. "Now the teams are even: five men, five women."

"Wait," she says with mock seriousness. "Are you counting Man with the men?"

We both laugh. "You're right," I say. "He's more likely to caucus with the kitchen staff."

We amble over to meet the Jerrys as they pull in alongside Laura's rig. We say our hellos and exchange a few pleasantries before heading up to the main house.

"I've been instructed," I tell them, "that because this is a special occasion—and the family rarely entertains guests—I'm to bring you all into the parlor for formal introductions."

"The parlor?" Man says with mock surprise. "Where are we, Big Valley?" Before I can respond he calls out in a dramatic voice, "Heath, come quick! Audra has swooned again!"

Laura and I laugh as Rigs elbows his husband. "Hey, best behavior, remember? These are simple folk. And they don't have TV, let alone Nickelodeon, so they won't get your cultural references anyway."

The four of us enter the parlor to find the lesser wives already waiting. They're seated on a single sofa looking like shy debutantes at the ball, decked out in their best gingham dresses. Seeing this, I have to admit that Man's *Big Valley* reference wasn't far off the mark. "Ladies," I say with a reflexive nod of acknowledgement. "Allow me to present—"

"No, no," Marilee interrupts. "You must wait for the Patriarch and the Lady of the House," she says firmly. "They will be here shortly."

"My mistake," I say, feeling an urge to bow and make light of it, but wisely deciding against it. As odd as some of their customs are to me, I really do have a tremendous amount of respect for these women. "Would you like to take a seat?" I say to our guests, extending my hand toward a second sofa facing the first. Laura and the Jerrys seat themselves and I remain standing. I'm just about to throw out some idle remark to fill the awkward silence when Tom and Rebecca enter from the hall.

"Good afternoon, ladies, gentlemen," Tom says with an air of authority that seems as out of place to me as the Sunday-best he's decked out in: an ill-fitting pinstripe suit that looks like a garage-sale find, complete with vest and pocketwatch. All that's missing is a bolo tie and a Stetson. His hair is slicked back with water. I know for a fact that no one in the household uses any hair products. In fact, almost everything they have is homemade.

Rebecca nods a greeting to the guests and seats herself in an armchair alongside the sister-wives' perch. Tom stands ramrod straight, puffing up his chest like a spring robin, and extends a hand to Rigs. "Good to see you again, Mr. Riggins," he says as though he's in a business meeting. Where does he learn these behaviors, I wonder. He's lived such a sheltered life, without TV, movies, or even role models outside the family. "Nick," Tom says to me, "would you like to present our guests?"

"Sure," I say, trying not to smirk at his earnestness. "You already know Laura, of course." Laura smiles and nods, as do the other women. "And Tom, Rebecca—you already know Rigs...uh, well, Mr. Riggins, I should say. Ladies," I say to the trio on the sofa, "Mr. Riggins is a long-time friend of mine, who also happens to be my attorney." All parties nod and smile.

"And this is Mr. Wong," I say, indicating Man, "Mr. Riggins's husband."

Man nods, first to the ladies, then to Tom. He's met only with a thunderous silence. The lesser wives are looking at their hands, which now seem engaged in adjusting cuffs or picking at imaginary threads on their sleeves. Rebecca alone remains motionless, wearing a polite smile that I can't make heads or tails of. What any of them are think-ing is anybody's guess, though it's now clear to me that the subject of Rigs's and Man's relationship has never come up before.

Only Tom fails to hide his astonishment. He's staring at the couple with an unabashed, unwavering gaze that would be considered impo-lite in any company. Whether he's appalled or merely curious is hard to say. His mouth hangs slightly open, as though he's been turned to stone in midsentence. Only his eyes move, flitting from Rigs to Man and back again.

The guests and I are shuffling nervously and looking from face to face, wondering who will speak first. My fear is that Tom will regain control of his tongue and issue some scathing religious pronouncement on Biblical morality. I'm relieved when it's Rebecca who breaks the silence.

"We're happy to welcome all of you into our home," she says with a grace and sincerity that don't feel at all forced. "Tom will be happy to show you around while the sisters and I finish our preparations in the kitchen. We'll gather in the dining room in fifteen minutes." She moves toward the hall as the sister-wives stand to follow. But Tom is in the way, glued to the spot from which he's still staring at the Jerrys. "Tom," Rebecca prods, placing a hand on his arm.

Only then is his trance broken. "Uh, yeah," he says, turning toward the front door. "I'll show you the grounds. C'mon." After some hesitation, the rest of us file out the door behind him. I throw Rigs and Man an apologetic smirk along the way. Rigs just smiles and takes it in stride. Man gives me a dramatic eye-roll and a wink.

Laura grabs my arm as we step off the porch. "I think you just kicked their ball into the Twenty-First Century in a major way," she says with a wicked grin.

"Hey, Rebecca invited them," I say in my defense. "I thought she knew."

✳   ✳   ✳

"Hey, look, I'm sorry," I say to Rebecca when I get her alone moments before the meal is served. Everyone else is already seated in the dining room, so my apology has to be quick. But I didn't want the incident to be hanging over the celebration all afternoon. "I thought you knew."

"It's not your fault, Nick," she says, taking my hand in a rare daylight gesture of affection. "We have set ourselves apart from the world of our own accord. We can hardly blame others when we don't understand them."

"Still, it should have occurred to me that maybe the subject hadn't been discussed. I just thought that since you had invited both of them that you knew."

"I only told Mr. Riggins that he was welcome to bring a guest. I didn't inquire as to his marital status. That was not my place," she says without any visible anger or annoyance. One more reason I'm so comfortable with her. She's the least judgmental person I've ever met. "In any case," she continues, "I'd appreciate it if you don't raise the subject in front of the children. We can just call Mr. Wong his 'friend.'"

"Absolutely," I say. "After seeing Tom's reaction, I wouldn't want to risk traumatizing any of the younger kids."

"You have to be patient with Tom," Rebecca says. "He has no experience with this concept," she pauses, searching for words, "a man with a man," she says at last. "It's something that has never occurred to him before. It may take some time for him to deal with it. It will for all of us, I'm afraid."

"Well, thank you for doing your best to understand," I say, squeezing her hand before disengaging. "You're a saint," I say with a wink. "A present-day saint."

Title 53

WE'RE SEATED ALONG JUST ONE SIDE of the head table, facing the four satellite tables occupied by the children, in a carefully considered arrangement: Tom occupies the center position, flanked on either side by two sister-wives. To his left, beyond Deborah and Marilee, sit Rigs and Man. To his right are Julie, Rebecca, me, and Laura. I feel like I should have a pint of grog and a slab of wildebeest before me, waiting for the jousters to enter the great hall on horseback. Instead, we're dining on stuffed hen and root-vegetable casserole, and there's no alcohol within miles of the place.

The absence of beer remains the greatest obstacle to my happiness here—and with a warrant out for me, it's now impossible for me to run down to Estacada to toss a couple back now and then. But I have to admit that I'm missing it a lot less than I thought I would. To my surprise, I'm enjoying the company of children more than I did the soused regulars down at the Safari Club. And, if I'm being honest, I'm also finding more satisfaction in the kind of arousal that Rebecca stimulates in me with just a smile, than I ever did from the overworked and overexposed dancers in town.

Normally during dinner I would enjoy some easy conversation with Rebecca. But with Laura isolated at the end of the table to my right, I spend the time catching up with her on the years since we knew each other in college. I want to confide in her my recently acquired feelings for Rebecca, as a gut-check if nothing else—an outside opinion. Of course, this isn't the time and place for that conversation.

When the main course is finished, the excitement among the children begins to grow. The anticipation of the cake has the younger ones squirming in their seats, while the older ones seem to be moving in double-time to clear the tables and produce the anticipated dessert. When it comes, the largest of the cakes—a double-layer cake—is placed before Tom, who has continued to be obsessed with Rigs and Man throughout the meal. Smaller single-layer cakes are set on each of the other tables. There are no candles, but an exuberant rendition of "Happy Birthday" ensues.

I don't know why exactly—maybe it's an emotional response to the singing or the comfort food—but I spontaneously reach over and squeeze Rebecca's hand as the song concludes. She looks at me with an expression that seems both shy and appreciative, and I see the color come into her cheeks. I return her smile and relish the moment; it feels so right to me.

Then it goes terribly wrong. Rebecca's is not the only gaze my handholding action has drawn. When I look just beyond her, Tom is boring holes in me with his eyes. I quickly withdraw my hand. Rebecca, reading my face, whips her head around to see the cause of my discomfort. Tom switches his disapproving stare from me to her, then back to me again. With the conclusion of the song, the room has fallen silent. I turn to find that all the children are watching Tom. I have no idea whether they too witnessed the moment of affection that Rebecca and I shared, but it's clear they're all waiting for the new Patriarch. Or maybe that's just me; they could be waiting for cake.

Tom eases out of his chair, still looking at Rebecca and me. Just when I think he's about to speak, he turns and bolts for the door. No one reacts, at least physically. I look at Rebecca for a clue as to what I should do, but she's watching Tom and provides me no help. At last I conclude that the only thing to do is go after him and apologize. It's clear now that he has been unaware of his mother's and my growing affection for one another. I don't know what the protocol for courting one's mother is in this society, but my unconsidered squeeze of Rebecca's hand has probably violated it. It's up to me to make it right.

I jump from my seat and follow Tom out the door. As I get into the hallway, I hear the back door slam shut. I race through the service porch and pursue him out into the yard; I'm just in time to see him disappear into the barn.

When I enter the barn, I call his name. There's no response. "Tom," I call again. "Let's talk." Still nothing. I move along the line of stalls, all of them void of the horses that once occupied them. Because of the arson investigation, the law requires a formal evaluation of the living conditions before the animals can be returned. As I pass each stall, I turn to look, but I don't see Tom. When I'm halfway through the barn, I turn to look up into the hay loft. I see no one, but if he's up there, he could easily be hidden behind stacks of hay.

"Tom," I call again. "C'mon. Let's talk. We can fix this." Nothing. I turn and continue beyond the last stall to the tack room. I turn the corner and walk right into the barrel of a rifle. It appears to be the same rifle that Father John began this whole wild ride with just weeks ago.

"Whoa! Back off, Tom," I say, instinctively raising my hands in the "shooter-dude" response I developed on the job. "C'mon, put that thing down before you hurt someone." I don't really think he'd shoot me, any more than one of my Census respondents would. But part of me isn't sure; the kid is an enigma, and his own brother says he frightens him sometimes.

"I don't want to hurt you, Nick," he says with a wavering voice. "Just go back to the house."

"Look, Tom," I say. "I'm sorry. I probably should have said something."

"No," he barks. "Don't say anything. Just go. You hear me? Go!" His voice rises in increasing desperation.

"OK. OK," I say, lowering my hands slowly and taking two steps back. "Just put that gun away and come back and talk. As soon as you're ready, OK?"

"You just never mind me," he says, still holding the rifle on me. "Now git."

"Right," I say, turning to go. "I'll be waiting for you at the house." With that I cross the barn and leave by the way I came. I don't look back. When I get to the house I stop. I'm not ready to go back inside. Who knows what chaos has followed Tom's sudden departure. I don't know if anyone blames me—it's certainly not in Rebecca's nature to hold any grudges—but I feel the need to sit and contemplate the meaning of it all before I face the family. I drop myself into one of the rockers on the porch and bask in the late-afternoon sun, trying to figure out what to do.

Title 54

I'VE BEEN HERE FOR ABOUT TWENTY minutes and I'm feeling guilty now about abandoning the party. Rebecca and the others must be worried about Tom; I should get inside and let them know I talked him down the best I could.

As I stand to go, movement catches my eye in the garden plot. I take a second look and discover Tom sidling through the cornstalks toward the lower reaches of the compound. He's still carrying the rifle. Maybe he's going to shoot some coyotes to work through his anger. He deserves as much, I guess. I'd probably want to do the same at his age. It was selfish of me to let my feelings for his mother upstage him on his big day.

Still, I can't help but wonder whether I ought not go after him. Rebecca would probably be more comfortable having him back inside. Besides, the party's for him, so it would raise spirits considerably if he were there for it. If Tom's as mercurial as Luke says, then the kids are probably used to these outbursts and nobody will make a big deal out of this one.

As Tom reaches the edge of the property, where Luke's favorite hiking trails head off toward Dubois Creek, I'm already in pursuit. I'm sure I can persuade him to return. By the time I catch up he'll have had plenty of time to cool off. Besides, now that he's officially responsible for leading the family, he'll have to shake this off quickly.

The cool of the forest shade is refreshing as I push past the property line and under the canopy of fir and maple. Patches of moss catch
the dappled late-afternoon sunlight, glowing antifreeze green. I neither
see nor hear Tom. He can't be that far ahead of me, unless perhaps he
ran once he was beyond my view. The air is so still that the only sound
comes from the wings of insects. It has a welcome, calming effect. I
hope that it affects Tom the same way. This is a good place for him to
walk off his anger. That's probably why he comes here. And why Luke
escapes here to write his stories.

Again I reconsider: maybe I should lay off and let Tom come back
when he's good and ready. That's probably what I'd want if I were in
his shoes. Still, I continue walking, not so much to find him now, but
because the forest draws me forward. The duff underfoot is thick and
spongy, massaging my feet with every step, and silencing my progress.
I suck in a deep breath of fir-scented air and force myself to focus on just
what it is I'm doing—not here in the forest, but in my life in general.

Am I serious about Rebecca? What about Beth? And Josiah, my
kid? How long can I hide out up here? Should I turn myself in and get
whatever's coming to me over with? One thing's for sure: I'm done with
the Census Bureau. Even if I don't get any jail time, I'm not going
back. I'm so over pissy supervisors and pissed off respondents. I need
to do something more noble with my life. Two possibilities are inescapable: fatherhood and this place. I don't know what role I can play in
Josiah's life at this point, but I at least need to try. As for Rebecca and
the clan, I feel an obligation to do something to make up for the loss of
Father John, even if it wasn't my fault. They can use a man around
here, and Tom hardly seems suitable as the only one. Besides, I think I
could get really comfortable here. If Rebecca will have me.

Suddenly it all crystallizes for me, as though I've just awoken from
a long obsession. I give up my pursuit of Tom and turn back, determined to accept reality. Beth and I will never work. Even if she'd have
me—and the restraining order were dropped—I don't want her any-

more. It's not just the parenting thing—hell, I'd be a surrogate father to two dozen kids if I stayed here. No, the real problem is that Beth and I no longer have anything in common, except perhaps a toxic cynicism and childhood obsession, long since impractical. She's spent too many years in the stranglehold of her parents, and I've suffered too many years of Angina. I'm tired of being bitter and cynical. It's time to start over.

I need to talk to Rebecca, I tell myself as I pick up the pace back up the trail. I need to know what we're dancing around. Is it a relationship? Or is it just a flirtation?

Before I can pursue the thought any further, something catches my eye. A glint of light. I can't immediately see the source, but I move off the trail to my right in the direction it came from. The firs are thinner here and the maples allow more light to reach the forest floor. It's a soft, warm, gauzy light tinged with green that causes the grove of maples before me to glow.

And there he is. I freeze in my tracks, not wanting to alert him to my presence. I consider going back, but that too might make too much noise. The last thing I want to do is disturb him now, so I just squat out of view and take in the scene.

Tom is kneeling, apparently in prayer, in a small clearing among the maples. The low rays of light stream in at oblique angles, catching him in an almost angelic spotlight. He's laid the rifle aside and his head is bowed. It's a touching scene, even to someone as jaded as me. The innocence it suggests is almost magical, even if it is at odds with the many other Toms I've gotten to know over the recent weeks. I can't help but wonder what he's praying for. Is he asking for help with his new responsibilities? Or is he praying that I'll leave his mother alone? Maybe it's just how he overcomes his anger.

After a couple minutes, I decide to retreat as quietly as I can. This just feels like too private a thing to be gawking at from the bushes. It reminds me of Figley and the pictures of Beth. Just the association of the two makes me feel like a Peeping Tom. I feel guilty.

Slowly I rise to my feet. I'm about to turn away when Tom does something totally unexpected: he picks up the rifle, props the butt of it on the ground, and puts the barrel in his mouth.

In a heartbeat I'm airborne across the clearing, lunging at the kid. "Tom! No!" My shout startles him enough to interrupt his plan. He snaps his head in my direction just as I grab the rifle from his hand and fall on it. It fires.

Title 55

AM I STILL ALIVE?

I must be, because my ears are ringing. But everything has gone dark. It takes me a second to realize that's because my face is buried in the ground. I don't think I've been hit. Jesus, with all the guns that have been pointed at me, I'd hate to think that I ended up shooting myself.

Then I regain my senses. Tom! Was he hit? I flip myself like a pancake, onto my back. Tom is standing over me with a look of horror. He probably thought I was dead, poor kid. Is he in shock? He's just staring, not moving.

"Tom? You OK?"

My voice activates him; he takes off running again. At least he left the rifle behind this time. I leave it too as I jump to my feet, spitting dirt and wiping detritus off my face. I take off after him, but the going is much tougher this time. Tom's opted to run straight through the forest without the benefit of a trail. He's also running directly into the sun. In an effort to keep from getting thwacked in the face by the branches that are springing back at me in his wake, I've got both arms up in front of me, further obscuring my vision.

"Tom, please stop," I yell. "Can we just talk for a minute?"

I'm wasting my breath. He's gaining on me and shows no intention of sitting down for a chat. Despite my protective strategy, I'm still taking stinging blows to the head—blood from my left ear is now trickling down my neck. There are spatters of blood on my sleeves, though I don't know from where or have time to care. Yet again I wonder if I should quit the chase. But I can't. Not after seeing him come this close to blowing his brains out. Whatever demons are in his head, I can't leave him alone with them now.

I turn my shoulder into the lead and run even faster, using it as a battering ram against the gauntlet of branches that stand between me and Tom, wherever he is. If he can make it through this shit, I sure as hell can too.

And then I catch air. *What the fuck?* Before I can answer my own question, I slam into a rocky slope, kidneys first. I'm sliding even faster than I was running just seconds ago. The incline is nearly vertical. Instinctively I grab at anything I can to slow my descent. A sapling fir. I get nothing but green-smeared lacerations on my palms for my effort. A tangle of tree roots. *Fuck!* I've broken at least two fingers. But that's still a secondary concern. I'm vaguely aware that there's a creek below, but I can't calculate the distance. I need to stop now. In another desperate attempt, I slam both my feet into a large boulder racing toward me from below. This stops my feet—at least temporarily—but not the rest of me. Now I'm flipping end over end until I'm flying headfirst toward oblivion. Now I'm fucked for sure.

Cold. The kind you feel in your bones. Only it's not static. It comes in waves. Is this death? All I sense is profound cold. Or is it heat? No, it's definitely cold. And wet. And pain. I try to locate it, but I have no sense of a body. Just pervasive cold and wet and pain. Later—is it a matter of seconds or hours?—I begin to feel suffocated. Then I'm moving, fighting back the sensation. Immediately the pain locates itself in my head and my eyes fly open to a sight more unexpected than death: I'm staring into Tom's panicked eyes at very close range.

I'm lying in Dubois Creek with Tom kneeling over me. And he's got me in a lip-lock. Instinctively I try to push him away, but my broken fingers scream from my right hand, and my left shoulder no longer seems to operate. It occurs to me that he's trying to give me mouth-to-mouth. Did I need it? Maybe he's been at it a while and that's the only reason I'm here now. Whatever the reason, I don't need it now. And I'm left with only my eyes to signal him that his effort is no longer necessary.

It's only a matter of seconds before he realizes that I'm alive and breathing on my own; he disengages. But before I can find out if my voice still works, he's kissing me again—on the cheeks, on the forehead, on the lips. Tears are streaming down his face and he begins to sob.

"Whoa," I try to protest, but it just comes out as a moan. I try to turn my head away from his labial ministrations, or whatever the fuck is going on, but a horrific pain explodes in my head and consciousness begins to slip away again. The last thing I hear is Tom.

"I love you, Nick. I love you. Don't leave me. Please don't leave me."

✳   ✳   ✳

I awaken in a hospital room. My awareness comes slowly and, ultimately, incompletely. I don't need to examine the source of the drip into my arm to recognize the effects of morphine. A motorcycle accident seven years ago introduced me to the stuff. In fact, most of what I perceive of my present surroundings could have been lifted from that earlier experience, when I spent three months in such a room as this one. The room, the machines, the traction; everything's the same. There's one new addition to this picture, however: Tom is scrunched up in a chair in the corner by the window, head back, mouth open, snoring.

The events of—when, was it just today, or was it several days ago?—come back in a slow ebb of recollection. Rebecca, the party, Tom with the gun in my face, Tom with the gun in *his* face, the chase, the fall, the pain, Tom's manifestations of love. How did it come to this?

Why did it come to this? All because I squeezed Rebecca's hand at lunch? The only thread of explanation that runs through all these events is—apropos of the last month of my life—is Tom. What the hell is up with that kid?

I lie in the dark in my morphine bliss, serenaded by clicks and beeps and snores, and try to put the puzzle pieces together. Tom was happy to have me at the compound, that much was evident. Rebecca and Luke both commented that his spirits were much improved since my arrival. We worked together, side by side, on numerous occasions without any sign of trouble. Rebecca and I would steal moments alone to talk and sip tea, but there was no hint that Tom was troubled by this. Could he have been completely unaware of how our relationship was developing? I suppose that's possible; we didn't exactly advertise it, and our moments together were almost always at night, after everyone else was tucked in for the night.

I suppose I shouldn't be surprised that I set him off with a tiny public display of affection. They aren't the most demonstrative people, after all. I wonder if Tom thought my action implied that we'd taken things farther; maybe it was his mother's honor he feared for. But suicide? What would drive him to that? Did he feel that as the man of the house he had abdicated his responsibility by letting a man take advantage of her? Is there some hara-kiri doctrine that says he must atone for such a lapse? I don't know. I'll have to ask Rebecca. Rebecca—does she even know I'm here? Does anybody know? They might still be looking for us... But I doze before I can finish the thought.

Title 56

WHEN I AWAKEN, TOM IS AT MY SIDE staring at me with a singular intensity, as though he's afraid I'm not going to wake ever again. This calls to mind the last words I heard from him before I lost consciousness: *Please don't leave me.* But why such emotion? And the kisses. What the fuck was that all about? I mean, one minute he's got a gun in my face, telling me to get lost; the next he's fucking kissing me, begging me not to leave him. Was he afraid he'd be blamed for my death? Like maybe he was responsible for Father John's death? I think it's time to get a few things sorted out with him.

"I'm so glad you're alive," he says when my eyes focus on him. "How are you feeling?"

"Not so hot," I try to say, only to find that I can't open my mouth. For an instant I wonder if I'm paralyzed from the lips down. But I can feel my extremities, so that's not it. I try again.

"Your jaw is wired," Tom says, answering the question in my eyes. "The doctor says you shouldn't try to move it."

Fuck. I've got a whole lot to talk about—important shit—and I've been rendered mute.

"Here," Tom says, putting a pad and pencil into my remaining good hand. Fortunately I'm left-handed, so I've got a fighting chance at communicating. The thing is, it's my right leg that's elevated in traction, and this is where I'm obliged to put the pad so I can see what I'm writing. It's an awkward reach, but I make it work.

How much longer? I scribble, nearly legible.

"Two weeks," Tom says.

What day is this?

"Sunday."

Does anyone know we're here?

Tom shakes his head. "The ambulance brought us last night."

You need to go home.

"I want to be with you."

This is a hell of a way to have an argument, and I just don't have the strength to keep this up for long. *I'm sorry about your mom,* I write, changing the subject.

Tom screws up his face. "Why?"

We didn't tell you about us.

Tom looks away. When he looks back his eyes are moist. "I thought..." he begins, then trails off. I keep my eyes on him, waiting for him to complete the thought. He tries again. "I thought you were my friend," he says, the emphasis on *my*. He looks away again.

I am, I jot.

"No, I mean... instead of hers," he says, still not looking at me.

I love your mother—I like you too.

"I wanted you to love me," he says, the tears now flowing.

Can't be your father, I write. *But can do my best.*

"I don't want to be your son," he says, his voice breaking. I'm trying to decide what the right response to this is, when he adds, "I want to be your... your husband." The last bombshell of a word is nearly lost in his blubbering, but that in no way lessens the impact. There's a full-blown crater in my head. Holy shit!

Suddenly all the puzzle pieces fall into place: Tom running away with me, moving into my house, squeezing the hell out of me on the bike, his efforts to please me, his funks when I didn't respond positively. Then there was his improved attitude when I moved to the compound, the joint projects he assigned, sitting next to me at meals. This also explains Tom's infatuation with Rigs and Man when I introduced them as husbands. Of course! Not to mention his reaction to my display of affection toward Rebecca. Nobody likes to think of their mother as a cougar, let alone to see her get hit on, especially by someone you've also got the hots for.

And finally, the suicide attempt. Jesus. I've always heard that something like half of all teen suicides are among gay kids, but all the gay guys I knew back at PSU were out and proud. I'd never known any of them to be anywhere close to considering suicide. Then again, maybe I was just clueless. That would be so like me. But hell, Rigs and Man have been together for a decade, and they've both been way happier than I have. I just don't have any personal experience with something like this.

Then I have an idea. *Call Rigs*, I scribble, adding his cell number to the page. But Tom's not looking. I nudge him in the shoulder with the pad.

Tom looks at the paper, then at me, then back at the paper. "Why?" he says, wiping his eyes on his sleeve.

Family worried. Need to know we're safe.

Tom takes the pad from me without saying anything. I point to the phone beside the bed. He looks at it, back at me, back at the pad. He repeats these motions in random order for about thirty seconds. A raise of the eyebrows is the only encouragement I can give. I can't even smile.

Finally, Tom gets up and comes around to the phone. He punches in the numbers, then hangs up. "It just beeps," he says.

I signal for the pad. *Dial 9 first.*

He tries again and the call goes through. Relying on just one half of the conversation, I use the pad to guide him through it. By the time he hangs up, we've got Rigs on his way to pick Tom up and take him home where, according to Rigs, the entire family stayed up all night searching and worrying. None of them knew of the accident or the 911 call from a passerby on the highway. I can only imagine what hell we've put them all through. I vow to make it up to them somehow, if I'm not dead or in jail before I get the chance.

✳ ✳ ✳

By the time Rigs has come and gone, I've made him promise to stop back by the hospital on his way home to help me straighten a few things out, not the least of which is the warrant for my arrest. It wasn't until Rigs arrived that I learned there was a deputy posted outside my room. Like I'm a flight risk or something. Idiots. Still, his presence is enough to remind me that, despite my present morphine vacation, I've got a few issues besides my health that need to be addressed.

Among the other things I've learned this morning is that I'm in the same ICU where Father John took his final breath. That's why Tom was admitted to my room without being a close family member: the duty nurse recognized him from our earlier visit. I have no doubt that he'd still be camped in the lobby had he not been admitted, given what I now know about the nature of his feelings for me. That knowledge also makes it creepy to think back to his kissing me in the creek when he thought I'd just come back from the dead. Here I thought it was some sort of transference thing, like I was a father figure to him or something.

But I'm working on the beginnings of a plan—not only for Tom, but for the rest of my life. I guess it's true what they say about a near-death experience reordering one's priorities. Either that, or it's the morphine. Oxycodone's got nothing on morphine. Oxy's like floating in the clouds; morphine's like flying above them. And from up here I finally have a clear view of my life—something that's eluded me for the past 32 years. I realize now that I've been stuck in adolescence my whole life; it's time to become an adult. When Rigs gets back I'm going to take the first steps toward doing that.

Title 57

I'M REELED IN FROM MY MORPHINE FLIGHT like a kite on a string. I open my eyes as I touch down; Rebecca is standing at my bedside, gently stroking my arm and saying my name. All I can do is smile with my eyes. She is a welcome sight. There is so much I want to say, but my present communication method imposes an economy of words. I pick up the pad from its default home on my lap and scribble a response: "Hi" followed by a smiley-face.

"I'm so sorry, Nick," she says, fighting back tears. "I shouldn't have let you go after him. He's not your responsibility."

Not to worry. Glad I did.

"He really respects you—you know that, I hope," she says with a smile.

If only she knew how far beyond "respect" it went. I want to discuss this with her, but besides my hampered communication skills, there's the issue of Tom's privacy. Nobody likes to be outed, especially to a parent. That's the kind of thing that has to be a firsthand conversation. I reply with a simple *Yes*. But there's also the suicide attempt; that's the kind of thing a parent has a right, if not a duty, to know about.

Did he tell you why I chased?

"No," she says, shaking her head. "Only that he was hiding from you when you fell over the rim."

Sit, I write, waving my pencil toward the chair in the corner. Rebecca drags it to the bed and sits beside me. I so want to kiss her and pour out my soul, but that will have to wait. She's looking at me expectantly. There's no easy way to break the news to her on a four-by-five notepad.

He had the gun in his mouth. I hesitate before showing the message to her, willing my eyes to convey empathy and soften the blow. Slowly I turn the pad toward her.

Rebecca's hand flies to her mouth and the tears begin in earnest. She squeezes my arm with her other hand and looks from me to the pad and back again. Then she starts shaking her head and sobbing. The word "why" finds its way out of her several times. I feel so helpless. My eyes begin watering too. For several minutes we just look at each other through moist lenses.

When at last Rebecca has wiped her face with several tissues from the nightstand—and handed me a few as well—she speaks. "I've known for a long time that he's been troubled. But I thought it was nothing more than a teenage phase, made worse by the conflict with John, of course. I was sure that things were getting better in recent weeks. You've seen him; he's been in such good spirits of late."

I nod as much of a yes as I'm able.

"I think he just needs a good male role model. Someone he can talk to about the troubles of a young man." She looks me square in the eye and adds, "Maybe when you recover you could sit down with him. He adores you."

Doesn't he though. I don't write this; I only think it and telescope an eye-smile instead.

"But in the meantime I just don't know what I'm going to do. I can't watch him around the clock." She pauses before adding, "But I'll have to confide in the sisters—and Luke as well. We need to do our best to keep him safe."

Hide the guns.

"Yes, I'll have Luke do that right away."

Will you talk to him?

"About this? Of course. A mother has no other choice. To say nothing and then have him..." She's unable to finish the awful thought. "It's unthinkable. I'll speak to him this very evening."

How about a therapist?

"No," she says without hesitation. "Psychotherapy is incompatible with our beliefs. Secular counseling is likely to do as much harm as good."

Her abrupt and unconsidered response makes me think that this might be knee-jerk conditioning. I press the issue. *Therapy can save lives,* I write.

Rebecca smiles, a sad smile. "I know, Nick. But so does the Lord. We've taught these children to trust in the Lord rather than the sophistries of men. To abandon those teachings in a time of trouble would be altogether the wrong message. Do you see?"

I semi-nod. Then I make a proposal. It's an idea I had while Tom was here, but I hadn't fully thought it out yet. Now it makes perfect sense. I write: *I'll have Rigs talk to him.*

"Rigs?" she says, musing over the idea.

Male role model, I write.

"But is he..." she begins, uncertain. "What I mean is, is it the right role model?"

Absolutely, I write, followed by three exclamation points.

"Oh, Nick, I didn't mean to imply... He's a very nice man. I have the greatest respect for him," she sputters, trying to make amends. "I only mean to say that perhaps he might not fully understand the needs of a boy like Tom." She looks at me, hopeful, her expression pleading with me to forgive her dissing of Rigs.

He'll understand. I underscore this twice for emphasis. Rigs is, in fact, the perfect role model for a confused gay teen. He's a gay man with a happy marriage, well-respected in his career, and he and Man are frequent foster fathers to troubled youth awaiting permanent placement, many of them also gay. I just wish I could tell Rebecca all this.

"It would be good if he had someone now," Rebecca concedes. "Until you're in better shape." She smiles empathetically and takes my hand. I drop the pad and pencil onto the blanket and squeeze back. For several minutes we sit in silence, thus engaged.

At length I let go and pick up the pad again. *We need to talk.*

"But we *are* talking," she says with a shy laugh.

About us.

She gives me a tender look that sets my Airedale tail a-wagging. My face hurts from trying to smile with a zipped mouth. I imagine myself looking like one of the kids in the film *Coraline* with their mouths stitched shut—nothing but two big button eyes gazing back at her.

Then she says, "Are we really *us*?"

I nod as vigorously as my one-inch range of movement allows me, and a tear rolls down my cheek.

Title 58

BETWEEN THE MORPHINE AND REGULAR visits from Rebecca, two weeks pass quickly. Others have visited too: besides Tom, Rigs, and Man, I've had two visits each from Laura and Beth.

Even Angie dropped by. For once I was happy not to be able to speak. I just let her prattle on to my morphine smile until she'd gotten everything off her chest. I wrote only two words to her in response: *Sorry*, when she asked if I could answer her many questions; of course, that didn't stop her from asking them. And I wrote *No* when she said the Census Bureau's inspector general had cleared me of any Title 13 violation and that I was welcome to come back to work as soon as I recovered. She blustered on for another five minutes before she realized that I had nothing more to say.

The doctor has just removed the wires from my jaw and is explaining how the at-home recovery process will go. It's the same on-call doctor that briefed us on Father John what seems like months ago, though it's barely been a month. When he's done he hands me a prescription. "Take these as needed for pain, no more than six times a day," Dr. Savage says.

I try to decipher the scribble, but fail. "What is this?"

"Oxycodone," he says.

I laugh. "No, Doc, sorry," I say, handing the scrip back to him. "That stuff makes me do some crazy shit."

"Suit yourself," he says, but refuses the slip of paper. "But keep it anyway, in case you change your mind."

I shove it in my pocket. "Hey, Doc. Mind if I ask you something else?"

He raises his eyebrows awaiting my question.

"It's not about me; it's about John Allred, the guy we came to see last month in ICU. You know, the one who died?"

"Yes, I'm sorry," Savage says. "My sympathies."

"Was there any funny business that day?" This, of course, is the question I've been unable to shake for so long, but it's even more relevant now, given Tom's recent mental state and capacity for self-violence.

"How do you mean?"

"What exactly was the cause of death?"

"Acute myocardial infarction."

"So he didn't suffocate?"

"Suffocate? No. What made you think that?"

"Oh, never mind. I probably just misunderstood."

Well, that's one less thing to worry about, I tell myself as the doctor leaves. At least I can cut Tom some slack on that count.

It also means I'm not an accessory to murder. The last thing I need is another warrant out for me. Rigs just barely got the last one rescinded. While I floated on planet morphine, he got the DA to meet with Beth and her parents to hammer out an agreement. Beth, of course, has always wanted it. Once her parents were assured that I no longer harbored a romantic interest in their daughter, and, perhaps more importantly, that I had no intention of getting DNA testing for Josiah or pursuing custody, they relented. I settled for informal visitation, but agreed not to tell Josiah I am his biological father until he turns 18, or until Beth decides to break the news.

I also had to give the DA something: I agreed to testify against Figley when his stalking and menacing charges are tried.

With all that ugliness finally behind me, and with a renewed ability to speak, I'm in good spirits when Rigs arrives to take me home. And I'm not even on morphine or oxycodone.

"Are the papers all drawn up?" I ask as we turn east onto the Interstate for the thirty-mile trip to Elwood.

"Yep. You're good to go," Rigs says.

"And she doesn't know, right?"

"Right," he confirms. "It'll be your surprise."

"Great, thanks," I say, enjoying the ability to smile for the first time in two weeks. In fact, it's probably been years since I smiled like this. I lost that ability when they charged me with statutory rape.

"I'll send you the bill, as usual," Rigs quips as he merges into traffic.

"Hey, how are things going with Tom?" I ask, remembering that I'm not the only one with problems to resolve lately.

"Hey, you know he's actually a good kid," Rigs says. "He's got a good heart."

"Yeah, well, the goal here is to keep it beating," I say. "It's the good who die young, remember?"

"It'll take time, but I think he'll pull through. He just needs to escape his isolation."

"Isolation?" I say. "Hell, he's one of twenty-five kids; if anything, he suffers from a lack of privacy."

"That's not what I mean, Nick. He's socially isolated. Do you know what it's like to feel all alone in a crowd?"

"Can't say I do."

"When you're different from everyone else, it doesn't matter how many of them there are; you're never going to feel totally connected. Part of you will always be alone."

"Huh. Never thought about it that way."

"Imagine if you were abducted by aliens—let's say they're friendly aliens. You learn their language and make a lot of friends, but you're forced to live on their planet the rest of your life."

"Might not be so bad," I say, "given what this planet's put me through lately."

"I'm serious, Nick," Rigs says. "In a situation like that you'd always feel isolated from people like you. There'd be no one you could talk to about human experience."

"So you're saying Tom needs to live on Planet Gay to be happy?"

"Not at all—a totally gay environment wouldn't be real either. But he does need to see life from other perspectives than the one he's got right now. The world view he's been saddled with there at the compound is pretty limiting."

"Yeah," I say. "I can vouch for that."

"Tom needs to learn that there are other ways of interpreting life; his family doesn't have the tools he needs to sort out his confusion."

"Rebecca's not going to send him away, if that's what you're thinking," I say, turning to Rigs to emphasize my point.

"She doesn't have to 'send' him; he can make his own choices. He's an adult now."

"In years, yes," I concede. "But in experience he's still a kid. He's her kid."

"I realize that," Rigs says as we exit the freeway onto the Estacada Highway. "That's why we got Rebecca's buy-in."

"On what?" I ask, snapping my head in his direction again. "What have you three been cooking up while I was strung up like a side of beef?"

"I proposed to her that Tom come live with me and Jerry, as soon as you're fully recovered and able to get along without him." Rigs glances at me to gauge my reaction.

"Well, shit, that's pretty harsh," I say. "Stealing my best farmhand and leaving me with all the heavy lifting." I flash him a look of annoyance, but he knows I'm just giving him a hard time.

"You've still got Luke; he's every bit as good as Tom. Hell, he's got more muscle anyway."

"Listen to you," I chide. "What are you doing checking out a sixteen-year-old's muscle?"

Rigs shoots me an annoyed look. "Don't even start. I'm happily married and I'm not into kids. But I'm not blind; Luke has the build of a Greek Olympian. Even you had to notice that."

"Yeah, I did. Puts me to shame," I say. "I was flabby before I jumped off the cliff; now it'll take me even longer to get into shape."

"You see," Rigs says with a shit-eating grin. "All the more reason you don't need Tom; you'll get more exercise without him."

Title 59

IT'S DÉJÀ VU WHEN WE GET BACK to the compound. It's as though Tom's birthday party never ended. The dining room looks much the same: decorations, the table arrangement, the food that's being served, as though we never actually ate it the first time. I wonder if the morphine is having a residual effect on me and I've lost time somewhere or maybe I've hallucinated the last two weeks. It's not until a chorus of voices shouts "surprise" and dozens of people pour in from the kitchen and work room that I understand that we're celebrating again.

And it really is a surprise: not only are the kids and sister-wives all there, but so are Man, Laura, Beth and the boys; even Angie. It's like seeing my life flash in front of me—which, just for the record, didn't happen when I was plunging to my near-death in Dubois Creek. It's a little unsettling to see the mingling of people in my life that I've tried to keep in separate compartments for the last decade: namely Angie and Beth. But I shrug it off. Beth is no longer a secret, forbidden longing and, well, my Angina is cured—I no longer care what she thinks.

Happy as I am to be back, I'm still weak. I have to get off my feet. Tom, attentive as ever, is at my side, ushering me to a seat at the head of the table before I even say anything. As he eases me into the chair he whispers, "I'm sorry about before, Nick. Thank you for understanding. I still love you."

I turn to him before he straightens up. "You know, Tom—I still love you too," I say with a wink. He blushes and returns to the crowd of well-wishers, each of whom is now moving to their assigned stations in preparation for the festivities.

The adults line up to file by my throne—all I'm missing is the raised dais—and offer their personal welcomes. "Not sure I like the new do," Laura wisecracks, referring to my recently shaved head, a result of surgery. "I can find you a crown if you'd like."

Angie stops to inquire if I won't reconsider coming back to the Census Bureau. When I decline, she can't help but remind me that I'm still sworn for life to uphold Title 13. "You know," I tell her. "That won't be a problem. I have no intention of speaking of the Census Bureau ever again."

Beth ushers the boys toward me, each of whom I give a pat on the head. She hands me an envelope. "Before I forget," she says, "this came from the State of Oregon."

I look at the envelope and recognize by the printing in the glassine window that it's a check—the bail refund check. "You'll have to give this to Tom," I tell her, handing it back. "That's his money. He'll need it to pay his room and board at the Jerrys' place."

Beth starts to move on, but I put a hand on her arm. "Hold on," I say, "I have something for you too." I reach into the breast pocket of my blazer and pull out the envelope Rigs handed me back at the truck.

"What's this?" she asks, taking it from me.

"Open it."

She does. She scans the first page, then looks up. "A Quit Claim Deed? I don't get it."

"It's the deed to the house," I say. "I've created a trust in Josiah's name and deeded the house over to it. You're the trustee."

"What? Nick, you can't be serious!" she blurts. "You're giving us the house?"

"I'm giving my son the house," I whisper. "Until he's 18 you get to live there as well. After that, it's entirely up to him."

"That's just... I... I don't know what to say," she says, breathless. "Thank you."

"You don't have to thank me," I tell her. "That was always 'our' house; I was just holding on to it until you came back." I give her a wink; she blushes.

Rebecca is the last to pay her respects. Everyone else is already seated and waiting. She shocks me with a demure peck on the cheek. I'm tempted to look around the room to see how others reacted, but I don't. I'd rather not take my eyes from hers. "Welcome home, Nick," she says. "You've been sorely missed around here."

"But not by you," I say with a coy smile.

"Of course," she says with mock indignation. "Just because I saw you nearly every day at the hospital doesn't mean I didn't miss you when I was here."

"Are you sure you wouldn't rather just keep visiting me?" I ask. "That's a lot different than living with me." I say this jokingly, but I really am probing the waters. I want to know if she thinks this arrangement can last.

"Nick, you are welcome here for as long as you want. Consider this your home."

"Do you mean that?" I ask her as earnestly as I can, searching her eyes for any hint that she's just being polite. But all I see there is a reflection of the love I feel for her.

"Absolutely," she says with a smile that makes even my good knee weak. If I didn't still have a cast on the other one, I might have slithered out of the chair.

Despite the cast, I struggle to get out of the chair anyway.

"Nick, don't," Rebecca cautions. "Where do you need to go?"

"Right here," I say as I drop clumsily onto my good knee with the cast-leg sticking awkwardly out in front of me.

Rebecca is fussing over me, looking flustered. "Are you sure I can't help you?"

"Actually, you can," I tell her. "Can you reach into my lower jacket pocket for me?"

She does. When she withdraws her hand she's holding a small, blue, velveteen box. She hands it to me.

I take it and open it. "Rebecca," I say for all the world to hear. "Will you have me as your husband?"

Epilogue

IT'S HARD TO BELIEVE IT'S BEEN five years since I became a part of the largest family in Clackamas County. That's half as long as I worked for the Census Bureau, yet that feels like an entire lifetime ago. And for as much physical labor as I've done during that time, it may as well have been sixty years. But I'm not complaining. I stopped complaining the day I sailed over a cliff trying to save the suicidal gay teenager I now call my stepson.

As it turns out, he saved me. If he hadn't jumped in my Jeep all those years ago, I'd still be a self-absorbed little prick up to my eyeballs in beer and strippers and regret. Now I'm the father of three—one by Beth and two by Rebecca—stepfather to two, and surrogate father to too many to count. And I love them all.

Tom's living with the Jerrys and loving his new life. He still comes around at least once a week to help out with the heavy-lifting projects, though I think he's really just checking up to see that I'm treating his mother right. I wouldn't dare do otherwise; I've seen what happens when he doesn't approve of her husbands. He's enrolled online at Oregon State getting his degree in Animal Husbandry. We all got a good laugh when he chose his major; I had to make sure that he knew it wasn't a course in finding a husband. If he's dating anybody, he and the Jerrys are mum about it. Rigs says that in order to function as a healthy adult Tom needs to have some partitions in his life. Works for me. Rebecca struggles with it at times, but we're both happy that he's happy.

Luke's also in college now, though he's attending in person at Mt. Hood Community. Like his brother, he wasn't quite ready to go away to college full-time. He and Tom had a bit of a falling out when Luke learned that his brother was gay, but, as I've seen over and over again in this incredible family, love always wins out.

Beth brings Josiah, now 15, and Micah, 13, up to the compound almost three weekends out of four. They insist. This is like their own personal 4-H camp. They love helping out with the animals and joining the other kids on hikes and projects. Sometimes they stay overnight and participate in the Sunday religious services that even I have grown accustomed to. Beth says she prefers the worship services here to those at her parents' church. She and Rebecca are now bff's. I sometimes think that if it weren't for Beth's and my sordid history, she and the boys would move in here as well.

Laura still comes by from time to time just to say hi. Sometimes she also brings "leftovers" from the restaurant, though I suspect that often she spends extra money at Costco and writes off the donation. After all, Clackamas County still lists us as a "Seasonal Camp: Religious." Hey, it's no lie—I sure got religion here.

✳   ✳   ✳

Oh, I almost forgot to tell you. The other day I was setting up the smudge pots out in the orchard when a pickup I didn't recognize came down the driveway. We no longer keep the gate locked—everybody's welcome here now. I hiked over to the house to see what was up.

"Howdy," the guy said, extending his hand. "I'm Dan Michaels from the U.S. Census Bureau. We're conducting the—"

"Dude," I said, interrupting him, "you really need to consider getting the hell out, right now."

"I'm sorry, sir," he said. "I'm required by law to be here."

"No," I said, correcting his misperception. "I mean you need to get out of the Senseless Bureau. That place will really fuck you up."

END

ABOUT THE AUTHOR

ORIGINALLY FROM THE SAN FRANCISCO Bay Area, Martin Bannon has lived in Oregon's politically schizophrenic Clackamas County since 1998. *Senseless Confidential*, a comedic romp through the county's backwoods, is his third book.

Bannon, who has lived in places as varied as Puerto Rico, Switzerland, and Utah, majored in Soviet Studies to pursue a career in intelligence. When he discovered that there was no such thing, he became a writer instead, where he has been living out cover legends ever since.

He is fluent in three languages and can make educated errors in a half dozen more. He has traveled to 38 of the United States and 19 foreign countries. He has been a tea guest of Her Majesty Queen Elizabeth II, pursued by Hungarian security forces, and questioned by East German authorities (all for unrelated reasons).

He has been adopted by a cat named Rudy, who is sometimes mistaken for a meatloaf.

Visit the author at:

author@martinbannon.com
www.martinbannon.com
@Martin_Bannon on Twitter
www.facebook.com/author.martin.bannon

Made in the USA
Charleston, SC
11 July 2012